Maggie's Marriage

Book Two in the Cloverleaf Series
Tales from Birch Valley

By Gloria Herrmann

Maggie's Marriage

Copyright © 2015 by Gloria Herrmann.
All rights reserved.
First Print Edition: January 2016

Limitless Publishing, LLC
Kailua, HI 96734
www.limitlesspublishing.com

Formatting: Limitless Publishing

ISBN-13: 978-1-68058-423-3
ISBN-10: 1-68058-423-5

Dedication

This book is dedicated to marriage. As a married woman, I have experienced the battles of compromise and utter frustration. I have also found my partner, my best friend, and an overall incredible human being. Marriage takes work, patience, and a tremendous amount of love. We both learned this from our parents, and only hope to set the same example for our children.

Traveling on this road toward the hopes of a successful marriage, we have enjoyed the times when it was smooth and scenic, we have encountered the bumps in the road and obstacles that life threw at us, but there is no one else I would want to share this ride with. I'm thankful to have married such a wonderful man; one who has patience, and who supports and encourages me regardless of my successes or failures, and who just gets me. I love you, Tim.

Chapter One

Maggie

Maggie Trembley clutched her queasy stomach. The pungent smell of the raw sea was not settling well with her today. She slowly sucked in the damp air through clenched teeth, trying to push past the urge to empty the contents of her stomach. She watched as her daughter got into line with the other students. The teacher tried to command the excited group of children, who were more interested in poking each other and giggling than listening to their teacher. Melanie, Maggie's child, was trying to follow directions the best a six-year-old could, but it helped that her mother's watchful eyes were targeted on her. Melanie's rust-colored, bobbed hair swung right below her chin. She sent Maggie a wide smile which showed she was missing her two front teeth.

Thick, angry, gray clouds threatened to burst open on that spring day in Seattle. Maggie felt the cool ocean breeze swim lightly in the salty air, blowing through her own chestnut-colored waves. She reached back, trying to smooth her tresses, and was thankful that the majority of this field trip was indoors. It wouldn't be the first time she or any of the residents in the city would get caught in an outrageous downpour, but who really wanted to be out in the rain? She wasn't in the mood for it today, that much was certain.

That was one of the drawbacks of living in this wet and busy place; it was nothing like back home in Birch Valley. Sure, Birch Valley had rain, it was probably even snowing there right now, but Maggie missed that wonderful little place that, at the moment, felt so far away.

In the almost eight years she had lived in Seattle, she still wasn't quite used to it. Recently, Maggie had been more homesick than ever before. She knew a lot of that had to do with the irritation she felt with her husband, Michael, and his constant absence at home. Michael, who was trying desperately to make partner at the law firm where he was a corporate defense attorney—the same firm where they had met and ultimately fell in love. Maggie knew there were more reasons why she missed Birch Valley, but right now, dealing with Michael never being around was ranking high on the list.

They had recently returned from a lovely weekend camping trip. Nestled deep in the woods of Birch Valley in their RV, sharing a nice time with her family, only made her longing worse. Coming back to the bright lights of the Puget Sound, the streets thick with traffic, and Michael leaving for the office only moments after they arrived home, reminded her just how lonely she was here.

The teacher announced to the children that they would be getting into different groups and were to be on their best behavior at the aquarium. Maggie smiled weakly at the teacher as she was given a handful of children to chaperone, Melanie clinging protectively next to her. The teacher passed a sheet to her and the other parents who had tagged along with the day's itinerary. Looking over at her daughter, Maggie announced to her small group of first graders that it was time to see some fish.

The tanks were filled with colorful fish that captured the attention of the children only briefly. As she eyed the little ones, Maggie was jealous of all the energy they possessed. She tried to keep up with the children; corralling them at various exhibits proved to be very difficult and exhausting. Their lunch break was a little calmer as the little ones enjoyed their sack lunches and shared what they loved seeing.

"Mom, are you having fun?" Melanie asked, taking a good sized bite out of her ham sandwich.

Maggie was nibbling slowly on a wheat cracker; it was all that her stomach could handle. "Yes, this is such a neat place. Are you enjoying yourself sweetie?"

"Oh yes, it's awesome. You don't look so happy, Mom." Melanie's green eyes flickered with concern for a brief second.

Maggie avoided Melanie's questioning stare, diverting her attention to the other children who were seated around them. Why did children always have to be so darn perceptive?

Maggie reached over for her daughter and pulled her close. "I'm so happy to be here with you, Mel."

That was enough to appease her curious girl, and Maggie was thankful as another wave a nausea swept through her.

The remainder of the field trip went as smooth as a field trip with a pack of six-year-olds could go. There had been some mild horseplay, tattle-telling, and plenty of restroom breaks. Maggie counted the minutes until they were all rounded up to get back on the bus to the elementary school. She enjoyed spending the day with her daughter, who was now thoroughly obsessed with sea creatures thanks to a fantastic tour guide and a not-so-amused red octopus.

Melanie chattered endlessly about everything she had seen at the aquarium on the ride home.

"What should we get for dinner?" Maggie asked as she weaved through the congested Friday evening traffic. The rain had let up, but left enormous standing puddles on the narrow streets.

"Whatever you want, Mom." Melanie was in the backseat, staring out the window.

"Fish and chips?" Maggie teased.

"Mom, that isn't funny. I love fish, but not to eat."

Maggie rolled her eyes. "I'm just kidding, Mel. How about pizza?"

"Yay, pizza!"

Maggie shifted the car and drove toward their favorite pizza place, which was near their neighborhood.

***

After reading Melanie her favorite bedtime story twice, she finally fell asleep. Maggie turned off her light and ventured out to the living room. Their small, two-bedroom condo was dark and quiet tonight. Maggie covered her mouth as she yawned loudly; she was completely exhausted by the time they got home from the field trip and pizza dinner. She stood by the large living room window and looked out at the glittering city lights of downtown Seattle. Where was Michael? She needed to talk to him. What she had to tell him couldn't wait much longer. She dreaded having this conversation with him, but knew she didn't have a whole lot of choice in the matter.

When they had been on the camping trip, she felt like there was hope for their marriage. They agreed on the drive back that he would put their family first, but once they had returned things instantly went back to how they had always been. Maggie was tired of feeling like she was the solo parent raising their daughter. These lonely nights, not knowing exactly where he was or when he would crawl into bed, were driving her mad, and she had had about as much as she could take.

Then there were those itching suspicions. Was he having an affair with the young, attractive receptionist who always gave Maggie a chilly welcome when she would stop in to visit Michael for an impromptu lunch date? How about the

5

paralegal with the legs that went on forever? Maggie knew her husband was still attracted to her, but she used to work at that firm. She wasn't stupid; she knew the types of things that went on there. It didn't help that Michael fit the tall, dark, and devilishly handsome type either. Maggie could recall different women at the office drooling over him right in front of her. She felt insecure, it was as simple as that. Sure, Maggie's figure took a little hit when she was pregnant with Mel, but she tried to fight Mother Nature and gravity by going to the gym several times a week. She remembered being the young, attractive receptionist at one time, the one with the toned and tight body that all the attorneys stared at. Michael used to lavish attention on her, spoil her downright rotten, and he'd charmed his way into more than her heart. Sometimes things changed after you have a baby. She had been warned by some of the other attorney's wives, who seemed so bitter and lonely, much like Maggie was now.

Maggie plopped down on the couch, misery quickly invading her thoughts, leaving her feeling empty. She placed her hand protectively over her belly. She had so much she needed to tell her husband.

***

Maggie's eyes fluttered open as a moment of confusion washed over her sleepy brain. Her body was stiff from falling asleep on the couch. The room was still dark as she sat up to get her bearings. She peered over at the clock; it was almost three. Maggie stretched and pulled away from the couch and moved toward her bedroom. The bed was still made, and there was no sign of her husband. Slipping under the covers, Maggie felt tears of anger stinging behind her eyelids. Another night without Michael by her side. She was asleep again before she knew it.

"Can I have cereal for breakfast?"

Maggie could hear her daughter yelling from the kitchen. She started to rise out of bed when she felt her stomach flip flop. Maggie moved with a quickness to the adjoining bathroom and emptied last night's dinner into the toilet. She could hear little feet scampering toward her.

"Are you sick, Mom?" Melanie's little voice squeaked.

Wiping her mouth, Maggie managed to say, "Mommy's okay."

"Can I have cereal for breakfast?" Melanie repeated. Maggie could only answer by nodding her head. That was enough for Melanie, who ran off to scarf down a sugary breakfast as fast as she could.

Sitting on the cold tiled floor next to the toilet, she knew why she had been sick and she wasn't the least bit happy about it. Well, that wasn't entirely true, a small portion of her sang with joy at the thought of having another baby. She just wasn't thrilled at the idea of Michael always being absent, and she wasn't so sure she could handle two children if she ever decided to leave him. Maggie had been feeling so conflicted lately, with far too many emotions bombarding her.

Morning sickness had become a daily ritual, and Maggie was well acquainted with every porcelain crevice of her toilet. She planned on seeing her doctor this week to confirm what a cheap test from the grocery store had already told her. She didn't even bother telling Michael her suspicion yet, and it hadn't been difficult hiding any of her symptoms from him either. With him trying to make partner, he spent more time at his office. She wanted to discuss the pregnancy and their marriage last night, but he had never come home.

"Mom, Grams is on the phone," Melanie announced from somewhere in the house. Maggie hadn't even heard the phone ring.

She climbed off the cold tile and managed to splash some water on her face before Melanie came running into the bathroom, shoving the phone into her hand.

"Hi, Mom," Maggie croaked, her throat still coated with lingering bile.

"Oh, sweetie, you don't sound too good," Mary O'Brien's voice said soothingly over the line.

Maggie knew she had to proceed with caution. Her mother was excellent at figuring out exactly what was going on with her children.

"I think it's just a little food poisoning," Maggie replied carefully.

"My poor dear, well, I won't keep you then. I just wanted to check in on you."

"Thanks, Mom. Yeah, I think I'll go lie down for a little while and will try to call you a later," Maggie promised.

After saying goodbye, Maggie sought refuge in

bed. Her body was exhausted, and she didn't recall being this worn out when she discovered she was pregnant with Melanie. This baby was definitely letting her know that him or her was in there. A shadow of a smile appeared along Maggie's mouth as she instinctively placed her hand over her stomach.

***

Maggie was busy rinsing off the remaining dishes from dinner when she heard Michael come into the kitchen.

"Sorry I missed dinner," he apologized as he bent down to plant a kiss on Maggie's slender neck.

She felt her back stiffen. "I'm surprised you're home this early."

"I know, I'm sorry about last night. I had a meeting that went on later than I expected, so I ended up just staying at my office," Michael said, pleading, his chocolate eyes begging her for forgiveness.

Maggie loved Michael, no question about that, but she couldn't ignore the annoyance she felt. The irritation she felt with him being gone, acting as a silent partner in their marriage, and a vacant father to their daughter, was starting to make being around him almost unbearable. On the rare occasions when he was home, things would be pleasant enough until the mounted tension and overall aggravation that had been swept under the rug surfaced.

"I heard today that they will be announcing who made partner at the end of the month. Rumor has it they are strongly considering me." Michael's eyes shone, a delirious grin on his lips. Maggie fought the urge to kiss him.

Maybe, once they announced who made partner at the firm, Michael would be home more, things would settle down, and maybe, just maybe, she could enjoy this pregnancy. But the nagging fear that he would only work more and be away more often, leaving her all alone, pricked at her.

"Michael, I really hope they see how hard you've been working, all the hours you slave away at that place."

"I'm pretty sure they know." Michael reached around Maggie's tender waist, pulling her closer to him. Nuzzling her neck, he whispered, "I've missed you."

Maggie wanted to let herself go and melt into her husband, but unresolved anger kept her guarded.

"You might want to go and say goodnight to Mel."

Maggie couldn't help the thoughts of her earlier conversation with their daughter. Melanie really missed her dad, and Maggie could only soothe her so much. She tried reassuring her daughter that things were going to get better soon and that her father loved her. What else could she possibly say?

Michael's chocolate brown eyes flashed with confusion. She could tell he had no idea how she felt, no clue at all. As he left the room, Maggie felt the familiar sensation of tears building up in her eyes. Crying—one the perks of pregnancy hormones.

***

"You almost ready for bed?" Michael asked, leaning against the archway leading to their living room. Maggie sat the book she had been reading down in her lap. Seeing him stand there, still in his work clothes, his navy blue tie loose around the collar of his crisp dress shirt, his gray slacks hanging perfectly on his toned legs, caused Maggie to feel pent-up desire for her husband. She hated being upset with him.

"Almost," Maggie answered.

"Well, I'm beat, I'm going to turn in." Michael yawned. He did look exhausted, the tiny crinkles by his eyes were heavy.

"Michael, can we talk?"

"Sure, babe, what's wrong?" Michael's furrowed, showing concern, and he approached the couch quickly.

Maggie swallowed hard. "I know you're working incredibly hard to make everything wonderful for us, but I just feel like you're never home."

"Maggie, we've been through this. This is the time when I need to sacrifice in order for our lives to be perfect later."

"I know, but it's so hard on Mel, she misses you so much. She needs her daddy." Maggie's voice grew rough as she tried to swallow back the pesky tears welling up in her eyes and choking her throat.

"I don't understand why you are so upset." Michael's calm tone was changing.

"You don't understand? Michael, you're never

home, literally, we see you for a couple of minutes here and there. This isn't what I signed up for." Maggie felt her stomach turn sick; the contents were like a small boat being tossed around a raging sea. She begged her body to keep calm, desperately trying to push away the wave of nausea.

"Oh, for Christ's sake, Maggie, you think I like not being home, or that I like spending almost every waking hour working? Come on."

"Of course, but Michael, Melanie is young and she misses you. I miss you. You need to be here more, it's as simple as that." Maggie could feel herself losing the battle.

Michael got up from the couch, Maggie could feel the emptiness as he turned and looked at her. "Everything I do is for us. It would be nice to have a little support, but instead every time we are alone you want to fight. As if I don't already have enough pressure and stress in my life, I don't need the added grief."

Maggie removed herself from the couch, throwing back the plaid throw that had been covering her. "I do support you. It wouldn't be a fight if you didn't work so much. I don't give a flying crap if you make partner. I want you to be my partner." Maggie felt like a child throwing a tantrum. Her thin arms were straight against her sides, her hands knotted up into tight balls. She imagined all she had to do was start stomping her foot, and she would look like a full fledged brat.

She felt her emotions spinning out of control; she hated herself for feeling like a crazy person. Lately, she felt like she had no hold on anything. Her emotions were all over the place.

"Maggie, that's enough. I'm not doing this with you right now. I'm worn out. I don't have the energy to fight." He turned away and went to their bedroom.

Maggie sank back on the couch feeling defeated and overwhelmed. What was she going to do? She knew one thing for sure; she couldn't keep this up much longer.

***

Maggie sat in the small office. The walls were covered in a modern, calm shade of teal and beige wallpaper. It made her nervous being locked inside the sterile room. Nothing was serene and inviting about it, not even the bleached starfish that were mounted sporadically on the walls. Maggie's mood lately hadn't gotten much better; she found herself overly emotional and just plain worn out. Cranky, that was probably a better word to describe it. Everything was annoying her, the inner rage that consumed her made Maggie feel disgusted with herself, but she tried to reason that this wasn't who she was. Then again, Maggie had lost sight of who she was a long time ago, and she wasn't sure about a lot of things now.

She had been waiting to talk to the doctor for close to twenty minutes. She felt herself growing anxious and irritated when a soft knock echoed off the door.

"Mrs. Trembley?" A man in a stark white coat and an obnoxiously colorful tie peered from behind the door as he entered slowly.

Maggie managed a tight lipped smile and a curt nod. *Try and be nice.*

The doctor took a seat on a small stool that was near Maggie. He pulled up to a computer that was on a portable desk and started to log into it. His eyes looked huge behind the thick glasses that kept sliding down the bridge of his nose.

"So, Maggie, can you tell me why you are here today?"

"I'm here today to confirm my pregnancy." Maggie groaned inside. *Wasn't it obvious when I peed in the cup today?*

"I see, yes, it says right here that we did send off a urine sample. Let me just check and see your results."

The doctor was an older man, his hair was primarily white and his face was lined with soft wrinkles. His voice was gentle, and that only seem to grate on Maggie's nerves more. Under normal circumstances, Maggie doubted she would feel such animosity toward him, or anyone for that matter. With the argument with Michael, Melanie's busy schedule, and now the pregnancy, Maggie felt overwhelmed and had a hard time just being polite.

The doctor cleared his throat, "Yes, here it is. Well, congratulations, Mrs. Trembley, it appears you are indeed pregnant."

Whoopie! Maggie imagined confetti falling from the ceiling.

Interrupting her thoughts, the doctor announced, "We will want to schedule you for an ultrasound to get an idea about how far along you might be. Do you recall the date of your last period?" He held up a small paper wheel that contained a series of numbers and months; he was spinning it slowly to figure out her approximate due date.

Maggie rattled off the dates as close as she could remember them. Satisfied with her response, he explained that her due date was around the start of fall. The doctor wrote a prescription for prenatal vitamins and asked her to schedule the ultrasound with the receptionist.

Well, it was confirmed. Maggie knew eventually she would have to tell Michael. He would be thrilled, of course, he had been pestering her for awhile about having another child. She had been putting it off for as long as possible, not that she didn't want another child, but to throw a baby into the mix now, when things were so difficult, wasn't something she had been interested in doing. She had hoped to add to their family once Michael got his priorities straight, once things settled down. Now it didn't matter what she was interested in doing or what Michael's priorities were, they were going to have a baby.

Chapter Two

The wind was starting to pick up as the sun strained against the cold day in Seattle, letting everyone know that winter was hanging around for a little longer. Maggie could feel the chill as she waited for Melanie to exit the school. Swarms of children came pouring out of the building as a loud bell sounded. Skipping and grinning around a mouth of missing teeth, Melanie's short red hair bounced happily as she saw Maggie.

"Hi, sweetheart, how was school today?" Maggie asked with heightened enthusiasm.

"It was great, we are going to have our spring concert on Friday. I'm so excited, Mom."

Maggie could see her daughter was thrilled about the idea of performing. She was the complete opposite of her mother. Melanie was so much like Michael, confident and almost showy. They loved attention, and jumped at any chance to capture it. Maggie, on the other hand, liked to keep under the radar and not draw too much focus to herself. Coming from a large family with three older brothers, it was fairly easy to get lost in the shuffle, but her mother, Mary O'Brien, made sure she kept a close eye on all her children. Her mother also respected that Maggie, her only daughter, was of the more quiet variety and liked her alone time.

Maggie had been attracted to Michael's confident manner. He wasted no time playing games, and when he saw something he wanted, he went after it. He was the polar opposite and they complemented each other well, at first. Over the last several years, after Melanie was born and Michael grew more insistent about his pursuit of success, Maggie felt herself again getting lost the shuffle of her own life. She had a hard time remembering who she was; she was known to everyone as either Michael's wife or Melanie's mother. There was no one who knew her as just Maggie.

She felt a tug on her sleeve, and looked down to see the concerned face of Melanie staring back up at her. Maggie's thoughts had sent her far away.

"Mom, I'm hungry."

"Let's head home, sweetie." Maggie steered her daughter toward her parked car.

***

"Daddy, I'm so glad you aren't at work right now," Melanie's voice chimed as she fiddled with her kid-sized chopsticks.

They were seated around their dining room table together, which was rare these days. Various large white paper cartons filled with Chinese food surrounded them.

Michael was serving himself some more beef and broccoli when he bent toward his daughter and gave her a kiss on her head. It warmed Maggie's heart to see him act so tender and sweet to Melanie. It was moments like these that made her fall in love with him all over again. These moments were fleeting, and she wanted Michael to see that.

"Mel, you want some more?" Maggie offered as she lifted a container filled with fried rice.

"No, I want to save room for my fortune cookie," Melanie answered as she struggled to grip her chopsticks.

"Daddy, are you excited about my concert on Friday?" Melanie gazed up at her father with the admiration that only a child can possess.

Michael looked at Maggie. "I can't wait to see you on that stage singing your little heart out."

Maggie said a silent prayer that Michael would live up to his promise of showing up to the concert, knowing how much it meant to their daughter. She couldn't bear the thought of how hurt Melanie would be if he didn't attend.

"Maggie, what time is the concert?" Michael asked from across the table.

"It starts a little after five." Suddenly the chow mein no longer agreed with Maggie as she fought a crashing wave of nausea.

"You okay, hun? You look a little green around the gills," Michael commented, concern present in his eyes as he narrowed them and watched her.

"Yeah, just getting over a little stomach bug," Maggie replied quickly as she bounded up from the table as gracefully as she could, given she felt like she was about to lose all their dinner.

Maggie heard Michael whispering in a soft, soothing tone to their daughter, "Mommy will be okay, sweetie. Let's clean up the table for her."

***

Michael was sitting at the table with his laptop out and open, a stack of files neatly stacked next to it. Maggie watched him as he hunched over the blue glint of the monitor and typed insanely fast, only to pause to rub at his eyes. The man was always working.

The house was quiet, except for Michael's rapid typing. He suddenly stopped. He must have sensed her presence.

"Feeling any better?" Michael asked softly.

Maggie shook her head, "A little. Did you put the food away? Where's Mel?"

"It has all been taken care of. Mel's in bed." Michael slowly stretched his long arms above his head and rose off the dining room chair.

He approached her slowly, with a great deal of caution. She inhaled the clean smell of his expensive aftershave. She wanted to smother her face in his chest and drown in his scent. She felt her body stir; she missed her husband.

Michael's arms encircled around her slender body as he pulled her closer to him, removing any space between them. "I'm sorry about the other night," he apologized in her ear as he left a trail of quiet kisses along her neck.

"Me too," Maggie answered, allowing herself to

be swept away in desire, swayed by the undertow of passion as Michael's hands roamed her tender body.

A nagging thought poked Maggie's brain, but her body quickly shoved it away. She desperately needed him. She brought his solid body to hers, and she hushed her thoughts, quieting them as she deepened the kiss.

Before she knew it, she was laying in the warm afterglow of some of the most passionate love making she had ever experienced. Maggie gazed at Michael. His eyes were closed, his sculpted, naked chest steadily rising and falling, almost hypnotizing her. His dark hair strayed from its usual combed style, lay messy on his head. This gorgeous man made Maggie feel almost maternal towards him. She could see bits of gray hair and tiny smooth lines on his face that weren't there a year ago. Her heart squeezed with love. Maggie laid her hand gently on his stomach and felt her eyes grow heavy. She said a silent prayer that they could figure things out.

***

Maggie kept looking at her cell phone. The auditorium was packed tight with families there to watch their children perform. Maggie had managed to snag a seat close to the stage, and she placed her purse on a vacant seat next to her to save for Michael. She had received several dirty looks for saving the seat. *Where was he?* The performance was going to start soon, and Maggie kept turning around in her chair to see if she could spot Michael. She had already sent him several text messages and hadn't heard back yet. She felt gnawing frustration biting at her when the lights in the large auditorium grew dim, and a group of children walked quietly onto the stage. Maggie spotted Melanie in her lavender dress, her red hair shiny against the stage lights. She smiled and forgot about Michael as she saw how lovely her daughter looked amongst her classmates. Music started playing, and the angelic voices of the first grade class filled the room.

Standing up along with the other overzealous, proud parents and relatives, Maggie clapped her hands as Melanie exited the stage after a beautiful display of singing and dancing. Maggie felt herself burning with anger at Michael. That rage became more inflamed as she saw the sad and confused look on Melanie's young face.

"Where's Daddy?"

"I'm not too sure, sweetheart." Maggie didn't want to have to make an excuse for Michael.

She was fed up with his failure to be there for important moments like this one. She did everything she could do to remind him; she texted him, left a voicemail, several in fact, and she slipped a Post-it note into his briefcase that morning. What more could she do, besides going deep into Seattle's downtown business district and kidnapping the man?

***

As Maggie sat in the heavy traffic, Melanie humming the songs she had just performed quietly in the back of the car, she thought about how to handle Michael's latest failure to choose his family over work. She was fuming by the time she was able to pull into the parking garage of their condo. The smell of rain mixed with car fumes turned her stomach as she got out and went to open Melanie's door. Melanie remained fairly silent. Maggie could sense her daughter's disappointment, and it only spurred her own anger further.

Once inside, Maggie made a plan, and it wasn't the most rational. Grabbing a small suitcase from the hall closet, she began to fill it with various clothing. Melanie sat on the couch and fiddled with her handheld game.

"Mel, how do you feel about seeing Uncle Liam?" Maggie asked.

The little girl's face beamed with a happy light. "Yay! I would love to see him. Can we see Grams too?"

"I think we might be able to arrange that," Maggie replied softly as she started to pack some of Melanie's clothing.

This impromptu trip was just what she needed. She felt herself ready to explode from all of the week's tension, and right now she needed to go home. Granted, no one had any idea she was coming to Birch Valley, but she figured she would make the five hour drive to her brother Liam's cabin. She could always talk to him, and he might be able to help her sort out things. She felt lost, and knew that if she were to see Michael right now she would be engaging in an all-out war with him. Maggie had hit her limits, and she needed some space to clear her head. There was no place better than her quiet hometown.

***

The highway leading Maggie to Birch Valley was quiet, even with the weekend travelers on the main stretch. Maggie already started to feel herself relax as she put the car in cruise control and sped along the main route back home. Melanie had fallen asleep; she'd been fairly quiet all evening, even with the excitement of going to see her uncles and grandparents. Maggie knew very well how upset her daughter was, and that only made her that much more angry with Michael, who still hadn't returned her texts or calls.

Thoughts about how she was going to deal with her husband when she got back plagued her. She hadn't told him about the pregnancy yet, and guilt was starting to set in. Maybe if she had told him he would have made more of an effort. At the same time, he should have been there for Melanie, regardless. Maggie knew that Michael deserved to know that they were expecting another baby, but for some reason she was reluctant to share the news. She had let her secret well up inside her, and now she was bursting to tell someone.

Driving through the dark mountain passes and keeping a careful eye out for deer, Maggie began to enter the rural town of Birch Valley. The main street was lined with lamp posts, and the ancient storefronts stood like quiet giants in the darkness. No other cars were driving on the roads. Everyone was tucked away, cozy in their little homes. Maggie continued to drive through town and continued on the highway toward her brother's cabin. He only lived about five miles away from the heart of the community where her parents and other brothers lived. Right now, she knew Liam was the one she wanted to see. She would go and deal with the rest of the family later. Maggie was close to Liam and knew that he'd welcome her no questions asked, no probing for information. He'd just be happy to see her. Liam was easygoing and liked to stay as far away from drama as possible. Maggie felt a twinge of guilt and regret showing up at his home this late. It was a little after one in the morning, she figured he would probably be asleep. Maybe leaving Seattle without calling ahead wasn't the best option, but she had to get away.

As her car handled the hairpin turn with complete ease, she pulled into Liam's gravel driveway. In the shadowy darkness she could make out the outline of the cabin nestled in the tall pine trees. There was a sting of cold in the air when she climbed out of her car. Melanie was still sleeping but started to stir now that the car had stopped.

"Sweetie, we're here." Maggie had opened Melanie's door and was unbuckling her daughter's seat belt.

The only light besides the moon that reflected off the small lake behind the cabin was a dim porch lamp. The yellow light guided Maggie up the walkway as she carried a groggy Melanie. She knocked softly on the door, readjusting the weight of her daughter on her hips. She waited patiently for her brother to open the door. She could hear the weight of his footsteps as he approached and opened the solid wood door.

"Maggie?" said a sleepy-eyed, confused Liam.

"Surprise!" Maggie announced.

Liam moved to aside to let Maggie in. "Yeah, it is."

Maggie worked her way to Liam's living room and deposited her sleeping child on the overly large, plaid couch that sat across from an enormous river rock lined fireplace. The comfortable, warm feel of Liam's home instantly made Maggie feel at ease.

"Want me to start some coffee, or maybe some tea?" Liam offered, rubbing the sleep from his face.

"That would be great." Maggie followed her brother into the kitchen.

Liam wore flannel pajama bottoms and had no shirt on, his bare feet padding on the wood floor. His shaggy, light brown hair was messy, and dark stubble covered his jaw. His emerald green eyes, which matched all of the O'Brien children, were sleepy and confused but far from judgmental.

"Aren't you going to ask why I'm here?" Maggie asked as she heard something behind her.

Liam's head turned. Maggie followed his stare and found Rachel standing by the doorway.

Her blonde pixie hair stood up at all ends, and her brilliant blue eyes shone with embarrassment. "Hi, Maggie," Rachel said.

At first Maggie had been a little unsure about the tan, petite blonde, but found herself connecting with her on many different levels and had started forming a new friendship with her. Rachel had moved up from Newport Beach, California, and had taken over as principal at the only elementary school in Birch Valley, the same one where Liam was a fourth grade teacher. The first time she met Rachel was during a cooking lesson at her mother's house. They hit it off right away, and she could see the chemistry between Rachel and Liam, though both continued to deny any attraction. The family went on their annual moose watching expedition, and her mother, Mary, had invited Rachel to join the family. Maggie found herself getting closer with Rachel; she was easy to talk to, and an overall sweet person. They had kept in contact with an occasional text or email, and made promises to hang out the next time Maggie was in town. She couldn't deny that she was a little surprised and taken off guard that Rachel was there at her brother's home. A part of her was happy for her brother. Rachel blended in so well with the family, and Maggie couldn't help but hope to have her as a sister-in-law someday.

"Rachel." Maggie hurried toward her and gave her a hug. She didn't really know what else to do, she was genuinely glad to see the other woman, but it was kind of awkward.

Rachel smiled and squeezed Maggie in a tight embrace as she looked questioningly up at Liam. Rachel released Maggie and began fussing with her short hair.

"I'm going to head home, but Maggie, maybe you want to get some coffee or come over and visit while you're here?" Rachel asked nervously, tugging at the flannel shirt that covered her thin body—Liam's flannel.

Maggie nodded, realizing how uncomfortable

Rachel must have felt. Rachel scurried down the hall, leaving the two siblings alone in the kitchen.

Once Maggie was sure the other woman was out of earshot, she swatted at her brother. "Wow, Liam."

Liam smiled. "I know, crazy, huh?"

"I'm happy for you. I really like Rachel," Maggie said as she heard Rachel making her way back toward them.

The petite blonde was now dressed in an over-sized gray sweater and jeans. She raised up on her toes and gave Liam a kiss on the cheek.

She moved to Maggie and gave her another hug. "I'm so glad to see you."

Maggie watched as Rachel carefully peeked over the plaid couch and gingerly patted Melanie's sleeping head. The small token of affection made Maggie's heart squeeze.

Maggie followed Liam's eyes, and she could plainly see that her brother was in love with the woman who just left.

Liam quickly turned back to the coffee. He grabbed two mugs out of the hickory cabinets and sat them on the granite countertop. He looked back at his sister and waited for her to make the first move.

Maggie cleared her throat and started to speak. "You are probably wondering why I'm here."

"Just glad to see you, though it's a little early. You want sugar or cream?" Liam asked as he poured the dark liquid from the French press. The aroma swam to Maggie's nose. She inhaled the rich flavor, and her stomach clenched, a reminder from the life inside her.

"You know, Liam, can I just have tea instead? Herbal, if you have it?" Maggie asked.

"Sure, no problem. I'm sticking to this stuff." Liam raised his mug and took a sip of the coffee.

Maggie felt the weight of the world melt from her shoulders as she sat there with her brother. A fire was burning slowly in the large fireplace, casting a soft glow along with the cold morning light in the living room. Earlier, Liam had moved Melanie into his bedroom, tucking his niece into the over-sized bed. The two siblings sipped on their hot beverages and discussed in great detail Maggie's dilemma.

Repeatedly dunking the tea bag, Maggie sighed. "I just don't know what to do, Liam."

Liam seemed cautious when he answered his sister. "Mags, I'm not really sure what to tell you. So you haven't told Mom yet?"

"No, I haven't said anything to anyone. I was going to tell Michael, but things have just been, well, I don't know, not good. It isn't like he's ever home for me to even talk to him anyway," Maggie reasoned.

"I can see how you're upset that he didn't show for Melanie's concert. I'm a little surprised he didn't at least let you know why he couldn't make it."

Maggie huffed loudly. "Does it even matter? The fact is, we are not a priority. I just don't want Mel getting hurt. You should have seen how disappointed she was, it nearly broke my heart."

Liam nodded. "I can imagine. But you have to

tell him about the baby."

"I will." Maggie yawned, her body was exhausted from the drive and lack of sleep.

"Let's get you in bed. You go sleep with Mel, I'll take the couch," Liam instructed.

"Thanks, Liam." Maggie looked lovingly at her brother. He was a good man, and she appreciated his kindness. Maggie was glad she had turned to him; she could always count on Liam.

Chapter Three

Maggie woke up confused. She could hear Melanie laughing in another room. Shaking away the heavy, sleepy fog in her brain, it took her a moment to realize she was at Liam's house. She tried eyeing the digital alarm clock on the dresser across the room. It was close to noon. Maggie could sleep more, her eyes wanted to close and drift away back to the warm slumber she had been tightly nestled in moments before.

"Shh, we need to keep quiet for your mom. Okay, sweetie?" Maggie could hear her brother say softly. Then she heard the obnoxious, loud ringing of a phone. Her brother promptly answered it.

"Hey. Yeah, she's here. Melanie too," Liam reassured the caller. Maggie knew it had to be Michael.

She heard her daughter beg to speak to the caller. Maggie felt the vibrations of Liam's heavy footsteps as he approached the bedroom.

A gentle knock. "Hey, Mags, you awake yet?"

Grunting, Maggie answered, "Yes. Come on in."

Liam filled the doorway with his tall figure. "Michael's on the phone. You want to talk to him?"

Maggie rolled her eyes. "Not really."

Liam shook his head. "Well, that's up to you. I'm not going to force you. But just an FYI, Mom called too."

"Oh, Lord, what did you tell her?" Maggie asked.

"I didn't say anything, but she heard Mel in the background. I told her you were here, that you guys got in late. I figured it's not my place to tell her."

She was glad she could count on Liam. He didn't divulge secrets, he'd been like that when they were kids too. He never wanted to get anyone into trouble, and everyone knew they could trust him.

"I'll tell her today," Maggie assured him as Melanie bounded into the room loudly.

"Mom, Uncle Liam made me French toast!"

Glad to see how unaffected her child was, Maggie felt gratitude toward her brother. "Well, that was very sweet of him. I bet it was yummy too."

"Uncle Liam saved you some too. You have been sleeping forever," Melanie complained.

"Okay, well, I'm up now. You want to go see Grams today?"

"Yes! I can't wait to go see everyone," Melanie squealed with pure delight.

Liam reached out for Melanie as the little girl started hopping on the bed. "Let's go and see if any deer are in the yard. Your mom still needs to get up."

Maggie appreciated Liam pulling the child off

the bed. The bouncy movements were creating harsh waves in her stomach. She sent Liam a look of thanks as she tried to settle the storm inside her belly.

***

Maggie was sitting in Liam's dining room, nibbling on a leftover piece of French toast when she heard a knock at the front door. Liam had taken Melanie outside to go visit the lake, leaving Maggie alone in the quiet cabin. Reluctantly getting up from her seat, she slowly shuffled to open the door, where Mary O'Brien, wrapped in her heavy, green wool coat and gray knit cap, stood.

"Mom," Maggie said as she let her mother inside the home.

Ridding herself of her coat and hat, Mary reached for Maggie, pulling her into a tight embrace.

"Maggie, sweetheart, I had no idea you were coming home this weekend," Mary said as she lead herself to the kitchen.

Maggie followed her mother, who was pouring water into the kettle to heat.

"Tea?" Mary offered.

"Um, sure." Maggie took her seat back at the breakfast nook.

"Now, I won't waste time beating around the bush, Maggie," Mary started. Maggie raised her hand to stop her mother.

"Mom, I know."

"Well then, you want to tell me why this

morning I received a frantic call from your husband?" Mary's stare burrowed into Maggie.

Maggie felt the salty tears emerging. "Mom, it's complicated."

Mary sat across from Maggie. "I'm sure it is. Can you imagine the fright I had when he called? He had no idea where you or Melanie were."

"Wow, I'm surprised he even noticed we were gone." Maggie's tone was vile with anger.

Mary reached for her daughter's hand. "Well, he did notice, and he was awfully worried, dear."

Maggie could only imagine how she would feel if she came home to find that her daughter and spouse were gone. But considering the stunt he had pulled on Friday with a no call, no show for the performance, she didn't have a whole lot of sympathy for her husband right then.

The kettle whistled loudly. Mary quickly got up to fill two mugs with the steaming hot liquid. She returned equally quickly to the table. It was obvious Mary O'Brien wanted answers.

Maggie reached for her mug. She inhaled the floral scent of the herbal tea, the warmth from which radiated through her hands, bringing the promise of comfort. It amazed her how a simple cup of hot water mixed with some tea leaves and a little honey had the ability to immediately soothe and calm her.

"Look, dear, I understand that you may be upset with Michael, but running off like this sure isn't going to solve any problems."

"Mom, things have been building up, you know that," Maggie said defensively as she took a

33

leisurely sip of the hot tea.

Matching her sip, Mary eyed her daughter. "Maggie, I realize that, but he's your husband, and what about Melanie? It isn't just about you, you know?"

"I told her we were coming to visit. Mom, you should have seen how upset she was that Michael didn't come to the spring concert." Maggie looked down, feeling the urge to say everything that had been trapped inside her. "There's something else I need to tell you."

"Oh, Lord, are you two getting a divorce?" Mary's eyes were wide with concern.

"No, we haven't quite got to that level yet. Well, it seems that our family is going to be a little bigger." Maggie watched as her mother's mouth twisted from a frown into a faint smile.

"Well, that's wonderful, dear. I mean, I can see with the current situation that this is probably not the best timing. God works in funny ways, doesn't He?"

"He sure does." Maggie paused. "I haven't told Michael yet."

Mary's eyes grew large again. "Oh, Maggie."

Maggie knew she should have told him by now, but honestly she hadn't really found the time. She sure as heck didn't want to spill the beans over a voicemail or text message. Maggie wasn't all that excited about telling Michael, considering how awful things had been at home lately, except for that rare night last week. The thought sent a silent ache to Maggie's core.

Liam and Melanie noisily entered the cabin.

"Hey, Mom, I didn't hear you pull up," Liam said as he grabbed some cocoa mix from the cabinet to make Melanie some hot chocolate. "Mel, you want any marshmallows, kiddo?"

"Sure, Uncle Liam." Melanie had propped herself in his recliner and started playing with her handheld game.

"I was going to make her and I some grilled cheese sandwiches, you guys want some?" Liam offered as he removed all the items he needed from his stainless steel fridge.

"I'm okay, thanks," Maggie answered as she swallowed another sip of tea. Her stomach was beginning to go a little uneasy.

"None for me, dear, I will be heading home. Maggie, you and Melanie come over for lunch tomorrow." Turning her attention to her son, she said, "Liam, let Rachel know if she wants to join us. I figure I can throw something together a little early so we have some time to visit."

Mary put her empty cup in the sink and gave Liam a kiss on his cheek. She strolled over to Maggie, bent down, and hugged her shoulders, placing a kiss on top of her chestnut hair. "I love you, sweetheart."

Maggie felt so much better now that she was back in Birch Valley. The support and love of her family was doing her a world of good. This was why she so desperately wanted to move back.

***

Maggie snorted as she tried to catch her breath;

she had been laughing uncontrollably for the last hour. God, she needed this.

Rachel had showed up earlier in the evening, unexpectedly, with a couple of pizzas and an arm full of board games and movies. They had played a couple games with Melanie until she couldn't keep her eyes open, then the adults sat on the ground around Liam's coffee table, sharing stories about growing up, mainly about the shenanigans that the O'Brien children got into. Maggie didn't recall the last time she had laughed so hard, it felt great.

"I'd better head home," Rachel announced as she slowly crawled up off the floor.

Maggie noticed Liam watch Rachel rise, and disappointment seemed to flood him as his eyes grew a shade darker, when moments earlier they were light and shining with happiness and something else. Maggie and Liam each rose off the ground, with Liam starting to help gather the games and movies.

"Thanks so much for coming over. I had a lot of fun," Maggie said as she rubbed Rachel's arm.

"I'm glad, I did too. I don't think I have ever laughed so hard in my life. You O'Brien kids are crazy," Rachel replied, a lingering giggle escaping her mouth.

Liam held a stack of board games. "Rachel, are you coming over to my folks' place tomorrow?"

Rachel bit her bottom lip. She eyed Liam, and said, "I'm not sure, your family may have a lot to discuss."

"I'm sure it will be fine," Liam said, clearly trying to convince her. Maggie could see he wanted to spend every moment he could with Rachel. She remembered feeling that way about Michael.

"Rachel, it's totally okay, you can come over if you want." Maggie attempted to reassure the other woman, but she could tell Rachel was still undecided.

"We'll see, I have some paperwork I need to do and stuff. I'll call you, Liam. Tell Melanie goodbye for me, just in case I can't make it over." Rachel reached out to Maggie and squeezed her softly.

"I will. She really likes you, Rachel. Thanks for all the treats you brought over, she had a blast."

"No problem, it was my pleasure. Well, I'd better get going," Rachel answered as she slipped her jacket on.

"I'll walk you out," Liam said, still holding the armload of games.

***

Rachel

Once outside, the chilly air slapped Liam and Rachel, stinging their cheeks. Their breath hung heavy around them. Rachel started her car to let it warm up, she popped her trunk, and Liam placed the huge stack of games inside. The days had grown warmer than when she first arrived in Birch Valley, but the evenings were still cold.

"Hey, thanks for coming over. I appreciate you bringing a smile to Maggie's face." Liam hovered over Rachel as she stood next to her silver BMW.

She looked up at Liam, wonder filling her eyes

37

as Liam bent down and kissed her. Rachel still wasn't quite used to it. Every time their lips touched, an electrical current surged through every inch of her. How did she get so lucky?

They had only been dating officially for a couple weeks since the O'Brien family had invited Rachel to go on their annual moose watching camping trip. It was there, in the majestic pine-filled mountains, near a partially iced over lake, that she finally let her guard down and accepted her feelings for Liam, feelings she had been fighting for a couple months. She didn't want to fall in love; that was not the reason she had moved over fifteen hundred miles away from the shimmering ocean community of Newport Beach, California. Rachel was cautious in their new relationship, especially considering she was his boss at Birch Valley Elementary. No one seemed to mind, except one teacher who plainly had the hots for Liam. Everyone else appeared happy that Liam and Rachel had finally ended their nonsense of denying their feelings for each other, especially the school secretary, Karen. Rachel was still a little uneasy about being open with their relationship, she wanted to make sure the school board would renew her contract as principal for following school year. Some state testing results would help decide that.

Liam pulled Rachel close to him, wrapping her tightly in his arms, trying to warm her.

"I'm not sure about tomorrow. I really feel like that this is something you guys need to work out with Maggie as a family," Rachel said firmly.

"Rachel, my family adores you and won't mind

if you're there. If they had their way we would already be married." Liam eyed her playfully, teasing her with a kiss on her forehead.

"Oh, stop. I'm serious, I kind of think this is a serious family matter."

"It'll work itself out."

"Liam, she's pregnant, she isn't speaking to her husband, and she left without telling him. I'm thinking it's a little more serious," Rachel countered.

"Fine, but she knows we are here to support her."

Rachel understood that Maggie felt safe amongst the O'Briens, but she couldn't help but think of how Michael must feel in the whole mess. "That's why she drove here, to your home. She knows you have her back."

"She knows that this is home, where she belongs," Liam added, his long arms moved loosely around Rachel's hips.

"But her home is in Seattle, with Michael. She needs to be there to figure this out, with him. I'm glad that she feels like she can come to you guys, but I don't think leaving him without so much as a message or anything was right, Liam," Rachel said.

"I know, but that's her call."

"Liam, that's not really the case when there are children involved. I really like Maggie, and think she's awesome, but she should have told Michael where she was going at the very least. That had to be pretty awful for him."

Liam sighed. "Okay, look, let's not get too worked up about this. Things will work themselves out. I'm here whenever she needs me. Last night, she needed me. So, basically, I'm not digging any further or casting judgment on what is the right call. She did what she thought was best at the time."

"Jeez, I'm not calling her out for the call she made, I just think she should have told Michael."

Liam's body tensed as he dropped his arms from her. "You're starting to shiver, you'd better get into your car. I'll call you tomorrow."

Rachel sighed. "Do you see why I think this is a family matter, and why I shouldn't be involved? I don't want to fight with you about your sister, you're a good brother, supporting her unconditionally, and I love that about you."

"You love me?" Liam teased. Rachel had still not quite fully admitted her love for Liam, only hinting that she thought she might love him.

"I'm going home now." Rachel sank into her car and smiled broadly at the man who she was indeed falling in love with.

***

Maggie

Maggie was lounging in Liam's recliner when he returned. "Boy, you were out there long enough," Maggie teased.

Liam stretched his long body out on the plaid couch. "Was just saying goodbye."

"So, how are things going between you guys?" Maggie questioned with a sly smile perched on her lips.

"We are taking it kind of slow, I guess. Mom and

Dad love her, so does Grandpa Paddy. Daniel and Patrick think she's great too. She really likes the whole family," Liam replied thoughtfully.

"Well, what do you think?"

"Think about what, exactly?" Liam asked quickly.

"Do you think you'll want to marry her?"

"I'm not sure, I mean, I care about her, but there are some things we don't see eye-to-eye on." Liam had a faraway look that concerned Maggie.

"I love her and think she's perfect for you. She is so nice and thoughtful. If I had to choose a wife for you, it would be her."

Liam smiled at his sister. "Glad that's been decided. I do care about her, and we are seeing where this goes. We still have the issue of her being my boss, so that is a hurdle we are still trying to climb over."

Maggie drew hand up and swatted the air. "Eh, it'll work itself out. She just needs to learn how things work in a small town."

"True. Karen down at the school is happy that we are dating each other, the teachers don't really seem to care or pay much attention. I tried to explain that to Rachel, but she is concerned the school board won't keep her on if they learn her and I are an item," Liam explained.

Maggie could see the dilemma. She remembered how it was for her and Michael at the law firm. She had only been a receptionist, not quite familiar with the large city. Michael was an up-and-coming hotshot lawyer from a prestigious family, and they had been an unlikely match. The firm frowned on employees dating, and they frowned even more when Maggie wound up pregnant and they had to marry quickly. She felt forced out of her job and ended up staying home with Melanie, while Michael focused on bringing his career to new heights. Maggie wondered if Rachel was worried she would get shoved out of her position. The likelihood in their small community was slim, but Rachel came from a large city. She wasn't stupid, she knew how things operated, so Maggie couldn't really blame her for wanting to keep their relationship quiet.

"She's so good with Melanie too."

"Mags, I don't need any more convincing, okay? God, you're starting to sound like Mom."

"Well, just adding my two cents." Maggie yawned.

"Duly noted."

"I'm going to head to bed, sure you are okay on the couch?" Maggie asked sweetly.

"That's why I bought it. One of the best couches to nap on." Liam's eyes were already closed as he answered his sister.

"Okay, well, thanks again for a really nice night. Please let Rachel know how much that meant to me too. Goodnight, Liam." Maggie strolled to Liam's bedroom, and slid under the thick warm comforter next to her sleeping daughter. She smoothed Melanie's hair from her forehead and planted a soft peck on her cheek. Maggie felt her body bend to exhaustion. She was asleep before she finished saying her prayers.

Chapter Four

When she went to Sunday dinner at her mother's, Maggie had almost forgotten how loud it could get in her childhood home.

Grandpa Paddy was seated at one end of the ancient oak table. He faced Maggie, eyeing her sternly. "Maggie, my darlin' lass, your mum tells me you're having another babe. About time." His brogue, thick as ever, was hushed so that the other members of the family dining at the table couldn't hear him.

Maggie swallowed hard and managed a smile. "Yes."

"I bet Michael is proud to be a papa again. Good for you two, wish he were here. I would make a toast to him for a job well done."

"Thank you, Grandpa." Maggie blushed and didn't quite know how to answer her grandfather. You never knew with Grandpa Paddy, he was such a character. He could be loud and boisterous, the rowdiest one of the O'Brien men, or as tender and warm as a saint.

43

One of his emerald green eyes, which were always filled mischief, winked back at her.

"Maggie, dear, you get enough to eat?" Mary asked sweetly.

"Yes, thanks, Mom," said Maggie.

"Kind of surprised to have you back in town, Maggie," Daniel noted as he scooped another helping of corn onto his plate.

"Yeah, I just needed to get away, and what better place than home?" Maggie answered. She sent Liam a glance, thankful he hadn't shared any of the reasons why she had returned home.

"When are you headed back?" Patrick asked, eyeing his sister with piqued curiosity.

"Mel and I are going to hit the road later this evening." Maggie glanced at her watch and saw that it was only around two in the afternoon.

"It's great you came out to visit, sweetheart," Maggie's father, Pat, added as he took a drink and held it up toward her. He gave her a wink as well, knowing what secret she held. Maggie wasn't surprised that her mother had shared the news about the pregnancy, but she did find it a little odd that Daniel and Patrick made no mention of it. Maybe her mother hadn't told them yet.

The family finished their late lunch, and the majority of the men retired into the den, leaving Maggie to assist Mary with the clean up.

Melanie was busy playing with her cousins, three-year-old twins Finn and Connor, who were Patrick's children. His wife, Beth, had been involved in a car accident when she was pregnant with the boys. Her passing had shaken the entire family. Doctors were able to save the boys by performing an emergency C-section and keeping them alive in the NICU at a large hospital over an hour away from Birch Valley. That was a dark shadow in time for the O'Brien family, one that still hovered over her oldest brother.

"Sounds like you guys had a nice evening yesterday." Mary broke the silence as she ran warm water over a set of dirty plates before placing them into the dishwasher.

"We did. Rachel brought over a bunch of fun stuff. Mel had the best time. She really adores Rachel, and so do I," Maggie answered.

Mary smiled. "Rachel is a sweet girl, we all like her a great deal. I'm hoping things continue to work out with her and Liam."

"Me too. I told Liam last night I think she's perfect for him."

"It is important to pick a spouse who complements who we are as a person."

Maggie felt it, she knew her mother was waiting for just the right moment to bring up Michael. She had set herself up; it was her own fault.

"So do the boys not know about the pregnancy?" Maggie held her stomach and motioned to her flat belly.

"I only told your father, who, of course, ran off and told Grandpa Paddy. I figured you might want to tell your brothers. I suggest you do it soon, before one of us slips up. Maybe you can tell them before you leave tonight."

Maggie understood, she didn't plan on hiding the pregnancy. It was just that she was now overwhelmed with guilt for not sharing the news with her own husband first. When she discovered she was pregnant with Melanie, she and Michael had sat and stared at a home pregnancy test together. They had sat in Michael's apartment, holding their breath, waiting to see the results. They spent the rest of the night making love, talking about their plans for the future, and reveling in the sheer joy of the moment.

"I'll tell them before I leave, I promise."

That seemed to please her mother. They continued to clean and organize the remnants of dinner until the kitchen was spotless.

Maggie was drying off her hands when Liam walked into the kitchen.

"Mags, you going to tell Patrick and Daniel?" He was filling up his empty glass with water.

"Yeah, Mom was just telling me the same thing. I'm kind of curious how Patrick will take the news, you know?" Maggie's voice was quiet.

Beth's pregnancy was the last one the O'Briens had, and Maggie knew it was bound to stir up some unpleasant memories for her brother.

"I'm sure it will be a little hard, but Mags, its been three years since Beth's been gone. He probably figures you and Michael would have more kids, he wouldn't fault you for that," Liam said.

"Yeah, I just don't want to make Patrick uncomfortable. I suppose that's why I wasn't in the biggest rush to tell him."

"It'll be okay, I promise."

Maggie moved past her brother and headed to the living room, Daniel was stretched out on his usual place on the leather couch. Patrick could be heard talking to their father in the den.

Plopping down next to Daniel, Maggie moved her brother's heavy legs, "Scooch over," She commanded.

"Ah, Maggie, I was comfortable," Daniel whined as he straightened up on the couch.

"Too bad. So, I have some news," Maggie started to say.

"Is that why you came home this weekend?"

"Kind of."

"So what's the news?" Daniel's eyes grew curious as he searched Maggie for an answer.

"I just found out that I'm pregnant," Maggie blurted out.

"Ah, that's great, Maggie. Oh, I bet Michael is thrilled." Daniel's joyful voice was loud.

Patrick was standing in the archway leading into the room, his tall figure filling the archway. His expression was a mix of things that Maggie couldn't quite figure out.

"That's really good news, Maggie." Patrick's tone was steady and even, but his emerald eyes held a wet sheen.

Maggie stood up and practically ran to Patrick. A sudden surge of emotional hormones were to blame as she wrapped her slender arms around her brother.

Patrick was stiff at first, but his resolve slowly melted away as he laid his head on top on Maggie's. They stood quietly together, leaning on each other for support and sharing a moment of mourning.

Maggie could feel her brother's sorrow leaking from his soul. She knew how much Patrick had loved Beth; they all had loved her. Patrick had been thrilled when Beth became pregnant after years of trying to conceive. They were overjoyed when they found out they were expecting twins. Patrick played the role of proud papa well, doting on Beth, helping decorate the nursery, even attending birthing classes. They had grand plans, charted out their course in life, only to have them dashed about eight months into the pregnancy. It had all happened so fast, Patrick never had any time to really grieve. He had suddenly become a widower and a father of two baby boys fighting for their lives in a NICU.

"I'm really happy for you," Patrick managed to say as he released Maggie from their embrace.

Maggie's eyes were filled with tears as she nodded. She found herself unable to speak. Liam had entered the living room and watched the interaction between his brother and sister. Daniel had fallen asleep and was starting to snore.

"I better gather my monsters and head home," Patrick announced. He hugged Maggie again.

Liam grabbed Patrick's shoulder as he exited the room. Patrick gave him a tight smile. The O'Brien siblings shared an immeasurable love for each other; their compassion and understanding was deeply embedded in their very souls. Maggie could feel the closeness in that room, even with Daniel sound asleep. It made her long to be back home. She now dreaded leaving Birch Valley more than ever.

***

Maggie's fingers tapped on the steering wheel, drumming along to a song that was playing on the radio. Melanie had fallen asleep after about two hours into the drive home. She felt uneasy with all the silence in the car. Maggie had scanned the radio for something upbeat and peppy to get her motivated for the journey home. Her insides cringed as she considered what was waiting for her in Seattle.

She could only imagine the confrontation that was going to happen when Michael saw her. He had tried calling her several times, but she had finally ended up turning her cell phone off. Maggie knew that was only going to make things worse. She wasn't exactly sure how she was going to handle things with Michael, but Maggie knew one thing for sure—she was in no rush to get home.

It was a little after ten when Maggie slipped into the parking garage of their condo. She gently woke up Melanie and started to retrieve their suitcases. Maggie's eyes searched for Michael's car. The overhead lights reflected off the shiny, black luxury sedan as she noticed it was parked in its usual spot.

Her belly became a tangled net of captured butterflies, fluttering wildly. Her nerves were raw from acting out how this confrontation was going to go in her head on the drive home. She contemplated every scenario, and was trying to prepare herself for all of them.

Maggie's hands shook as she tried shoving her key into the door. Once she finally opened the door, a sleepy Melanie pushed past her and veered toward her bedroom. A table lamp cast a low light in the living room, the window exposing the view of the city below, which allowed some street light to filter in. Then she saw his figure in the muted light, shadowy as he sat there. Maggie felt her body tense, a thick, nervous knot forming in her throat. Her stomach bubbled in anticipation.

"Glad you decided to come home."

Maggie shoved her suitcase further into the hall, dropping her keys and purse on the table. She approached him slowly.

"Michael," Maggie started to say, her voice uneven, matching the tormented waves in her stomach.

"Stop, Maggie. I have some things I want to say first." Michael's tone was firm and direct.

"I don't really think you have the right, Michael."

"Oh, but I do, especially when you decide to leave town with our child without so much as a note or phone call. Then you decide not to answer your phone, which forced me to track you down."

Maggie inched closer, her nerves turning into rubber. "Michael, I'm surprised you even noticed that we were gone."

Michael stood up and glared hard at her through the semi-dark room. "Are you kidding me? So you think what you did was totally just?"

"Do you think it was okay that you didn't call or text me that you weren't coming to Melanie's performance? She was so disappointed, Michael," Maggie countered.

"I couldn't get away, there an emergency meeting we had with one of our top clients. I had no choice, Maggie."

"But you could have called or let me know."

"There wasn't an opportunity to do so. I have to sacrifice things right now, they are deciding who will be made partner at the end of the month."

"So sacrificing your family, especially our daughter, after you promised her you were going to go, is completely okay in your book?" Maggie felt her nerves tightening, her body gathering strength as her anger flared.

"Maggie, what you did was a little different. Taking our child away from our home without notifying me is not okay. I was so close to calling the police," Michael argued.

Maggie felt a twinge of vile anger spill from her as she spewed, "Well, I didn't just take our child, I took our children."

She wasn't sure why she announced the pregnancy, especially like that. She wanted to retract her words the second they soared from her mouth, but it was too late. Michael's face contorted into silent confusion.

Time stood still as Michael digested her words. Maggie could hear the city traffic below the window, and she could feel her heart pounding violently against her ribs. She wondered if Michael could hear it too. Suddenly, Maggie's brain swirled. Ringing rammed loudly in her ears, and then, darkness.

Her eyes fluttered open. Maggie's mind was twisted and confused.

"Maggie, are you okay?" Michael hovered over her. Her hands reached to her sides and felt carpet;

she was on the ground.

"I don't know," Maggie answered. Her body felt stirred, all mixed up and out of place.

"You fainted." Michael's voice was laced with concern, but his serious demeanor kept his body rigid.

She could feel his tension as her brain righted itself, and she started to push past the fog that had settled there briefly. She had fainted before when she was pregnant with Melanie, but this had hit her suddenly.

"How long have you known?" Michael asked firmly.

"Known about what?" Maggie was still a little dazed and wasn't sure about the root of his question. She wracked her mind to recall the last bit of their conversation, before she went down like a ton of bricks. She had no idea what she had said to him.

"Maggie, about the baby?" Michael's face was stoic, his eyes almost unforgiving as they stared into her.

"Oh, God." Tears immediately started streaming down her cheeks.

"How long, Maggie?" He pressed further. "How long have you known you were pregnant?"

Maggie felt trapped. Did she tell him she only just found out, or that she had suspected it for almost a month? She stalled, blinking away automatic tears.

"Were you not planning on telling me?" Michael accused as he moved away from her and sat back on the chair he was in earlier.

"No, I wanted to tell you," Maggie said as she tried to figure out how to crawl out of this mess of a hole she gotten herself into.

"Well, that's considerate."

"Michael, that's not fair. Of course I was going to tell you."

"So, you must have just found out then? Does anyone else know?" Michael asked, tapping his fingers hard against the arm of the chair, his frustration oozing from him.

"Well, I went to the doctor last week," Maggie confirmed. Her thoughts blistered as she tried to determine if telling that was enough to satisfy his question. She had told her family. Everyone knew, except Michael.

"Maggie, did you tell everyone at home?"

A long sigh escaped Maggie. "Yes." There was no point in denying it.

"I see."

"I wanted to tell you, but God, Michael, it's not like you are ever home," Maggie said defending her reasoning.

"So, when I was home last week, and we spent the night making love, you didn't think that maybe then might have been the perfect time, assuming that you just found out," Michael said, in true form to his attorney persona. "I'm guessing you knew long before then. The question I have is why you would keep that from me, your husband?"

"Because honestly, Michael, you hardly act like a husband anymore. You are barely there for Melanie, and the thought of bringing another child into our life is terrifying to me."

"Are you serious? I do everything I can to provide for this family. I can't believe you would even say such a thing." Michael's brown eyes burned with an inner anger Maggie had never seen before.

"Michael, your priorities when it comes to our family are all screwed up. Melanie wanted you there at her concert, she needed that support from you. Instead, you chose work over her. You always choose work."

Michael rubbed his jaw. "I choose work to support this family."

"Well, I don't think there is anything else to say. I didn't sign up for this kind of marriage. I can't live like this." Maggie stared Michael down. "I won't."

"I think you are being a little dramatic."

Maggie leaped from the ground and stood in front of him. "Michael, just so it's clear, I'm going back to Birch Valley and I'm taking Melanie."

Michael stood to face his wife. "Are you saying you want a divorce?"

"No, but I'm saying you need to get your priorities straight."

"You are being ridiculous. I'm going to the office." Michael brushed past her.

"Surprise, surprise. Glad to see you're really working on those priorities," Maggie snarled.

"Maggie, you and Melanie are all that I have in this world. Everything I do is for the two of you."

"Can't you see we don't need to live in this fancy condo, or drive those expensive cars? You don't have to work so much. We could even move back to Birch Valley." Maggie's voice softened as she offered her solution.

"Are you kidding me? Maggie, I have worked so hard, and I'm about to finally make it. You can't expect me to throw that away."

"So you would rather throw us away?" Maggie asked sadly.

Michael rolled his eyes. "There is just no winning with you. You can go back home to Birch Valley if you want, but I'm staying here, in our home, where you and our children belong."

"Why should I stay when you aren't ever here?"

"Then go."

Maggie's heart broke, her insides shriveling at the thought of leaving her husband. What made it worse was that he was willing to let her go. Standing there, Maggie watched as Michael grabbed his briefcase and keys and sailed through the door.

***

Melanie smiled as she happily waved goodbye to Maggie before skipping into the large school. Maggie watched her join the other students, feeling her heart break at the thought of having to disrupt her daughter's life. School would be ending in June, over three months remained. Maggie knew she couldn't wait that long to move back to Birch Valley. She knew that the fighting between her and Michael was only going to continue, and she didn't want it to start affecting their daughter more than it already had.

Typing a text to her husband, extending a virtual

olive branch, she waited to hear back from him. Her phone buzzed, he simply wrote back that he was working. Maggie exhaled sadly as her eyes absorbed his message. So that was it, he had made his choice, so she made hers.

Leaving the school parking lot, she headed in the direction for one of her favorite spots in Seattle, a quiet little park that was tucked away in an older neighborhood. The park had a fantastic view of the Sound. Located right on the sand of a cozy inlet of water, it offered her the solitude she needed right now. When Maggie arrived, not a soul was there. She headed toward the faded, green painted metal stairs that led down to the beach. An enormous, washed up log that sat alongside pieces of driftwood stood out to her. It looked like the perfect spot to sit and stare out at the salty sea water. She trudged through the thick sand, the wind tangling her long hair as it whipped all around. She wrapped her sweater tighter around her, pulling it close to her chest, and she sat and let out a huge sigh.

Her phone rang. After a brief conversation, Maggie hung up the phone. She had finished talking to her mother, who surprisingly was not at all on her side. Maggie stated her case, explained her side, but Mary remained firm that leaving Michael was not the best course of action. But in true Mary O'Brien fashion she offered for Maggie and Melanie to move in, and offered any help she could lend. She may not agree with Maggie, but she was still lending her support.

It was decided that Maggie would pack up some of her and Melanie's belongings and move to Birch

Valley by the following weekend.

***

The week carried on. Michael stayed away from their home for the most part, coming in late and leaving early. He avoided Maggie and only interacted with Melanie on the few evenings where he was home at a decent hour before their daughter's bedtime. The chilly distance and tension was almost unbearable.

Maggie attempted several times to reach out to Michael on the morning she was leaving, hoping he would beg for her to stay and fight to change her mind. He never did. She loaded her car with several suitcases, her heart aching as she filled the trunk. Maggie was worried that this might be the end of her marriage.

Chapter Five

Melanie had been complaining all morning from the backseat; she was not at all thrilled about this new adventure they were embarking on. The drive had taken its toll on Maggie, her nerves were shot, and she silently prayed for strength.

"I don't want to go to school in Birch Valley, Mom," she whined.

"Mel, it might be fun. I went to that school when I was your age, so did all of your uncles," Maggie said, hoping to reassure her child.

"Yeah, but I like my school. I want to go back home."

"Melanie, we're going to go and stay with Grams for a little while." Maggie felt awful, regret was starting to sink in as she got closer to her destination.

Why hadn't Michael stopped her? Why couldn't he see that all Maggie wanted was for him to be home, and that she needed him to be present in their lives? She knew how hard he worked. He didn't have to, she wasn't the kind of woman that expected him to hand her the world on a silver platter. She only wanted him.

The highway was fairly clear, it was midmorning, and there weren't too many cars on the road. The sun was shining in front of them as they headed eastbound toward the thick line of trees where Birch Valley lay nestled.

Maggie cruised onto the street where her childhood home proudly sat. Pulling along the curb, she heard Melanie let out a huff.

"It will be okay, sweetie."

"I just to want to see Grams," Melanie said, her tone dismissive and cold, not much different from Michael's.

Mary was standing on the porch of the Craftsman style home, wearing her favorite apron and smiling wide. Melanie fled the car and bounded up the stairs to her grandmother. Maggie watched as her mother practically scooped up Melanie.

"Daniel's home, want him to help unload the car?" Mary offered, Melanie clinging at her round waist.

"That would be great, Mom." Maggie unlatched the trunk and started pulling suitcases out and setting them on the street. She felt energized despite being emotionally worn out. The morning sickness had been slowly improving, and Maggie was grateful to the little one for laying off.

Daniel ran toward Maggie, a concerned look on his normally jovial face. "Hey, don't be lifting all those suitcases."

"Daniel, I'm not helpless. Just pregnant."

Daniel snatched the suitcases effortlessly, his

strong arms hoisting up several of the bags as he went to the house.

Maggie followed, slightly annoyed, carrying only her purse and a small bag.

Mary was standing in the entryway to greet her. "I cleared out the sewing room, and am setting that room up for Melanie. The boys set up a bed for her. You can stay in your room, I figured you might want your own space."

"Thanks," Maggie replied as she hugged her mother, the threat of tears stinging in her eyes.

"It'll be okay, love," Mary promised quietly.

"I know, Mom, it's just so hard. He didn't speak to me all week, he pretty much stayed away from the house, Melanie is so mad at me for moving us here," Maggie rambled, her emotions going every which way.

"Melanie, it will be okay, but you can't blame her for being upset. Give her time," Mary continued. "As for Michael, same thing I suppose. He's hurt too, and you just need to give it all some time."

"I'm hurt too, Mom. I didn't want this, I feel like I had to do something to try and get him to take me seriously. It's like he doesn't even care."

Mary frowned. "Maggie, of course he cares. I have the water on for some tea. Why don't you go freshen up and meet me in the kitchen?"

That was always her mother's way of solving things: tea and some sort of scrumptious baked good. Maggie felt alone in her feelings, no one seemed to understand where she was coming from. Her husband and daughter were upset with her, her mother sure as heck didn't agree with her, and Maggie realized there was probably only one person who might actually be on her side, and that was Liam.

"Mom, I'm thinking I might go over to Liam's, if that's okay. Do you mind watching Mel for a little bit?" Maggie asked.

Maggie could hear Melanie's feet running toward her.

"Why can't I go to Uncle Liam's house?"

"You can a little later," Maggie answered as she tried to reach out for Melanie.

Melanie glared at Maggie. "But I want to see him now."

Maggie wasn't used to her daughter acting out, it was completely out of character, but she couldn't deny she had a great part in it.

"I need to run a couple of errands, you just stay here with Grams."

Melanie rolled her eyes and shuffled to the living room.

Maggie turned to her mother and offered her an apologetic glance. "Sorry."

"She'll be fine," Mary reassured her. "Can you tell Liam to please invite Rachel to dinner tomorrow?"

"No problem, Mom." Maggie kissed her mother and hurried out the door.

***

Maggie turned into Liam's gravel driveway, the tiny rocks crunching under her tires. The tamarack trees were turning a brilliant green, the yellows of fall and winter almost forgotten. The pines stood proudly in their constant state of evergreen, and as Maggie got out of her car, she could see Liam's frozen lake had just about melted, and several large Canadian geese sat like buoys in the cold water.

Liam emerged from his cabin and announced, "I thought I heard someone pull up."

Maggie hugged Liam, who towered over her.

"You doing okay?" Liam asked.

"I guess so, I mean, not really, to be completely honest," Maggie replied, wrapping her slender arms across her chest, a sudden chill rippling through her.

"Have you talked to him yet?"

Maggie shook her head. "Not yet, he really didn't want much to do with me last week. Melanie is giving me some trouble now too. Oh, Liam." The tears started before she finished.

Liam reached for his sister again. "Things will work out, Mags," he whispered.

"I hope so."

"You want to go to lunch?" Liam offered.

Maggie looked up at her brother. Why was food always the O'Brien solution to a problem? Her stomach growled at the invitation.

"Herrick's?"

"Where else?" Liam grinned.

***

The bell on the weathered piece of yarn chimed as they entered; that same bell had hung over the entrance to Herrick's ever since Liam and Maggie could remember. The diner was a popular eating spot for pretty much the entire town. The atmosphere might be dated, but the food was excellent. As usual, the place was packed, but Liam managed to find a booth near one of the large windows that let in an ample amount of sunlight.

A waitress approached and took their order, quickly returning with their beverages.

Maggie tore open a sugar packet and dumped it into her iced tea. Liam took a long sip of his cola.

"So, how are things going with you and Rachel?" Maggie inquired, looking out at the other customers in the diner.

Liam smirked. "Good, I guess. We didn't see too much of each other this last week."

"Yeah, sorry, probably my fault," Maggie commented, feeling a twinge of guilt.

"Nah, usually at work Rachel tries to avoid me. Granted, it did throw us for a loop when Mom said you were moving back."

"I know, but I didn't know what else to do. Michael has hardly talked to me, Melanic hates me right now. I feel like Mom is so disappointed in my choice. I guess I'm a little overwhelmed."

"Well, I'm glad you are back. I just wish things were a little different and that Michael was here too."

"Me too," Maggie said, her eyes filling with relentless tears.

"So, you going to have Mel start school this Monday?" Liam quickly changed the subject.

Maggie cleared her throat. "That's the plan. She isn't thrilled about it."

"Well, I think once she sees me, and maybe even Rachel, she'll be singing a different tune."

"I sure hope so."

The waitress arrived with two plates piled high with golden French fries and large sandwiches.

Maggie's eyes bulged at the amount of food being placed in front of her. "Wow, have their servings always this big?"

"Yep." Liam grabbed his enormous roast beef sandwich.

Grabbing her club sandwich, she bit off a large mouthful. "This is so good."

Liam nodded in agreement.

Maggie felt much better after lunch with her brother. They chatted about a lot of things, enjoying their meal, and sharing a number of laughs. Maggie started to feel better about her decision to move back home.

***

Arriving back to the O'Brien house, Maggie entered quietly. She could hear distant chatter emitting from the kitchen. When she peeked in, she saw her daughter and mother elbow deep in some sort of batter. The smile on Melanie's face caught Maggie's heart. It felt good to see her smiling. It also swarmed Maggie with guilt.

She let out a false cough. "Hey, what are you guys up to?" Maggie asked.

Mary smiled. "My girl and I decided to make a pie for dessert. She has the dough for the crust just about mastered."

"Wow, good job, Melanie," Maggie praised.

Melanie's smile started to disappear when she locked eyes with Maggie. "Grams and I are having a lot of fun cooking."

"Well, that's good. I think you are becoming a much better cook than me."

Mary laughed. "I tried my hardest to teach you, Maggie. You were more interested in painting or playing in the river."

"Can you blame me? Not like I get to do any of that now," Maggie replied.

"One of the gals from my book club mentioned that the community center is going to be offering a painting class. Maybe you should look into it," Mary suggested as she removed clinging dough from her hands.

"Maybe, probably not the best time right now." Maggie motioned to her daughter. Her mother seemed to understand.

"Well, something to consider eventually."

"I guess. I'll let you guys finish with that pie. I might go lay down for a bit," Maggie said. To say she was exhausted would be an understatement. This pregnancy was proving to be a whole lot different than her first.

"Okay, dear, I will check on you when dinner's ready," Mary stated, turning her attention to her granddaughter. "Melanie, you ready to roll this dough out?"

Melanie nodded her head in excited agreement. Maggie stole a glance at her before heading to her bedroom.

***

Maggie slept most of Saturday away. Mary kept her promise and did check on her. She was too tired to even think about eating, opting to remain sheltered beneath the warm blankets. Maggie continued to sleep for the rest of the night.

Before she knew it, morning light filtered through the room, forcing Maggie's eyes to open. Regardless of how much sleep she had yesterday, her body cried out for more. She could hear some activity down the hall, and remembered it was Sunday. Her parents and Grandpa Paddy were probably getting ready to head out to church, something she hadn't done since she lived here as teenager.

Melanie burst through the bedroom door with an energy that only a six-year-old could possess that early in the day.

"Mom, are getting up yet? Grams is going to take me to church. Do you want to go with us?" Her small face was hopeful.

"Maybe next Sunday. I still feel super tired, I think I might stay in bed a little longer."

Her daughter's disappointment was apparent. "Okay. Grandpa Paddy says we are going to breakfast afterward." Maggie could tell her daughter was trying her hardest to persuade her.

"I think maybe next Sunday, sweetie. I think all that driving really tuckered me out. Have a good time and eat a pancake for me." Maggie welcomed the hug that Melanie offered. Breathing in the warm scent of her child, she squeezed Melanie lightly and whispered, "I love you."

"Love you too, Mom." Melanie ran off in search of her grandmother.

Maggie yawned and felt her eyes grow heavy. Before she knew it, her mind had wandered into a dream.

***

Sunday dinner at the O'Brien house proved to be even louder than usual. In the large living room, Melanie and her cousins, Finn and Connor, had their Uncle Daniel pinned on the ground like professional wrestlers. Liam had brought Rachel over to partake in the craziness that was their family. Patrick was in the den with the older O'Brien men, going over business dealings.

Maggie helped Mary in the kitchen, gathering dishes to set the table. Rachel was quick to volunteer to help, leaving Liam to be tackled by one of the three-year-old twins.

"Good grief, was it always this wild here for dinner?" Maggie asked as she placed bowls around the large family table.

Rachel laughed and added silverware by each bowl. "I like it. Growing up, my house was never like this."

Mary smiled as she busied herself stirring the contents in an enormous stainless steel pot, adding a dash of spices. "When you were younger, Maggie, you and your brothers were always running around here like a pack of wild animals."

"Funny, I don't remember that," Maggie said.

Rachel chimed in, "At my house, my dad was always working, and my mom was usually out with her friends. My brother was busy getting into trouble, and I just hung out and read loads of books."

Mary turned off the chili, which had been simmering most of the day. She pulled out a cast iron pan filled with cornbread. "Dinner is ready, if you guys want to round up the family."

Everyone approved of the delicious meal. The children gobbled down their food and ran off to play. Most of the adults were working on their second helping of chili, laughing and sharing stories.

Maggie felt the familiar vibration of her cell phone as it buzzed in her jean pocket. Reaching awkwardly in her seat to retrieve it, she saw that it was Michael calling. She had ignored him for the last two days and hesitated to answer this one. Excusing herself from the table, she answered, "Hello."

"Maggie."

"Michael, what do you want?" Maggie instantly felt herself annoyed with him.

"I'm actually surprised you picked up. I have been calling you for almost two days," he complained.

"I don't really know that there is a whole lot to discuss right now. I needed some time to think."

"How's Melanie?" Michael asked softly.

"She's doing fine, busy playing with her cousins right now. Do you want me to get her so you can talk to her?" Maggie offered.

"It's okay, I really just wanted to check in with you."

"I'm fine. We're fine," Maggie retorted, but she wasn't all that sure she was fine. She knew that their daughter wasn't exactly fine either.

"I don't know if I'm fine. I think you guys need to come home. I miss you both."

Maggie could hear the loneliness in her husband's voice, and a part of her wanted to run right back home, but to what? To Michael never being there, to basically being a single parent, to living a lonely existence?

"Michael, I think we still need some time to figure things out."

"Can't we work on things here?" he pleaded.

Maggie countered, "Isn't that what we've been doing?"

She could hear Michael release a long sigh. "I don't know. I just feel like you should be home, here in Seattle."

"Well, I disagree. I'm sorry, but I need you to figure out your priorities. That is something I have been asking you to do for a long time."

"Maggie, I don't feel like you are being fair. Everything I do is for our family. You are pregnant with our second child. You are keeping our daughter away from me. What do you want me to do?"

"Michael, I've got to go. I don't want to discuss this anymore right now/" Maggie hung up the phone, and she felt a mixture of guilt and irritation as she started to return to the kitchen.

Her mother was at the sink rinsing dirty, chili-encrusted bowls as Rachel was wiping down the large table.

Looking at Maggie, Mary asked, "Everything, okay, dear?"

Rachel stopped cleaning and waited for Maggie's reply.

"I don't know." Maggie's answer was honest. She had no clue how to handle this whole mess with Michael.

"Was it Michael that called?" Mary asked cautiously, turning the faucet off and facing Maggie. Rachel approached, concern etched on her face.

Maggie nodded. "Yeah. He wanted to talk, but I don't know, I just can't."

"Was he asking you to come back home?" Rachel inquired as she reached out to stroke Maggie's arm.

"He wants us to come back. Of course I feel guilty because he brought up the pregnancy and Melanie. I don't know, I just don't want to be there anymore."

"I understand, but it has to be lonely for him without you or Melanie there," Mary pointed out, taking her daughter's hand in her own. "I know you weren't happy there, dear, but running away isn't the answer."

"Mom, I'm not running away. I have tried to make it work for a long time," Maggie said defensively.

"Maggie, I was thinking it might fun to grab dinner one night," Rachel suggested. She must have sensed Maggie's discomfort.

Maggie smiled. "That would be great, I'd really like that."

She was thankful that Rachel was trying to redirect the conversation, she wasn't in the mood to defend her actions to her mother, who plainly didn't agree with her. This was her battle, her mess to figure out.

The evening started to wind down; the home was no longer the loud and rambunctious place it had been only hours ago. Patrick and the twins had left, and Daniel vanished shortly after to go hang out with a couple of his buddies. Liam and Rachel were in the process of leaving, still lingering over tea with Mary and Maggie in the dining room.

"Mary, you are making me fat," Rachel claimed as she finished a homemade scone.

"Nonsense, you could use a little meat around those bones."

Turning to Maggie, Rachel asked, "Is Melanie going to start school this week?"

"I'm going in tomorrow to register her."

"Is she excited at all?" Rachel asked cautiously.

"Honestly, not really." Maggie knew Melanie wasn't thrilled at all about starting school in Birch Valley, she knew her daughter would much rather be at home, at her old school.

Liam looked back at her, concern sitting in his eyes. "You know, we just need to give her a little time."

Rachel patted Liam's arm. "I think she will love going to the same school her uncle teaches at."

"She's pretty fond of you too, Rachel," Liam said as he looked lovingly at Rachel.

Maggie watched the interaction between the two. She was happy for Liam, and truly hoped this new relationship turned into a marriage. Not that she could talk, as her marriage was in complete shambles.

When she looked at a thin silver watch on her wrist, Maggie saw that she needed to get Melanie ready for bed. "I better go tuck in Mel. Good night you guys," Maggie said.

They smiled at her and in unison said, "We'll see you at school tomorrow." Maggie could hear them giggle as she left the room.

Chapter Six

"I don't want to go," Melanie stomped her foot hard against the concrete sidewalk just outside the elementary school.

"Melanie, please don't act like this. Uncle Liam and Rachel are here, and they're very excited about you going to school here." Maggie was frustrated, the entire morning had been one battle after another with Melanie. First, breakfast, her daughter didn't want the oatmeal her grandmother made her, then, when it came time to get washed up and dressed, she flat out refused to cooperate. Maggie was at her wits end with this child.

"I don't care, I want to go home."

"Look, Mel, we came to Birch Valley to see how living here might be. Think of this as a science experiment. Remember how much you love science?" Maggie was trying desperately to coax her daughter into the school as she heard a loud bell ring in the distance. Students rushed past them, hurrying inside. "Come on, sweetie, let's give this a try." Maggie offered her hand to Melanie.

Melanie pouted her lip, accepted Maggie's hand, and they entered the school.

***

"Well, if it isn't Maggie O'Brien, oh wait, it's…" Karen, the school secretary, said as she made her way towards them.

"Trembley now," Maggie answered as she was hugged.

Karen crouched down to Melanie's level, smiling. "This must be Melanie. Your uncle told me that you might be coming in today."

Melanie nodded. "He's a teacher."

"I know, and a very good one," Karen responded, then continued, "Did you know I worked here when your uncle and mom were kids?"

Melanie smiled. "That's neat."

"Well, I think it's pretty neat that you are going to start school here too." Karen started to lead Melanie to a counter that was just across the foyer. Maggie trailed after them, watching Karen quickly earning Melanie's trust.

Maggie took a moment to absorb her surroundings. Little had changed since she was girl here. On the large wall was the same Lewis and Clark expedition mural, the framed pictures of the staff proudly mounted on another wall, and the polished concrete floor that reflected the overhead lights, which seemed to sparkle. The building smelled exactly the same as she remembered, an ancient wood smell mixed with food being cooked in the cafeteria that was directly to the left of the foyer. It did feel strange being back, let alone having her child start attending class here. Who knew, maybe the child inside her would also be a student here?

Karen's sweet voice broke Maggie away from her nostalgic thoughts. "Now, Maggie, if I could have you start filling out some of these forms, I'm going to take Melanie on a mini tour of our school." She grabbed Melanie's little hand in hers and started to lead her toward the cafeteria.

Maggie went to work on filling out the paperwork that Karen had left for her. She couldn't help but notice how permanent this seemed. She was partially through the first form when she saw that Rachel was headed in her direction.

"Maggie, how's it going?" Rachel flashed a smile of stark white, perfect teeth.

"Just filling out these forms that Karen gave me."

"Good. Where is your little cutie pie?" Rachel asked as she scanned the area for Melanie.

"Off on a tour of the school. You wouldn't believe how much trouble she gave me this morning."

"Really? I'm sorry. I was hoping she'd be a little more excited." Rachel frowned, her blue eyes sympathetic.

"It'll be okay," Maggie said, changing gears. "So I have been wanting to ask, how are things going with you and Liam?"

Rachel rolled her eyes and let out a sigh. "You know, it's hard. We are trying to find the balance between work and play, if that makes sense. I don't feel comfortable acting like we are a couple at work, your brother feels differently."

"Well, lucky for you, you live here now and folks don't really worry about stuff like that," Maggie said, trying to convince her.

"I don't know, I still feel uncomfortable. We are just trying to take things slow and sort of see how it all plays out."

Maggie nodded. "Understandable."

"So how are you holding up?"

"It changes by the minute." Maggie let out an awkward, uncomfortable laugh.

Rachel rubbed Maggie's arm tenderly. "It has to be rough. I'm hoping things work out."

"Me too."

Another bell sounded, and Rachel glanced at the thin, silver watch on her delicate wrist. "Crud, I've got to get going. I have a meeting with the district later." Rachel started to turn back down the hallway where her office was located, but then she turned back around. "Maggie, I'm really glad you're here now. Let's make sure we get together this week for dinner."

"You bet, that would be great."

***

Maggie waited patiently for school to let out. She stood outside the large glass double doors along with a string of parents that had lined up to pick up their children. The day almost felt normal, except it was anything but. She had signed up Melanie for school, which went surprisingly well, and she had

Karen to thank for charming her little daughter into falling in love with the school. She really owed that woman. Leaving Melanie at the school and coming to pick her up felt normal, but after getting into another argument over the phone with Michael it reminded her that things were not the norm. She wasn't in Seattle, she wasn't home, no, she was staying at her parents' house. She was married, yet her husband wasn't with her, and after their argument she wasn't sure if she saw herself being married for much longer.

The loud shrill of the school bell tore Maggie's thoughts away. She searched for Melanie as students started to emerge from the large brick building. A feeling of dread started to form in her stomach as the number of students leaving the building became more of a trickle. Where was Melanie? As Maggie was about to go inside the building, Melanie appeared, holding hands with her uncle. Liam towered over his niece, his long legs having to take half steps so that the girl could keep up with his stride. As she eyed her daughter coming in her direction, she could tell Melanie looked happy. Maybe things would work out and be okay.

"Hi, sweetie, how was school?" Maggie asked in an upbeat tone.

"It was good." Melanie looked up at Liam, who stood happily next to her.

"She did good, recess rumor is that she made a lot of friends," Liam said, causing Melanie to giggle.

"That's great, honey. Why don't you go to the car? I wanted to chat with Uncle Liam for a minute." There were only a couple of cars in the parking lot, mainly belonging to staff. All the buses had already left for the day. It amazed Maggie how quickly the school became eerily quiet, almost like a ghost town.

Melanie looked both ways before stepping off the curb toward their car, which was parked only about twenty feet away.

Maggie turned to Liam and asked, "So how did she do?"

"Good. She seems to really like her teacher. The kids were working on St. Patrick's Day decorations for the town celebration, and her teacher said Melanie dove right in," Liam answered.

"I have been so worried about her all day. She was in quite the mood this morning, and then I had it out with Michael today."

"Yeah, she's going to be okay. I showed her my classroom, she says it isn't nearly as pretty as her teacher's room."

Maggie laughed. "Oh, really?"

"All in all a good day, I promise you. It will get better, Mags. You've got to have faith, especially if you felt that moving back was the right call," Liam said, trying to reassure her.

Maggie turned to check on Melanie, and she saw that her daughter was buckled in and reading a book. She turned back to Liam and said, "I saw Rachel today."

"I see her almost everyday," Liam teased.

"I know you do, but it was nice for me to see her, Liam."

"It's nice for me too."

Maggie lightly slugged her brother in the arm. "Stop being a brat." She smiled as Liam rubbed his arm, feigning injury. She continued, "As I was trying to say, I really like her. Rachel and I are going to try and have dinner this week."

"Can I tag along?" His eyes were hopeful.

"Nope. You see her every day, remember?"

"Yeah, but it's way more fun to see her away from this place." He gestured toward the school.

"The answer is still no. Well, I'd better get Melanie home. Thanks for letting me know how she did." Maggie hugged him and then walked to her car.

***

Melanie and Maggie survived the rest of the week. Melanie was beginning to make friends at school, and had even been invited to a play date that weekend. Things were finally beginning to look up. Maggie did find herself a little restless; there was only so much she could do at her mother's house. If staying here was going to become permanent, she needed to come up with a game plan and figure out a way to support herself and her children.

Maggie pulled up next to her parents' home when she saw her brothers out in the driveway. They were standing around and talking, grins plastered on their faces. She had just finished with Melanie's play date at the park and had done a little grocery shopping on the way home.

"Hey, guys." Maggie waved and started to open the trunk of her car, and her brothers all jogged toward her to help. Melanie got out of the car quickly and ran to give each of them a hug before scurrying off toward the house.

Each man grabbed a couple of bags and followed Maggie into the home. They deposited the groceries in the kitchen, and Maggie worked on putting them away. Her brothers plopped down around the dining table.

"So, how was the play date?" Patrick asked.

"I think she had a good time." Maggie folded a paper sack in half and started a pile as she emptied each bag of its contents.

"That's good. Finn and Connor love having her around too," Patrick said.

Liam cleared his throat and cautiously asked, "Mags, any word from Michael?"

Maggie rolled her eyes. She hadn't talked to him all week, and when he had called she'd given the phone over to Melanie. Maggie didn't have a whole lot to say to him, but she didn't want to deny Michael or Melanie their time. Michael had made himself quite clear that he was unhappy that Maggie had already enrolled their daughter in school. He was more than a little upset, to say the least.

"I haven't really talked to him, why?"

"I don't know, we were just curious how things were going," Liam continued. "I know Mel is settling in nicely at school, and we were sort of curious about what your plans were."

"My plans?"

Daniel chimed in, "Yeah, like do you think you might need a job?"

"Well, eventually, I suppose. I don't really know

what's going to happen." Her voice was turning shaky. Earlier, her mind had been working out the details of her new life, but she knew at some point decisions were going to have to be made.

Patrick spoke next. "Maggie, we wanted to see if you would be interested in possibly coming to work down at the shop."

"What happened to your receptionist?" They had her attention now. At first she thought her brothers were just meddling, but they were actually trying to throw her a lifeline.

"She's moving to Spokane, I guess she met some guy out there or something," Daniel answered. "What's for dinner by the way? I'm starved. Did Mom say when she was going to be back?"

"No, she didn't say, she's with her book club ladies. I was thinking of making spaghetti. You good with that?" Maggie offered as she started to set out the fixings for dinner.

Daniel nodded in agreement. "Yeah, that sounds great."

"So do you think you might be interested?" Patrick asked.

"Maybe, I mean I can work up until the baby is born for sure. I'd be happy to help you out. At the least until you find a replacement."

"Great, we would appreciate the help for sure. I remember when you used to help out down there when we were teenagers, so it'll be a piece of cake." Patrick seemed happy that Maggie was agreeing to work there.

"I actually appreciate you guys offering the position to me, I have been kind of going a little nuts here. There isn't a whole lot for me to do while Mel is at school."

"Well, that's perfect, we're helping you, and you're helping us. Everyone wins," Daniel said as he stretched and rose from his chair.

Maggie started dinner as Daniel and Patrick got up to leave. "I'll let you guys know when it's ready. Patrick, are you sticking around for dinner?"

"Yeah, the boys love spaghetti." Patrick smiled as he followed Daniel.

Liam remained at the table. "Do you need any help with dinner?"

"Um, you can help with the salad I guess, and maybe open these dang jars of sauce." Maggie was straining as tried to twist the lid off. She smacked the bottom of the jar, but to no avail. Liam got up and took the jar from her, and her gentle giant of a brother took the lid off with ease. "Thanks."

"So that's pretty neat about the job, right?"

"Yeah, it's sweet of you guys to think of me. I guess I just feel like that might make this whole thing with Michael real." Maggie could feel her voice catching on the lump forming in her throat.

"I know, it's weird having Mel go to school here. I see her in the halls, and she comes by my class sometimes on her way to recess. It's great and sort of how I had always hoped it would be, but I've got to admit it's a little strange," he said.

Maggie nodded. "Dropping her off at school the first couple of days was really hard. You know, when we are here it just feels like when we used to come and visit, except now she has her own room."

"What are you and Michael going to do?"

"I think time is really the only answer for now. He's welcome to come here. I want him to be in our lives. I still love him, Liam," Maggie said. She could feel hot tears burning in her eyes.

Liam scooped her into a hug. "I know you do. I can't imagine what you are going through, but I hope things get better."

Maggie hugged her brother back, wiping the wetness from her cheeks. She took the jar of sauce, adding it to the large stainless steel pot. "Enough about me. How are things going with you and Rachel?"

"Good. Her friend is coming up to visit next month. She was supposed to get in this week, but I guess she is known for changing her mind. I'm a little nervous to meet her, to be honest."

"Really? Are you talking about her friend Chelsea? Rachel told me all about her, she sounds like a fun girl and one of Rachel's best friends," Maggie responded as she stirred the simmering contents in the pot, the sweet, tomato laden aroma filling the kitchen. She took out a tablespoon from the drawer and sampled it, then went in search for some herbs to add to the sauce.

"Starting to smell good," Liam commented as he pulled out an enormous serving bowl to put some salad fixings in.

"Anyway, I wouldn't be too nervous about meeting her friend."

"I know, it's just our relationship is pretty new and…"

"Are you worried because it's someone from California?"

Liam started chopping away at the head of lettuce and looked like he was considering what Maggie just said. "Maybe a little. I mean, at first I wasn't so thrilled with Rachel being from there."

"Well, I'm sure her friend is kind and wonderful just like Rachel, otherwise how could they have been friends this long?"

"I guess you're probably right."

"Besides, I'm sure Rachel is excited to show you off." Maggie hoped the little confidence builder was enough to reassure her brother. She could see his cheeks blush a soft pink.

***

The morning before St. Patrick's Day was cold, the sky a wicked gray with thick white streaks of angry-looking clouds. Rain drops started to splatter the windshield of Maggie's car as she went to take Melanie to school. Maggie prayed the weather would improve, the town would be holding its annual celebration of the holiday that weekend. The Pacific Northwest's spring weather was well known for the storms that would violently pass through, only to have the sun come out fighting, shining brightly as though not a raindrop had been spilt. You just never knew what to expect.

After waving good bye to Melanie, she drove toward her brothers' shop. It was only a few blocks away, and by the time her car pulled next to Patrick's truck the sun was out and quickly drinking up the wetness left behind from the passing storm.

"Morning, guys," Maggie announced happily as

she hung her lightweight coat on the metal hooks by the entry.

Patrick leaned against the counter, coffee mug securely in hand as he gazed at a small stack of invoices. "Morning," he replied, not even looking up. Maggie could tell he hadn't had enough caffeine yet to actually interact with others.

Daniel was gathering several tools to load into the work truck for the job they had to do that day. "Hey, Maggie, is it still raining?"

"Nope, it's already clearing up."

"Good, it looked nasty out there earlier." Daniel smiled as he spoke.

Maggie worked her way behind the counter and sat at the desk. She turned on the computer monitor and looked at her brothers. They were both so different: Patrick, always moody and serious, Daniel, joyful and happy. She wondered how these two men were able to work so well together, when they were such complete opposites. She had been helping out at the shop for a little over two weeks and she'd been able to watch her brothers in action. Patrick ran a tight ship, much like their father and Grandpa Paddy had. He was all business. She would catch him laughing, but only after Daniel had finally cracked his professional exterior. Daniel ran around the shop with an efficiency she didn't know he possessed. He knew where every single tool was kept, what its purpose was, and tried teaching Maggie things when times were quiet and he was busy organizing everything. Maggie enjoyed her part in the whole operation, answering phones, setting up appointments, and making sure there was plenty of coffee waiting for the guys when they returned from a job. Granted, she handled invoices and other paperwork, but a lot of the time she sat at her desk letting her mind wander with games of solitaire on the computer. She was thankful her brothers offered the job to her. She was starting to squirrel away a little money and felt satisfied that this could be a part of her future.

The shop was quiet after Daniel and Patrick left. She knew they would be gone most of the day today, and she prayed the weather would be kind to them. She was stapling some statements together when the phone rang.

"Good morning, thank you for calling O'Brien Construction, how can I help you?" Her voice was professional and warm.

"Good morning, dear," Mary replied.

"Hey, Mom, how's it going?"

"Splendid. I was hoping I could steal you away on your lunch?"

Maggie smiled. With her working during the day, she found herself spending less time with her mother, and was actually starting to miss her company. "Sure, Mom."

"Herrick's?" Mary offered.

"Sure, sounds great. You want to meet me here?"

"I'll come by the shop, say, around one. Will that work for you?"

Maggie looked at their large, white dry erase board. They used it to keep the day's work organized so that way everyone was on the same page and knew what was going on. The board looked clear for one, and for most of the afternoon.

"One is fine, Mom. See you then." Maggie hung up the phone. She was delighted to spend her lunch hour with Mary. Her belly was already growling for food, she could almost taste one of Herrick's golden fries, cooked to absolute perfection. She eyed the clock above the dry erase board; it was only a little after nine.

***

Maggie had just beat another round of solitaire on the computer when her mother arrived at the shop.

"Hello, dear," Mary said. "You ready to get some lunch? I'm starved."

Maggie smiled. "Great, let me grab my coat. You want to take my car?"

"That's fine, or we can walk?"

"It was pouring earlier, I don't trust this weather," Maggie replied.

Mary nodded and followed Maggie out to her car. Once they were inside, Mary ran her hand slowly against the caramel-colored leather interior. "Such a lovely car, Maggie."

"I remember when Michael picked it out, I told him I was fine with my other car, but he insisted that I needed this one." Maggie felt sick at the memory. She recalled them purchasing her previous car only a couple of years before this one. That car was equally stunning, and it had been her first actual "new" car. For some reason Michael felt like she needed the one she drove now, it was more expensive and had so many features that Maggie never even touched. She regretted the purchase because she knew what the car payments were like on this type of luxury sedan, and that meant her husband had to work harder to provide something she didn't really need.

"Have you talked to him lately?"

Not bothering to reply as she drove a little faster to the dinner, Maggie worried that this was what their lunch date might entail. She knew her mother only wanted the best outcome and was considering everyone involved. Maggie knew she was acting a little selfish, and it tore her up inside keeping Melanie away from Michael. But the door was open, and when he finally figured out that family meant more than work, she would be waiting.

They pulled into the parking lot of their favorite place to eat. When Mary took hold of Maggie's hand as they walked to the door, it reminded Maggie of when she was a child. Once they entered the aging building, the warm smells and loud chatter of the customers greeted them. They worked their way to a booth near the large windows that looked out to the street.

"What do you suppose you will have today, dear? What does that grandchild of mine in there want?" Mary said as she motioned toward Maggie's belly.

Maggie laughed. "I was craving some fries, but now I'm thinking I may go with their chowder." She shivered. Warm soup sounded excellent on this stormy day.

"You know, that sounds wonderful. I think I could go for a bowl of that myself."

The waitress appeared shortly and took their orders, promising to return with two glasses of water for them.

Mary sighed. "I know you don't feel like discussing Michael, but I really feel like we should."

"Oh, Mom, I'm not quite sure what to say. I just started working at the shop, Mel's in school now and making friends. Things are going pretty well, considering."

"Maggie, I'm glad you are helping your brothers, but I'm trying to look at the future, the bigger picture." Mary smiled at the waitress as she returned with their drinks.

"I'm not looking too far into the future because honestly I have no idea what that will hold. For now, I know a couple of things: I'm here in Birch Valley, Mel is in school and around people who love her, and that I want a future with Michael, just not in Seattle." Maggie's tone was firm.

"Well, no use discussing it any further I suppose. We love and support you, but I do hope you can work things out with Michael."

Their soup came to them steaming hot, contained in large homemade bread bowls. Maggie inhaled the sharp scent of the clams, and dug right into the creamy goodness that sat before her.

"This soup is amazing," Maggie said as she savored the rich flavors.

Mary nodded in agreement. Lunch continued with more neutral conversation, which was an enormous relief. Maggie drove them back to the shop and Mary got into her own car after hugging her tight. There was no shortage of love in her family.

***

The sunshine was out on full display the next morning, which also happened to be the morning of St. Patrick's Day, as Maggie and Melanie walked to the school. Maggie was a little hesitant to make the trek to school considering yesterday's temperamental weather. As they entered the aging brick building, the inside was fully decorated with various shades of green garland, there were leprechaun cut outs and shamrocks of every color of green imaginable clinging to the walls. A banner with a giant painted rainbow made up of children's handprints which lead to a glittery pot of gold made Maggie smile.

"Mom, isn't that so pretty?" Melanie was in awe of the decorations. The community was primarily made up of Irish-Americans, and they went all out for St. Patrick's Day. The town celebrated with a fun parade and activities for the residents. Grandpa Paddy didn't see what all the fuss was about, back in his home country of Ireland they didn't celebrate the holiday the same way as Americans did. Suffice to say, green beer, corned beef, and cabbage were not something Maggie's grandfather grew up on, at least not until he arrived in America.

After gazing at and enjoying the decorations with Melanie, Maggie saw Rachel leaning against the counter chatting with Karen.

Karen smiled and excused herself to answer a

phone call back at her desk.

"Good morning, Miss Melanie. You look positively gorgeous in that green sweater," Rachel said happily and then went to hug Maggie. "How are you doing?" she whispered in her ear.

"I'm okay," Maggie answered as she pulled away. She was starting to get tired of everyone asking her how she was doing. She knew Rachel meant well, they all meant well, but she was sick of answering the question.

"Are we all ready for class today?" Rachel asked Melanie, patting the girl's rust-colored hair.

"I love her hair color," Rachel told Maggie as she ran her own slender fingers through her cropped blonde hair.

"Yeah, something we both inherited from Mom." Maggie swept her long chestnut hair back into the ponytail that was coming undone.

"Well, I think you both have beautiful hair," Rachel said to Melanie. The bell rang out loudly, and Melanie waved goodbye to both of them.

"So are you coming to the St. Pat's Day festival this weekend?" Maggie asked.

"Liam has been talking about it all week, so yes, we will be going." Rachel laughed.

"Great, I know my brothers have been working on a float for the parade." Maggie glanced at her watch and realized she needed to hurry to the shop. Her brothers didn't demand she be there at an exact time, but she did consider this job an actual job and didn't want to take advantage of their kindness either. "I'd better get to work. See you this weekend."

Work, it sounded funny coming out of her mouth, it had been such a long time since she had said the word.

Rachel smiled. "Well, I'll catch up with you later."

Maggie headed for the double glass doors. She waved at Karen, who was still on the phone, who returned the wave with a smile.

***

Maggie watched as Grandpa Paddy held Melanie's small hand, and their faces were amused and smiling. She could feel her heart swell as she gazed at them instead of the parade they were watching with much enthusiasm. Her parents each held the hand of one of Patrick's twins. The boys were not as interested in the parade; they were at that age where running around and jumping on everything had much more appeal. Maggie loved that their town did neat things like the parade, and she had tons of wonderful memories growing up in Birch Valley. She pulled out her cell phone and snapped a picture of her family without them noticing. The moment was too perfect not to capture.

She felt a sudden tap on her shoulder, and turned around to see Liam. Rachel was tucked behind him.

"Hey, guys," Maggie said, hugging Liam then Rachel.

"Wow, so this town doesn't mess around, this is quite the little festival," Rachel commented, her blue eyes wide as she took in her surroundings.

Maggie scanned the main street, seeing all the vendors set up on both sides. Residents dressed in various shades of green were lined up watching the parade. Shamrock-shaped green, white, and orange balloons were strung everywhere. Rachel was right, Birch Valley did a great job hosting such an event, but she hadn't seen anything yet. This was just for St. Patrick's Day. Wait until Rachel saw some of the major holiday celebrations.

Maggie caught sight of her brothers' float. They had volunteered their time decorating one of their flatbed work trucks to sponsor the high school. The truck was decked out in sparkly green and gold, and someone in a costume was dancing around dressed like a leprechaun on it. Maggie had to see Grandpa Paddy's reaction. She looked over and saw him laugh and grimace at the same time as he bent down to tell Melanie something.

"Oh, wow." Maggie giggled as Irish music blasted from the truck. She waved as she saw Patrick driving and Daniel tossing out candy out into the street for the children, who had been gathering sugary loot for the past twenty minutes.

Liam pulled Rachel close and asked, "Want to grab dinner later, Mags?"

She turned her head to look up at him. "What did you have in mind?"

"I don't know, maybe Herrick's or Antlers. I figure somewhere will be serving corned beef tonight."

"Rachel, what do you think?"

"You know, I haven't eaten corned beef before, so I'm game to try it," said Rachel.

"It's really good," Maggie assured her. The thought of the peppery taste and cabbage made her stomach growl. She was thankful that it didn't have the opposite effect. Lately she had had an insatiable hunger. Oh, the joys of pregnancy.

***

Maggie huffed as she looked at the rain pelting against the window of the shop. It had been raining for the last couple of weeks. She was tired of it, simple as that. It slowed work down for her brothers; they were helping construct a barn for a ranch, and this rain hindered their progress. Patrick had complained to the point where Maggie got the message loud and clear that she was not the only one sick of the constant drizzle.

Other than being frustrated with Mother Nature's torrent of precipitation, Maggie was somewhat starting to enjoy her new life, or at least making the best of her circumstances. She had been having dinners with Rachel, and sometimes Liam. Her friendship with Rachel made all the difference. That, and her job at the shop. Without her job, she would probably be moping around, dwelling on the fact that she was starting to really miss Michael. Maybe it was the surge of hormones, but as she slept at night she wished he was next to her. Perhaps it was because she was hanging out with Liam and Rachel, and seeing their interaction that made her crave that with Michael. Plus, seeing her parents display their love to one another only illustrated what her future with Michael should be like. Maggie was irritated that her marriage had been reduced to an occasional text or call for him to speak to Melanie. This was not how her life was supposed to turn out.

Chapter Seven

Spring was in full bloom in Birch Valley. Maggie could hear birds chirping loudly, the sky was a happy blue, and the sun shone brightly. That was the most important element about spring in Birch Valley. It meant no more snow, which also meant Maggie and Melanie could walk to school. She kept her fingers crossed that the rain would continue keeping its distance for a little while so they could enjoy the gorgeous weather.

Back in Seattle, they lived a good distance from Melanie's school, so Maggie would drop Melanie off, hit the gym, and run errands. She had stopped working out for the last month due to feeling like she was going to lose her breakfast at any given moment, and usually she did. Today, however, Maggie decided to take advantage of living close to the school and work, and getting a little exercise in felt great. It helped tremendously that her morning sickness had passed, and she was starting to feel human again. Maggie was thrilled when Melanie actually liked the idea of the two of them walking to school. Melanie's overall mood was pleasant this morning too, which was another bonus. Her mood had been improving slowly each week since they left Seattle. The only times Melanie seemed a little sad or upset with Maggie was when she would get off the phone with Michael. She knew it had to be terrible to be so far from her father.

"Can you hear all those birds?" Melanie asked sweetly.

"I can, aren't their songs lovely?"

"Yes, I love when birds sing. It's so pretty here, Mom." Melanie was practically skipping as she held onto Maggie's hand.

"I'm glad you think that. I loved growing up here." Maggie started to wonder why she had been in such a hurry to leave Birch Valley when she graduated high school.

"I wish Dad was here, though." Melanie's voice turned a little sad, but the light did not leave her eyes.

"I know, honey. Maybe someday," Maggie said as she steered them toward the school, which was only a couple blocks away.

Kissing her daughter goodbye, Maggie watched as Melanie scurried into the school with the other children. She felt the familiar vibration of her cell phone in her pocket.

"Hello?"

"Hi, Maggie."

"Good morning, Michael." Her tone was solid, not warm.

"You just take Mel to school?"

"Yes. Are you at work?" She was a little

surprised that he was calling her, especially this early in the day.

"Um, no, I'm at home today," he answered quickly. *Too quickly*.

Maggie started to walk away from the school. "Everything okay?"

"Actually, no. My dad died."

"What? Michael, oh God, are you serious?" Maggie felt her stomach bottom out.

Michael's family was quite different than the O'Brien clan. The Trembleys were a wealthy and prestigious family who originally hailed from Vancouver, British Columbia. His father was a well-renowned cardiologist, and his mother, who was a high-profile attorney, had only had Michael, no other children. His parents regretted bringing a child into their busy and hectic lives. Michael was raised by a constant string of nannies who came and went, and he had learned rather quickly to fend for himself. Luckily, Michael wasn't one to get into trouble. He'd developed a strong love for reading, and excelled in school. He decided to pursue law, like his mother, and worked hard to gain her respect and approval. She was pleased when he followed in her footsteps, and constantly pushed him to succeed further. His father was less than pleased that his son didn't choose medicine, and Michael often felt shunned by him, and what little interaction they had was icy.

Years passed, Michael gained entry into a very prestigious firm in Seattle, and there he had met Maggie, who was a young, naive receptionist from a tiny town he had never heard of. Their affair was fueled with desire and lust, then ultimately they fell in love and found out they were pregnant. Michael's parents felt that this was going to hold him back in his career, but he wanted to prove them wrong. They married and started their lives as a small family. Eventually, things improved as his family learned to love Maggie. After all, she had given birth to their only grandchild, a child that they doted on and spoiled beyond anything Maggie had ever seen. Sometimes their overindulgence caused some friction in her marriage.

Melanie was a toddler when tragedy struck the Trembley family, Michael's mother was traveling to Europe to represent an important client when the chartered private jet crashed. Maggie watched as Michael and his father waded through their grief; it was heartbreaking to see them suffer the loss of a woman who had meant so much to them. The loss and pain brought Michael and his father closer, the years of cold distance had melted, and a new relationship had formed. Their bond became strong, they tried to find the time even with both of their hectic schedules to partake in activities they both enjoyed, such as meeting up for a game of chess, or a round of golf, sometimes just dinner and drinks. Maggie envied the great lengths and effort that Michael put into spending time with his father. Why couldn't he do that for her and Melanie?

"Oh, Michael. I'm so sorry." Maggie felt stinging tears piercing her eyes. She sat down on a curb about a block from the school, she was in shock and didn't know what to say or what to do. Guilt reared its ugly head again, she should be home to comfort her husband.

"Maggie, can you and Melanie come home?" She could hear his voice breaking. She knew he was holding back tears, and it splintered her heart.

"Yes." That was all that needed to be said. He needed her right now, and she at least owed him that. Regardless of her feelings about the way things were between them, she loved Michael, she knew she always would. Maggie assured him that she was going to go her mother's house and pack, then pick up Melanie and come back home.

***

Maggie drove toward Seattle, her eyes raw from crying. Melanie was asleep in the back seat. Her daughter didn't quite understand why they were headed back home. Maggie had tried explain that her grandfather, Michael's father, had passed away. But Melanie seemed to only understand one thing, that they were headed back home. Maggie didn't bother explaining to Melanie that they would be going back to Birch Valley, and that going to Seattle was only temporary. Birch Valley was now home.

She grew restless as the highway started to fill with traffic as they approached Seattle. It was mid-evening, the sun was already gone, and the twinkling lights on the horizon felt odd to Maggie. She had made this drive a number of times, but tonight it felt different. Easing her car toward the direction of downtown Seattle and their condo—well, Michael's condo—she found her old parking spot empty. She had been gone for almost a month, but all of sudden it felt much longer.

"Melanie, wake up, love bug," Maggie said softly after she shut the car off.

The girl stirred, rubbing her eyes, looking around a little confused. "Where are we?"

"Seattle, sweetie, remember?"

Melanie's eyes grew wide. "We're home!" She jumped out of the car with incredible speed.

"Wait, we are still in a parking lot," Maggie scolded. "Here, take your suitcase." She handed off a bright pink suitcase decorated with kittens.

"Is Daddy home?" Melanie asked, her voice perky as she accepted her small suitcase to carry.

Maggie nodded, she had already seen his sedan in the large parking garage of the condo. Her nerves were jumbled as she wrestled with an array of emotions. Maggie led her daughter to the elevator across the way and they arrived at their door. She hesitated. She almost knocked on the door, but thought better of it. Using her key to unlock it, she noticed the home was quiet and the lighting dim as she entered.

She called out, "Michael, we're here." Melanie rushed past her in search of her father. Maggie dragged her own suitcase toward the living room to find Michael's long body stretched out on the couch that was against the large window, which gave them a terrific view of downtown Seattle.

He raised his head, groggily throwing back the cream-colored throw that was covering him. Maggie couldn't get over how exhausted he appeared; his handsome face was unshaven, swollen bags had formed under his chocolate eyes. Her heart broke as she looked down at him.

Practically falling on top of him, Maggie reached for him as he remained on the couch, his arms wrapping around her. "I'm so sorry, Michael," Maggie whispered in his ear.

Melanie ran full speed after discovering them in the living room. "Daddy," she squealed.

"My little girl." Michael scooped her up. Maggie moved to the side, making room for their daughter. It felt nice having them all snuggled close together. Maggie realized how much she missed Michael.

After Melanie got her fill of cuddling with Michael, they got her ready for bed and tucked her in. As they stood in the doorway of her bedroom, Melanie said, "It is nice being in my old bed. I'm glad we're home now." Her eyes closed as she started to drift off to sleep. Maggie felt horrible. Of course her daughter missed being home, hell, she did too. Why did life have to be so darn complicated?

Michael turned back toward their living room, Maggie trailing behind him. Things now felt a tad awkward.

Not quite knowing how to handle things, Maggie offered to make some tea.

"Maggie, I think we should talk, don't you?" Michael's eyes were sad.

"I came back to be here for you because of your dad. I don't think we should really discuss us right now," Maggie pleaded softly as she worked her way into the kitchen and started to heat a kettle of water on the stove.

Michael followed her into the small kitchen and leaned against the counter. Maggie felt her heart race. Even when he was grieving, the man still managed to look sexy. His dark hair was tousled, his white dress shirt unbuttoned slightly, his charcoal colored slacks hugging his muscular thighs. He had always had this effect on her. She steadied herself and tried desperately to reign in her senses as Maggie grabbed two mugs out of the cupboard and sat them on the shiny, elegant, granite countertop.

Turning to Michael, she swallowed as she watched him looking down at their tiled floor, deep in thought.

"How are you holding up?" Her tone was quiet and cautious.

He rubbed his stubble-covered chin. "I don't know. I mean, it is what it is I suppose."

His words confused her, she expected more emotion and further explanation of what he was feeling.

"How did he pass?" They still hadn't gone over the details of his death since he called her earlier that morning. Maggie wasn't quite sure how to ask. She had been with him when they had received word of his mother's untimely passing.

"He was actually performing surgery when a brain aneurysm ruptured." Michael's voice wobbled. "At first the other surgeons and nurses thought he had just fainted, they said it happened so quickly."

"Wow, so what now?" Maggie asked as she reached for Michael's arm and rubbed it.

Michael managed to smile at her, seeming to appreciate her tenderness towards him. "Well, I got the call early this morning, I actually had just came home from the office, so like almost four."

Maggie wasn't surprised to hear he was still working ungodly hours at the firm. Nothing had changed in the weeks since she had left. She pushed her angry thoughts aside, right now she needed to focus on Michael's grief. He still appeared to be in shock, still digesting the fact that his father had died that morning. Maybe that was why he didn't have a whole lot to say about it, he was still probably numb.

"So what can I help with?" Maggie asked as the kettle whistled loudly.

"Just you being here, bringing Melanie back home, means a lot. I mean, of course we need to figure out funeral arrangements and stuff like that."

"Well, let me know what I can do to help," she said as she turned the stove top off and carefully removed the kettle.

"Dad already had his funeral arrangements secured shortly after Mom died, he went in and handled everything. He has a will for his estate, but that is pretty cut and dry considering he had me draw it up." Michael laughed, but it was a sad laugh and sounded weird coming from his mouth.

Maggie poured the hot water into their mugs, dunking the small bags to steep, which quickly dyed the water brown. After she returned the kettle to the stove, she glided toward Michael. She worried about how he was actually handling this, he seemed different than the time his mother had died. Maggie stood in front of him as he continued to rest against the counter in a daze. She moved in slowly, placing her head on his chest, he felt warm against her face. She breathed him in, taking in the scent of his aftershave as she wrapped her arms around his lean waist. Maggie couldn't help herself, she knew she should have resisted the temptation of bringing their bodies close. She also knew she was sending him the wrong message, but right now she only wanted to love him.

Standing up on the tips of her toes, her hands flat against his chest, moving up to his neck, her mouth sought his. Michael groaned as he leaned into her, welcoming her as she parted his sensual mouth and explored with her tongue. His strong hands grabbed at her back, pulling her hard against him. She didn't resist or fight the rush of feelings that flooded her body. Maybe it was the hormones or the emotional torment they were going through, maybe a mixture of both, but right now she needed Michael as much as he needed her. She knew this wasn't going to solve their problems, in fact, it would probably only create more. But at the moment, she saw the situation as an avenue to help ease his pain, and possibly even hers.

With their tea forgotten, passion surged between them, their chemistry still intact. Michael's hands wandered all over her body. He paused and looked down at her. "Are you sure?"

Maggie replied by crushing his mouth with hers. She didn't want to think or deal with reason. That answer sufficed for him as he carried her off to their bedroom.

***

Feeling Seattle's early gray sunlight penetrating the room, Maggie's eyes fluttered open. She could feel the pleasant weight of Michael's arm as it rested on her hips. She backed up against him, their naked bodies spooning, she sighed. *Why couldn't things just be okay?* Thoughts plagued her; she tried to think of ways to try to solve their marital problems, she wondered how they could repair things and be a family again. She thought of the new life slowly growing inside of her, she thought of Melanie and how quickly she was growing up. Life as an adult was so complicated and messy, and was nothing like she'd imagined.

Maggie sensed that Michael was stirring. The sound of his content breathing had changed, and his hand started to roam over her, cupping her breast and pulling her closer to him. She sighed again as she felt his body harden against her. She welcomed him as he prodded her gently, her body still tender from the night before.

"Oh, Maggie." He moaned in her ear. She felt her body heat up as desire warmed through her. Pleasure soared through their bodies, emotional release contracted in their muscles. Spasms lingered in their afterglow. Spent and sated, they fell asleep in each other's arms again.

***

Maggie heard their bedroom door opening, and pulled their comforter tighter around her naked body. Melanie peeked in and asked, "Mom, I'm hungry, can I have breakfast?"

"I'll be right out and will make us all some. You sleep okay, sweetie?"

Melanie nodded. "Yeah, I slept okay." Maggie could tell her child seemed a little out of sorts.

"Everything okay, Mel?"

Melanie's bottom lip jutted out a little. "I thought I would be happy that we are home. I sort of wish I was going to school today."

"Like school here or in Birch Valley?"

"Birch Valley. I miss Grams and my friends at school."

They hadn't even been gone a full day, and it was Saturday, so it wasn't like Melanie would even be at school. That certainly was a change of events. Maggie felt a sense of relief that she had made the right call moving them back to that special, rural community.

"I bet they miss you too, sweetie. Do you know why we are here?" Maggie decided she needed to discuss this again with her daughter.

Melanie nodded, her expression sad. "Grandpa died."

Maggie felt tears emerging. That was why they were there, it as what brought them back, brought her, back to Michael. She felt her husband move next to her, he must have heard them speaking.

"Good morning, sweetie," he said to Melanie.

"Morning, Daddy. Mom says she is going to make us breakfast." Melanie's expression quickly changed as she smiled widely at him.

"Well, let's get out of bed and get dressed,"

Maggie said, clutching the thick comforter even tighter.

"Aren't you wearing pajamas?" Melanie asked, a confused scowl crossing her face.

Good grief, thought Maggie as she was filled with embarrassment. She could hear Michael let out a laugh as he told Melanie, "We'll meet you in the kitchen in a minute. Can you see if we have any eggs in the fridge?"

That was clever. Melanie happily skipped out of their room. Michael grabbed Maggie's waist and turned her to him. "Did I thank you for coming back?"

She watched as his lips curved into a sexy grin. "Yes, several times now." She couldn't help laughing. Here they were on the verge of their marriage ending, yet they were naked in bed.

Maggie memorized his face, the faint wrinkles and creases near his eyes, the shadowy stubble that outlined his strong jaw, and his slightly swollen lips from the heavy kissing the night before.

She felt his hands slowly run down her spine as he leaned in to kiss her full on the mouth. God help her.

***

The mood shifted when reality decided to invade. They were seated at the dining table eating a breakfast of scrambled eggs and toast, and Maggie had recovered some frozen sausage links that were tucked in the back of the freezer. Her cooking talents were limited, but she could manage a simple meal like this. They were working on their second cup of coffee when Michael's phone rang. He left the table to answer it and came back minutes later explaining he had to go to the office, but would return as soon as he could. He showered and dressed in record time, and Maggie reluctantly kissed him on the cheek as he headed out the door. The scene was all too familiar.

After clearing the table of their dirty dishes, Maggie showered, her body still sensitive from her and Michael's love making. Letting the hot water beat hard against her shoulders, she felt more confused than ever. Last night, and even that morning, being with him in their bed felt so right, like it was where she belonged. Then when he left her to go to his office, she felt abandoned again. Sure, he promised to be home early, she would give him the benefit of the doubt and see if he actually did. In her heart, she knew that wasn't how Michael operated. But last night felt completely different, as they lay in bed together, flushed from their intense and powerful love making, they talked. Really talked. Michael opened up about the feelings he was struggling with, how the grief hadn't really settled in yet, and that he was worried about when it finally did. Maggie comforted him, holding him in her arms as they both cried in the darkness. For the first time in a long while she had actually felt hope, hope that their relationship could be mended. If only she could convince Michael to leave Seattle and come to Birch Valley, maybe they could still be together and be a happy family like she had always dreamed.

***

The evening sky had turned an even more dismal gray color, which suited Maggie's mood. She kept eyeing the clock. She had sent a couple messages to Michael to check in with him, only one response came that he was going to be a little late. Of course he would be. Maggie stood and gazed out the large window of their high rise condo, watching the cars below move at a snail's pace. She could hear the distant sounds of horns of frustrated drivers.

They had already eaten dinner, Melanie was in her bedroom playing with dolls, and Maggie sat waiting like she always had when she lived here. This helped remind her why she couldn't move back to Seattle, and it cemented her reasons for leaving. Lost in a tangled web of angry thoughts, she heard her cell phone ring.

"Hello?"

"Hi, Maggie," Rachel said on the other line. Maggie was surprised but happy to hear from her.

"Rachel, how's it going?"

"Fine here, just wanted to see how you guys were all holding up. Liam told me about Michael's dad, I'm so sorry." Her voice was soft as she offered her condolences.

Maggie appreciated Rachel thinking of her and Michael; it showed what a decent and kind person that woman was. She really hoped that someday Rachel would become her sister in-law, but for now she would settle for her being a good friend.

"We are doing okay, I guess," she paused and wondered how much detail she could go into with

Rachel. She threw caution to the wind and started to explain everything that had happened since she had arrived back in Seattle.

Rachel let out a long breath. "Wow, I can't say I really know how to advise you on this. I mean, on one hand, he's your husband, so obviously wanting to be with him is natural, but on the other you guys are sort of at war about things. If you add in the grief and shock I'm sure you both are feeling, damn, I mean, I wouldn't even know how to handle that."

"Trust me, that's why I'm venting to you. I don't know what to do. Like I said earlier, I love him, I honestly do. I really thought maybe we could work this out and save our little family," she said as her hand drifted protectively over her belly.

"Okay, here's where we can start, let's handle this thing with his dad first. Try and get through that. When's the funeral?" Rachel asked. Maggie frowned, Michael hadn't been home all day, and she had no idea who was handling things.

"Gosh, I don't know. Michael mentioned last night that his dad had alrcady sct up his funcral arrangements, but I have no idea when the funeral is being held." This made Maggie feel a little more anger towards Michael. How could he ask for her to come home, and then run off to the office, leaving her stuck, not having any idea as to what was going on?

"Maybe you need to work out the details with Michael when he comes home tonight," Rachel suggested. "Maggie, try to go easy on him, this is a lot to deal with. I'm not excusing his behavior, he should be home grieving, with you and Melanie by his side."

She was right, Maggie had to admit. Her husband didn't really know any other way, he had always thrown himself into his work. He said it was for them, but she knew that it was because that was what he had always done, long before he had even met her. Maggie wished Rachel a good night and thanked her again for calling before hanging up.

Maggie was chatting with Melanie as she brushed her teeth and got ready for bed when Michael came home.

"Are you guys here?" he frantically called out.

"In the bathroom," Maggie answered.

Michael appeared in the doorway. He looked exhausted, his dress shirt was partially un-tucked and wrinkled, and his eyes looked raw but relieved to see her and Melanie.

Maggie let Michael tuck in Melanie and read her a bedtime story. She heated up some leftovers for him and waited at the dining room table. Moments later he joined her, and he looked grateful as he eyed the food.

"So what happened today?" Maggie asked as Michael forked in a mouthful of noodles.

He swallowed. "A lot of things actually. I have been working on this case for the last month or so, and had some last minute deposition changes." Michael forked another bite of food into his mouth and took a drink of the cold iced tea that Maggie had poured for him. "Then I spoke with the people down at the mortuary." His eyes glazed over with a wet sheen. Maggie realized it wasn't the first time her husband had cried that day.

She reached out to him and rubbed his arm soothingly. "So what did they say?"

"Well, I guess Dad has picked out everything from his casket to floral arrangements, if you can believe it. God, I can't imagine being able to do that, you know?" His voice trembled.

"He was actually just trying to make it easier on you, sweetie. He knew you would be distraught, just like you both were when your mom died."

Michael dropped his fork and placed his head in his hands. "I know, but God, Maggie, it's just so hard."

She witnessed the reality of his father's death starting to sink into Michael. He was no longer in shock, he was fully absorbed in his grief. Rachel was right, this was a lot to deal with, and she did need to go easy on him. Maggie stood up and walked over to him, she reached for his head and brought it her belly and held him close to her. She could hear Michael sob as he wrapped his arms tightly around her. Seeing him so vulnerable chipped away at her resolve. She just wanted to hold him and make the pain go away.

"Have you felt the baby move yet?" Michael asked quietly. It was the first time he had brought up the pregnancy since she had returned. With tears swimming in her eyes, her heart sank.

***

Maggie was laying on their bed. She had suggested Michael go take a hot, relaxing shower.

He emerged from the adjoining bathroom, steam following him as he entered their bedroom. His dark hair was wet, and he had on only a towel that hung low on his hips as he neared the bed. Maggie felt a bit guilty for the aroused feelings that were overcoming her. She needed to be his pillar of strength and support.

"You were right, I feel a lot better," Michael said as stood near her.

"I'm glad. You want me to make you some hot tea, or can I get you anything else?" Maggie offered, trying hard to keep her eyes off his sculpted chest and the towel that looked like it could fall at any moment. Her heart raced with anticipation, hoping it would.

"No, it's okay. I think I might just go to bed." Michael yawned. He did look exhausted, but there was something else that sparkled in his brown eyes. Maggie recognized it; she was more than familiar with the stare of desire he was giving her.

"Michael, I want you to know that I'm here for you. I want to support you as you deal with your father's death, but this doesn't mean I'm back home for good." Maggie was gathering all her inner strength to not strip down and relive their passion from the night before.

Michael towered over her as she sat up in the bed. "I know. To be honest, being with you helps me forget everything that I'm dealing with. I miss you." His voice grew raspy, rich with desire. Maggie could see her husband wanted her. God knew she wanted him equally, but it was only complicating matters.

"Maybe we should talk?"

Michael ran his hand through his wet hair. "Right now?"

She could tell he was frustrated, but she wanted to figure things out before she continued letting her heart and body become more entangled with him. "Yes."

He sat down on the bed and then stretched out. "Fine, let's talk."

"Michael, I love you, but I want to be able to make love to you without feeling like it's the only time we connect. I want to feel secure when we are together, I want to know if we are even going to stay married."

"So what do we do?" he asked, his voice low.

"Honestly, I don't know. I think right now we need to cool things a bit." Maggie touched him and instantly regretted putting her hands on him. The smooth, taut muscle of his flat stomach begged her to stroke it, her eyes followed the light spray of fine black hair that traveled from his navel to other regions she was more than familiar with. She gulped, trying to swallow some air to cool the heat that was starting to simmer inside her. The devil on her shoulder told her to just enjoy this physical need, to give in to the pleasure she knew she would share with him.

As Maggie struggled to gain her composure, Michael looked longingly at her. "I know we need to, but I can't think straight when I'm around you. I never have been able to." He moved from his position on the bed and slithered closer to her, the pesky towel now pooled to his side, leaving his body fully exposed.

"Oh, Michael." Maggie felt her internal heat rising. The angel on her other shoulder pleaded with her to reconsider, that this was not the way to get her point across, that she needed to be strong and not be ruled by her desire. She shoved that angel aside and let the devil lead her into temptation, and welcomed Michael's fully nude body as he draped his toned leg over her thighs, pinning her gently his large hands, snatching her wrists and holding them over her head as his tongue traveled down the length of her body. Maggie found herself hopelessly giving in, and their sheets were quickly tangled around them.

If he had been home more and spent more nights like this with her, Maggie wouldn't have moved to Birch Valley, and they probably would have had many more children.

Chapter Eight

Rain splattered hard against the living room window, and Maggie poured herself another cup of coffee. Melanie watched cartoons and ate a bowl of some sort of sugary cereal that made Maggie feel pangs of guilt each time she allowed her to eat it. Michael had left again, but would be returning that afternoon after tying up some loose ends. The funeral was scheduled for tomorrow. Maggie hoped this rain would pass, but every service she ever attended was gloomy and full of drizzle, as if funerals weren't sad enough already.

Maggie felt a little restless in the condo. She cleaned the place from top to bottom, she had spoken to her mother a couple of times, and she had had another chat with Rachel, which was a nice distraction. She itched to get back to Birch Valley.

Michael and her had had a long drawn out discussion the night before after another round of passionate love making, which wasn't helping with the tension and anxiety she already felt. The conclusion of their conversation wasn't pretty, but it was decided, although not mutually accepted, that Maggie would return to Birch Valley the day following the funeral. She offered to hang around a little longer, and she wasn't quite sure what spurred her to make that offer, but Michael rejected it, saying that if she wanted to go she could leave at any time. It didn't feel right, leaving Michael before the funeral; she wanted to see how he coped after the final heap of dirt covered his father's casket. She wanted to be there to comfort him, to make sure he was going to be okay.

The day continued to drag on, and Maggie ran out of things to occupy herself. She strained to focus on the book that was in her lap as she sat on the couch when Michael arrived through the front door.

"You're home."

"Very observant, Maggie." His chilly tone was snarky. She knew he was still pissed at her. She blamed herself, all too aware that she had sent him false hope each time they wound up in bed together.

"Hi, Daddy," Melanie chirped from inside the dining room where she was coloring.

"My little girl," Michael said, his hand ruffling her russet-colored hair, which caused Melanie to laugh.

Maggie watched as he started for the fridge in search of something to eat. "I was thinking we could order a pizza or something, I wanted to wait until you got home to see what you wanted," Maggie said as she closed her book and set it gingerly on the end table. She got up from the couch.

"Whatever you guys want. I'm not that hungry."

His back was to her, she could see the muscles tense at the sound of her voice. "Okay, that's fine."

If this was how the evening was going to be, he might as well have stayed at work. Maggie sat next to Melanie and grabbed a crayon. Melanie looked up at her and smiled. "I'd like pizza for dinner."

***

Maggie reached for Michael's hand as they stood under the canopy that shielded her father in-law's casket from the constant rain. He almost flinched from her, which broke her heart even more. They were among a great deal of people dressed in various shades of black and gray, sharing black umbrellas, who were there to mourn Michael's father. His casket was a shiny, deep, mahogany wood, lined with gold handles. A simple spray of white flowers sat neatly on top. The hired preacher didn't know the man he was praying for, but his words were thoughtful and kind, and Maggie wasn't the only one moved by him. The rain never let up, it pounded the bright, green grass and made the soil muddy and squishy underneath Maggie's heels. The air was chilly as the storm swept through, bringing more misery to an already awful day.

The service ended, their friends all left to get in dry in their cars, and the men who operated the large, yellow backhoe to fill the hole that her father in-law now occupied waited patiently beneath a nearby sycamore tree. Michael just stood there, looking down at the ground. He hadn't spoken much at all. Maggie wanted to touch him, to reassure him that things would be okay, but how could she when she was going to leave him the next day, alone to handle his grief, without her or Melanie? She felt cruel and awful, but his cold demeanor and silence cut her deeply.

***

Maggie woke up early. It was still dark outside, but the rain had finally stopped. She felt like that was a good omen. Michael had already left, but she wasn't all that surprised. After the funeral he basically shut down. He quit speaking to her and just spent time with Melanie while Maggie packed their bags. She even loaded the car with more stuff than she had brought the weekend before. This was going to be permanent. She was going to return to Birch Valley, to her job, to her family, to her new life, and there would be no going back to Seattle.

The drive to Birch Valley was quiet, except when she chatted with Melanie, who was quite excited to go back to school the following day. They pulled into the small town fairly early; it wasn't even ten yet. They had made excellent time, but Maggie felt exhausted. It wasn't the journey that had wiped her out, but the emotional last couple of days she had spent in Seattle. She prayed she never had to go back there.

"Grams!" Melanie shouted as she exited the car and leaped into Mary's arms.

"My precious little one." Mary hugged her tight and planted a kiss on top of her head.

Maggie gave her mother a weak smile.

"I just put the kettle on for some tea," Mary said as she led them both into the home. Maggie felt like crying. It felt wonderful to be back in the cozy O'Brien home, the place of her childhood, but she also couldn't help but feel like it wasn't her home. That was something she had to figure out.

Melanie spotted her Uncle Daniel and bolted in his direction, leaving Mary and Maggie. They headed to the kitchen, where Mary placed two large cups on the dining table. She set out some Earl Grey tea, cream, and sugar.

"Sit," Mary instructed Maggie, who quickly plopped down. "How are you, dear?"

"Oh, Mom." Maggie knew the tears were coming. Mary captured her daughter in a secure hug, only releasing her when the kettle started to whistle.

"Tell me everything, sweetie."

Maggie brushed away the large droplets that were trailing down her cheeks as her mother poured the hot water into the cups. "I don't even know where to start."

"Well, you went to your husband, you were there for him in his time of need. And somehow you came back here." Mary had an unhappy look on her face.

"I know."

"Oh, Maggie, love, I wish you could have tried to work it out with Michael."

Maggie felt a sudden burst of anger erupt inside her veins. "I did try, Mom. I begged, I pleaded, and I loved him with every inch of my being, and have

121

done just about everything in my power to save my marriage."

Mary frowned and added cream to her tea. Maggie couldn't stand the disappointed look on her face. She got up from her seat and stormed to her bedroom.

Maggie didn't leave her room for the remainder of the day. Instead she hid under her blanket, nestled in its warmth. She could stay there forever, but her bladder begged her to get out of bed. After relieving herself, she spied down the hall to see if any of her family were out and about. When she didn't see anyone, she snuck back into her room. There she slept until the room grew dark as night took over.

She heard the door handle jiggle loudly, and Melanie's little round face peeked in. "Mom, are you awake?"

"Yeah, sweetie."

"Grams says that dinner is ready, and it would be good for you to eat. She said that there's a baby in your tummy that might be hungry." Melanie wore a confused expression.

Thanks, Mom. Maggie gritted her teeth quietly. She hadn't told Melanie she was pregnant yet, especially with everything that was going on. She worried it might be too difficult for her daughter to understand. She waved at Melanie to join her on the bed. After Melanie cuddled up close, Maggie circled her arms around her, placing her head on top of her daughter's. She could smell the lingering scent of a fruity child's shampoo, inhaling it deeply, she said, "Mommy does have a baby in her tummy."

"Really?" She could feel Melanie pull away to look at her. "Wow, so Grams was serious when she said I was going to be a big sister. That is so cool, Mom."

Maggie was thankful that her daughter was happy, at least for now, with the prospect of having a sibling. Maggie had been the youngest in her group of siblings and never got to experience how it felt to be a big sister.

"So is that why we moved here, Mom?"

Maggie considered her daughter's question for moment. A distinctive yes was all that came to mind. "I think it is a big reason why we are here. I think it's important for you and this baby to be around family."

"What about Daddy?"

Maggie knew this was coming. "Well, we need to pray that he can join us here." What else could she have said? Maggie felt like all of their futures were up in the air.

"Mom, I'm excited that we are having a baby, I wonder if it will be a boy or a girl," she said as she softly rubbed Maggie's flat belly. "So will your tummy get really big?"

Maggie chuckled. "Yes, it will. I was huge when I was pregnant with you. As far as what the baby will be, that is part of the fun, it's a surprise." They didn't find out Melanie's gender when they were pregnant, and took it as the one complete surprise that life offered. They couldn't describe how exciting and thrilling it had been to find out when Maggie made her final push in the delivery room.

Maggie and her daughter lay on the bed together and discussed all the things Melanie wanted to name the baby. She came up with some really silly ones, but one stuck out that was quite promising. Maggie would keep that one in mind.

***

Maggie was thankful to be back to her new, real life. Melanie had linked arms with her as they practically skipped their way to the school. The air was warming up and filled with floral scents as flowers everywhere bloomed into colorful displays. They arrived at the school, happy and ready to take on the day. Melanie led Maggie into the building, chattering away. Maggie caught sight of Rachel behind the counter talking with Karen.

"Good morning, ladies," Karen said as she gave them a wide smile.

"Good morning," Maggie and Melanie replied in unison. Melanie let out a giggle.

Rachel's brow bent with concern as she gave Maggie a tight-lipped smile and hugged Maggie. "How are you guys doing?" she whispered in Maggie's ear.

"We're doing okay."

"Well, hello, Miss Melanie, are you ready to do lots of learning today?" Rachel asked, her voice pitched high as she squatted down to Melanie's level.

Melanie nodded happily as a loud bell chimed throughout the building. Before she scurried off toward her class, she gave Maggie a tight squeeze.

"Have a good day, love you," Maggie called after her.

Rachel stood close to Maggie and watched as Melanie joined the group of children headed to their classrooms.

Rachel's eyes focused in on Maggie. "So how are you feeling?"

"Fine."

"I mean like the pregnancy and stuff?" Rachel asked carefully.

Caught a little off guard, Maggie answered, "I guess that is going fine too. I don't feel nearly as sick now, so that is a relief."

"Well, that's good, right?"

Maggie nodded in agreement. "Rachel, do you think you'd ever want to have kids?"

Rachel's mouth twitched. "Gosh, I honestly don't know. Like, when we went camping together and the kids were in that RV with me, I thought, wow, I could totally be a mom. But that's quite different, I was really more of a babysitter." Rachel laughed uncomfortably. "You already know how my mom is, so I'm not really sure I would be a good one."

Maggie considered that for a moment. "I think you would be wonderful. You are a loving person, and look at how amazing you are with the kids here at the school. They adore you, Rachel."

"Do you think Liam wants kids?" Rachel asked.

"Probably, he's always talked about settling down someday." Maggie was curious where all these questions were coming from.

"Well, coming from the type of family that you

guys are from, I'm not all that surprised."

"I think he would make a great dad," Maggie added.

"I bet he would. Well, I'd better get back to work," Rachel said as she glanced at the thin, silver watch on her wrist.

"Me too."

Rachel paused as she started to turn toward the hallway. "Maggie, my friend Chelsea is visiting, you want to come over tonight?"

"Sure, that sounds like fun," Maggie said. Something struck her as odd with Rachel, but she couldn't quite put her finger on it. She hoped everything was going well between Rachel and Liam.

"Great, see you tonight." Rachel strolled down the hallway toward her office. Maggie watched her disappear, and then headed out of the school, giving Karen a wave before she exited.

***

Maggie arrived at the doorsteps of Rachel's little yellow-painted home. It sat across the street from a park that Maggie recalled playing in when she was a child. In the door was a pretty stained glass depiction of a hummingbird flying among some purple flowers. She heard voices behind the door as she knocked. Rachel appeared a moment later, greeting Maggie with a huge smile.

"Come on in," Rachel said as she opened the door, allowing Maggie to enter. The inside decor matched Rachel perfectly. The warm tones of her furniture, splashes of colorful art on the walls, and the lovely smell of fragrant candles filled the air. Maggie enjoyed coming to Rachel's home; it was inviting, and they had shared dinner and many laughs there over the last month.

A slender, tall blonde popped up from one of the couches, an unsure smile on her face. "Hi, I'm Chelsea," she said, extending her hand. Maggie ignored her hand and scooped her in for a hug.

"Great to finally meet you, Chelsea. I have heard so much about you."

Chelsea appeared to be taken a little off guard by the simple gesture of affection. Rachel quickly ushered them to sit down in the living room. Chelsea took her place next to Rachel, as if to say she had been Rachel's friend first and that she hadn't quite warmed up to Maggie yet.

"So, you are Liam's sister, right?" Chelsea asked.

Maggie nodded as Rachel added, "And she is Patrick and Daniel's sister too." She looked at Maggie. "I can't wait for her to meet your family, Maggie."

"When did you get in, Chelsea?" Maggie asked politely as she found herself mesmerized by how beautiful and movie star-esque Rachel's friend looked.

Chelsea looked up toward the ceiling as if searching for the answer. "Two days ago, I think."

"What do you think of Birch Valley?"

"It's a pretty little place. Very different from where we're from," Chelsea explained. "I can't get over how blue the sky is here, and the trees, wow, there are so many of them."

"Yeah, it's a great place."

Rachel nodded in agreement. "I love it here."

"It wasn't that long ago you almost wanted to come home, so I'm thinking it's something more than all the scenery."

Maggie couldn't help but laugh at Chelsea's remark. "I have to agree with you." The ice was starting to break between Chelsea and Maggie, which came as a huge relief.

Rachel huffed. "Okay, okay, I admit it's more like someone has made me love it here, but it's still very pretty and totally different than Newport."

"Well, at least she admits it now. Trust me it took her a while to admit that she was even interested in Liam," Chelsea said.

Rachel got up from the couch and as she headed toward the kitchen she asked, "Can I get you guys anything to drink? Maggie, what would you like?"

"Whatever you have is fine," Maggie answered as she suddenly felt a ticklish sensation flutter in her belly. "I think I just felt the baby move."

"No way! Oh, that's right, you're preggers. Congrats!" Chelsea squealed, her eyes wide with excitement.

Maggie smiled. "Yeah, I'm a little over four months along."

"You have a daughter, right?" Chelsea asked

"Yes, Melanie, she's six."

"Oh, I bet she is thrilled about becoming a big sister," Chelsea said as Rachel returned with three large glasses of iced tea.

"What did it feel like, you know, the baby

moving just now?" Rachel asked, and Chelsea moved in closer as if Maggie were going to share the biggest secret ever.

"Well, to be honest, it almost feels like gas. Gross, I know, but it feels like a tiny bubble or something," Maggie explained. She wished she could have made it sound more enchanting, but the truth was it did feel like gas, at least in the early stages. Later on it would feel like there was gymnast living inside of her, flipping and tumbling.

Rachel seemed even more curious as she asked, "When will it start really kicking?" Rachel and Chelsea's eyes were glued to her.

"Well, with Mel, I really felt her later on the pregnancy. We could even see her move. Michael would be sitting across the room, and he could actually see her outline as she was moving around."

"Uh, that's kind of creepy, sort of like an alien inside of you," Chelsea blurted out.

"Yeah, I guess so." Maggie didn't quite view it that way, she was more amazed and excited when they could see their baby. Feeling her baby move had also reassured her that the baby was healthy.

Suddenly, the mood got heavy in the room as Rachel let out a long sigh. Maggie could see that Rachel looked uneasy. Rachel was about to speak when Chelsea blurted out, "We think Rachel might be pregnant."

Maggie coughed as she almost choked on her drink. "What?"

Rachel rolled her eyes. "Thanks, Chelsea." She looked at Maggie. "Okay, so that's partially why I invited you here tonight. Chelsea thinks I should take a test."

"You haven't yet?" Maggie asked. "Have you told Liam you think you might be pregnant?"

"No, to both questions. I don't even think I am, I mean, I would know, right?"

Chelsea patted Rachel's leg. "You see, Maggie, my dear little friend here hasn't been feeling well for a couple weeks. She thought she had a touch of the flu, or maybe just a little under the weather. Then when her period didn't show up, like it does religiously every single first of the month since we were twelve, she called me, and here I am."

"Rachel, I think you might be. You really should take a test." Maggie watched as tears started to form in Rachel's blue eyes. "Oh, Rachel, it'll be okay," Maggie said as she got up from the opposite couch to hug her friend.

"I know, it's just, I don't know if I want to be pregnant. Liam and I are still trying to figure things out and are barely starting to date," she babbled as the tears trickled down her face.

Chelsea looked at Maggie as she enveloped Rachel in their arms. "I bought a test from the grocery store when Rachel was at work. I have been trying to convince her to pee on it since she got home."

Maggie took hold of Rachel's petite shoulders and softly said, "Rachel, why don't you take the test since we are all here now?"

Rachel nodded. "I don't know if I want to know. It changes everything, Maggie. What if I am, I mean, God…" She broke down again.

Maggie could relate to the fear that Rachel felt.

Granted, when she became pregnant with Melanie, she and Michael had been together for several months. Liam and Rachel were barely scratching the surface of their relationship, and her heart went out to her friend. Maggie also knew what it was like to be pregnant and stuck in uncertainty; she still didn't know what was going to happen in her own marriage.

"Rachel, it will be fine," Maggie said, attempting to sound reassuring as she stroked and patted Rachel's back.

"Probably something in the water up here, I mean, look, Maggie's pregnant, now maybe you. I'd better stick to bottled water while I'm here," Chelsea teased as she tried to lighten the mood.

Both Rachel and Maggie laughed. "Okay, I'll go and take a test."

Chelsea practically leaped from her spot on the couch and ran down the hall, only to emerge within seconds carrying a plastic bag. She pulled out a small box that contained two tests. It wasn't all that long ago that Maggie held a similar box. Tearing open the package and pulling out the contents, Chelsea started to read the directions. She handed Rachel one of the two white test sticks.

"Do you want us to be in there with you?" Chelsea asked.

Rachel shook her head no as she got up and made her way down the hall to the bathroom.

It felt like a lot of time had passed, and Chelsea looked concerned. "You think she's okay?"

"Should we go check on her?" Maggie asked.

Just then they heard the bathroom door open and

watched as Rachel appeared. Her eyes and nose were a little red from crying. Maggie and Chelsea hurried to her. Rachel was clutching the stick tightly in her hand.

"I just don't how this is possible." Her voice wavered, and she started sobbing.

"Well, I can tell you how it happens, if you want," Chelsea joked. Maggie could tell that Rachel's friend always tried to keep things light and fun, as if anything serious made her incredibly uncomfortable.

Rachel released her strong hold on the test, handing it off to Chelsea, who stared in shock at the two pink lines behind the plastic window of the test.

"Rachel, it'll be okay," Maggie soothed. Granted she wasn't a hundred percent certain it would be, but she knew her brother would probably be excited. At least she hoped he would be, for Rachel's sake.

"I want to take another one. Maybe it's broken, don't false positives happen all the time?" Her blue eyes searched Maggie's.

"False negatives are a little more common, but let's take the second test just in case," Maggie said as she gently rubbed Rachel's back.

Rachel nodded, and Chelsea ran to get the other test, quickly giving it to her. "Don't wait in there so long this time, maybe just bring it out with you, and we can all wait together," suggested Chelsea.

Maggie watched as Rachel hurried back to the bathroom and closed the door. *Poor thing, how scared she must be.* Chelsea joined Maggie back in the living room, and they sat across from each other on opposite couches. "Wow, huh?" Chelsea said, still a little shocked.

"I know."

"I honestly didn't think she was going to be pregnant, I was sort of just kidding. She had complained about not feeling so great, and then her period was late, she said it was probably just all the stress at work. I feel so bad for her, I mean, no offense to your brother and stuff, but I don't know how she is going to handle this," Chelsea rambled.

"I'm worried about her too. You know, we just had a conversation about my pregnancy, and then she told me how she didn't think she would make a good mother, she even asked if Liam wanted kids. So, looking back on it, I'm thinking she might have suspected she was pregnant, or that this is a really funny coincidence,"

Rachel came down the hall as Chelsea was about to speak, and placed the test on the coffee table. She dropped her head in her hands, Maggie looked down at the test, and two clearly visible lines stared back at her. The room was quiet, except for the sobs coming from Rachel.

Chapter Nine

Maggie opened the door to greet Rachel and Chelsea. Mary had insisted that Rachel come to Sunday dinner and for her to bring her friend along, so the family could meet her. Maggie gave Rachel a nervous smile. "How are you doing?" she asked, then glanced at Chelsea and gave her a kind and polite smile.

Rachel nodded. "I'm okay, well, no, not really, but I'm trying to be."

Chelsea rubbed Rachel's back. "She's still a little in denial, but we are working on it."

"Have you told Liam yet?"

Rachel shook her head. "I haven't, I want to make sure that it really is positive, you know?"

Maggie gave her a tight lipped frown. "You need to kind of let him know."

"I know, and I will, I promise, please don't say anything, Maggie," Rachel pleaded.

"I won't, it's yours to handle. I'm just advising you to say something soon. He deserves to know, and he'll be there for you."

"What if he freaks out?" Chelsea asked, her eyes wide and filled with concern.

"My brother's a good guy, besides he's never felt this way about another woman before," Maggie said, defending Liam. Granted, her brother had never been put in this position before, but it wasn't like he was a young, ignorant kid. He was reaching thirty-four, and as a grown man he should have taken precautions to prevent something like this.

Mary made her way to the entry, where the three women were deep in conversation. "Rachel, how lovely to see you," Mary said as she embraced Rachel.

"Mary, this is my best friend, Chelsea," Rachel introduced her friend. "Chelsea, this is Liam's mother, Mary O'Brien."

Chelsea offered her hand to Mary, who ignored the outstretched hand and scooped Chelsea up in a hug. Chelsea's reaction was a little less surprised this time, but her body was still rigid. Maggie and Rachel held back their laughter as they followed Mary.

Mary looped her arm through Chelsea's and led her toward the living room. "Chelsea, dear, I would like you to meet the rest of the O'Brien family."

Maggie could see that Chelsea looked nervous, but she flashed her Hollywood smile and put on a good show.

Liam stood up and moved toward Chelsea. They had already met, and after Chelsea gave him the interrogation of a lifetime, she decided she absolutely adored him. She thought he was perfect for Rachel to date. Liam gave Chelsea a slight hug from the side, and then maneuvered so he was standing next to Rachel, instantly wrapping his long arms around her waist.

Daniel practically bounced up from the leather couch and raced over to meet Chelsea. "Hi, I'm Daniel." He stood tall and was puffing himself up to look larger, a male peacock trying to show off his wares.

"Nice to meet you," Chelsea said, looking beyond him. Maggie could see that something more interesting had caught her eye.

Patrick reluctantly got up from his spot as he moved toward them. "I'm Patrick." His tone was cool and flat, but Chelsea's eyes sparkled with interest.

Maggie was used to women always acting goofy or attempting their most sexy glares when they came into contact with her oldest brother; it had always been like that, even when they were kids. Granted, who could blame them? Patrick was incredibly handsome. His dark hair set him apart from the rest of the O'Brien siblings, but he still had their emerald green eyes.

"I'm Chelsea, so nice to meet you, Patrick," said Chelsea, her words leaving her mouth slowly and seductively. Maggie could see Daniel was annoyed, and he excused himself politely.

"Let's have you meet my husband and his father, they're in the den," Mary said to Chelsea as she pulled Rachel's friend away from the living room, leaving the rest of the group.

"You guys want to sit down?" Liam offered as he ushered them toward the couches.

Patrick sat next to Maggie, and Liam with Rachel on the opposite couch. Maggie couldn't help but feel bad for Liam. There he sat next to a woman who was pregnant with his child, and he had no clue. Yet she had a lot of sympathy for Rachel, who wasn't unlike herself, unsure and scared out of her mind. Maggie just hoped that Rachel told Liam soon; it was starting to make her feel uncomfortable.

They sat around for a little while, discussing mundane things until Mary returned with Chelsea in tow and announced that it was time for dinner.

Everyone sat at the enormous table, but Mary had already fed the children, and they were now in Melanie's room playing.

Chelsea's steady gaze on Patrick made Maggie a little irritated. Did this woman have to be so obvious? *We get it, he's gorgeous, move on.*

"Chelsea, what do you think of Birch Valley?" Grandpa Paddy asked as he added a helping of vegetables to his already full plate.

Not taking her eyes off of Patrick she said, "It's beautiful here, I can see why Rachel loves it so much."

Daniel smirked as he loaded up his plate with pot roast. "We're glad Rachel moved up here."

Oh boy. Maggie felt bad for Daniel's bruised ego, but this wasn't the first time a lady had passed him over in order to get a chance at Patrick.

"I'm glad she did too," Liam added, looking lovingly down at Rachel, who sat next to him. Her cheeks turned a pale pink.

The conversation continued. They learned a great

deal about Chelsea, mainly from stories about Rachel and her growing up. Maggie wasn't too impressed as she listened to the tales, and now that she was getting to know Rachel's friend a little more, Chelsea seemed a bit shallow and completely different than the Rachel she knew. She hoped Patrick wasn't interested, as Chelsea kept flirting with all her might to get his attention. Patrick was used to women practically throwing themselves at him. Maggie didn't notice one flicker of desire, in fact, he seemed bored.

Once the table had been cleared of their dinner, Mary served everyone homemade peach pie with tea. It wasn't long before the men excused themselves and left the women alone at the table.

"Chelsea, dear, what exactly do you do back in California?" Mary asked sweetly, genuinely curious.

"Well, you mean like a job?" Chelsea replied.

Rachel quickly jumped in and said, "Chelsea and her mother are well taken care of. I have told this girl she needs to go to school and find something she loves doing." Rachel looked at Chelsea and grinned.

Maggie knew what Rachel was trying to do: soften the blow that Chelsea was a spoiled brat who never worked a day in her life. She was probably one of those girls who relied on daddy for everything, and spent her days spending his money with reckless abandon. Maggie couldn't explain the irritation she felt toward Rachel's friend. Maggie worried that if Rachel was best friends with a person like Chelsea, what was Rachel really like?

Was she a snob too, like Liam originally suspected? She silently prayed that Rachel was the real deal. Maggie liked Rachel so much, and now that she knew that her friend was pregnant with Liam's baby there was a good chance she would be her sister in-law soon.

After chatting for a while, only pie crust remained, and tiny crumbs were left on their plates. The ladies cleared the table again and prepared to leave. It was already turning into night as everyone said their goodbyes. Rachel practically had to drag Chelsea away, but she managed to give Liam a quick kiss before they left.

Patrick gathered his twins and was headed out the door when Maggie went up to him. "Wow, Chelsea sure thought the world of you," she said, teasing him.

"Not my type, so don't get any funny ideas," Patrick responded as he hefted up one of his sons.

"Just making sure you aren't interested."

"Trust me, I'm not. She's cute enough." Patrick paused, as though he was choosing his words carefully now that he realized that Maggie must not be Chelsea's biggest fan. "I'm actually surprised they're friends, to be honest."

"Yeah, I know, I kind of thought the same thing when I first met her, but she seemed okay. Tonight, though, I feel like I really got to know her, and I'm not sure I care for her." Maggie grimaced as she recalled listening to Chelsea talk all evening.

"Well, don't worry, little sister. I don't have any plans to see her, though she did ask me if I would take her to dinner while she was visiting. Maybe I should show her what Birch Valley has to offer." Patrick gave Maggie a rare mischievous grin.

"Get your wicked butt home, Patrick," Maggie said as she lightly slapped at him. He laughed and headed out the door.

Maggie went back into the living room, Daniel was stretched out on one of the couches, he had turned off most of the lights, leaving on a single table lamp.

"Hey, Daniel, you doing okay?" Maggie asked quietly.

"Yeah, I'm good."

Maggie could see the stinging remains of Chelsea's rejection still bothered him. "So, that was Rachel's friend."

"Yep, not sure why Rachel would be friends with a girl like that, but whatever," Daniel stated as he closed his eyes, trying to escape in a nap.

"Rachel is a lot different. I just hope those are her true colors, you know," Maggie said. She hated even questioning Rachel's character. She knew deep inside from the time she spent with Rachel that she was kind and caring, but when she saw her friend interact with Chelsea, there had been a glimmer of snootiness that couldn't be mistaken.

"Rachel's a good person, Maggie. But I know what you mean. When Chelsea was going on and on about all their adventures, I saw Rachel a little differently. I mean, they grew up as a bunch of rich kids, their dads are both plastic surgeons," Daniel explained.

Maggie suddenly worried that maybe Rachel was terrified to tell her parents. She remembered Rachel telling her how much her mother wanted her to marry someone that held enough value in their social circle. Liam couldn't be further from that circle. He was a country guy, not interested in material things, and didn't like having to play up to people. He drove an old pick-up and fished, he got his hands dirty, and he would hardly be the type to run around with Rachel and Chelsea's crowd back in California.

"Maggie, you okay?" Daniel asked, breaking into Maggie's thoughts.

"Sorry, I kind of spaced out there. Pregnancy brain, I guess. Well, let's not worry too much about Rachel, she's been more than sweet to us, even to you, you big goof." Maggie socked Daniel's shoulder playfully on her way out as she headed to tuck in Melanie and go to bed herself.

***

Maggie was humming along to a song on the radio while filing some papers at the shop when she noticed Chelsea saunter in. *Good grief.*

"Hi, Chelsea, how's it going?" Maggie asked kindly.

"Hey, Maggie, I was just seeing if Patrick was around." Chelsea had a wicked Cheshire Cat grin on her lips, and it threw Maggie for a loop. Maybe Patrick was going to explore Chelsea's invitation after all.

"He's out on a job with Daniel, was he expecting you?"

Chelsea shook her head, her pale blonde ponytail

swished back and forth. "No, but I wanted to see him before I left. My flight leaves tomorrow, and I thought maybe I could steal him away for a bite to eat."

Thank God. Maggie was relieved, she was worried for a moment that her brother had taken the bait.

"Well, I can tell him you stopped in," Maggie offered, but she had no plans to even mention that Chelsea had stopped by.

"I appreciate it. So, what do you do here?" Chelsea was peeking over the counter at Maggie's desk, and looked to be taking in the environment.

"I just help my brothers out with some paperwork and stuff."

"You're married, right?" Chelsea questioned, apparently suddenly interest in Maggie.

"Yep."

"Where's he at? Does he work here too?"

Apparently Rachel didn't share with Chelsea any of the problems that Maggie was having with Michael, and that instantly helped remedy her ill feelings toward Rachel. She appreciated that her friend had kept their conversations just between them, and that proved more than anything that Rachel was indeed the real deal, a real friend who Maggie could trust and rely on.

"Actually no, he's an attorney." Maggie tried to stay as vague as possible; she couldn't quite get a good read on what Chelsea was after.

Chelsea turned to Maggie, "Really? So why are you working?"

"Because I want to help my brothers out."

Chelsea let out a sigh. "So does Patrick own this shop?"

Ah ha, there it was, she was sizing up Patrick, wanting to see if he was worth more than just his good looks.

"My grandfather, who you met on Sunday, started the business and it has stayed in the family ever since."

"That's nice."

An awkward silence floated above them until Chelsea cleared her throat. "I'm just looking out for Rachel, she's my best friend in the whole wide world, and I love her to death."

"She's a great person," Maggie said, waiting for what was going to come out of the debutante's mouth.

Chelsea squared her stance as she face Maggie. "When Rachel tells her mother that she's preggers, Evelyn is going to flip out. My mom and her mom are very close friends as well, and Evelyn asked me to check things out up here."

"Okay, so, I'm not quite following you."

"Well, you see, Liam isn't exactly what Evelyn wants for Rachel. Granted, I think Liam is great, but I worry how he will fit into her family, if that makes sense?"

"Chelsea, they don't have a lot of choice in the matter now. I don't know what Rachel and Liam plan to do once he learns about this pregnancy, but I can tell you one thing, my brother will make an honest woman out of Rachel, if that is what her family is worried about." Maggie felt her cheeks get warm as anger started to bubble inside of her.

"I don't think you understand, there is no way that Evelyn will allow Rachel to marry someone like Liam. I can't imagine that Rachel would want to either. She has to think about her future."

"Someone like Liam? What the hell do you mean?" Maggie knew very well what that little spoiled brat was saying, but she wanted to hear her explain it, for the words to actually come out of her mouth.

Chelsea rolled her eyes in frustration. "I'm saying that Rachel's parents want her to marry someone who can provide for her and take care of her in the ways that she is used to. I know she moved up here to prove to everyone that she didn't need their money and that she could survive on her own. We didn't think she'd be here this long. They are expecting me to convince her to come back home, Maggie."

"What? But she can't, I don't even think she would want to."

"Come on, Rachel and I are not made for the kind of life you have here. Not that it's terrible or anything, but it's just so simple and boring."

Maggie felt like she had been punched in the stomach. "Wow, are you serious? Maybe you don't know Rachel anymore, because the Rachel I know seems to love it here, with Liam."

"I'm not saying that your brother isn't good enough for her to date or anything, I even encouraged her to start seeing him. I thought it would be good for her to get out there again after what happened with her ex. I just didn't expect her to get knocked up."

"I didn't expect Liam to fall for Rachel as hard as he did, and I sure didn't expect them to end up pregnant either, but it happened. They seem happy, and I can tell that they both love each other, even this soon into their relationship. Once Liam learns that she is carrying his child—" Maggie squared her shoulders as she prepared for a verbal battle with Chelsea.

Chelsea interrupted Maggie. "Well, she needs to come back home. It's as simple as that. Her parents will help figure out this pregnancy stuff out, and then things can go back to normal."

"I can't see Rachel doing that, especially after the stories she has told me about her family. She's becoming a part of our family now, especially since she is pregnant with my brother's child. My mother will want her here, Evelyn doesn't even call Rachel unless it's to complain."

Chelsea tried to rebut. "Yeah, but…"

Maggie cut her off. "No, there is no but, it's up to Rachel to decide where she wants to be, not her family, not you or I."

"Obviously we aren't going to see eye-to-eye on this. You think you know Rachel, but I have known her since we were kids."

Maggie was beyond irritated at Chelsea. Her childish claim on Rachel was no surprise. She had acted territorial the moment Maggie met her. Maggie tried to be welcoming and polite, but now she wanted nothing to do with Chelsea and prayed Rachel's friend would just turn around and leave.

"Maggie, you have a nice little life here with your family, but Rachel doesn't belong here. So you need to really stay out of this, don't get too attached to her." Chelsea's tone was dismissive and patronizing. She knew nothing about Maggie's life, and this sent bolts of anger through her veins.

"Chelsea, I really think maybe you should leave, considering there isn't anything here for you."

"That's fine, but I want you to know I will do everything to protect Rachel." Chelsea turned on her heel and stormed out.

Maggie sat down at her desk, trying to wrap her head around what just happened. She felt the need to confront Rachel and warn Liam, but how could she when she held a secret that could change Liam's life forever? Maggie grabbed her purse and headed to the school to see Rachel.

***

Karen greeted Maggie as she entered the school foyer. "Maggie, how are you today, dear?"

"Great, thanks," answered Maggie impatiently.

"Did you need to pull out Melanie?" Karen questioned.

Maggie shook her head. "Is Rachel in by chance?"

"Yes, in her office. You want me to call her?"

"No, it's okay. Can I go back there?"

Karen smiled. "Of course you can." The telephone next to Karen rang, and she waved Maggie on as she answered it.

Maggie walked cautiously down the hall. She had never been in trouble at school, but the fear of going to the principal's office had always been

146

there. Or perhaps it was the dread of having to confront Rachel.

She knocked lightly and then opened the door slowly, but first she saw Liam standing over Rachel. "Oh, sorry, I didn't know…"

Rachel tried smoothing her skirt flat, her face flushed, as was Liam's. "It's fine, how's it going, Maggie?"

"Good," she said, turning her attention to Liam, arching her eyebrow. "Shouldn't you be teaching right now?"

"Recess. Also, Rachel found out some terrific news." Liam smiled.

Thank God, Rachel told him.

Panic rose in Rachel's eyes, and Maggie became confused as she heard Liam speak. "The district office came back with the testing results for our school. We did great, and they offered Rachel a contract to stay on as principal. Isn't that awesome?"

"Fantastic news. Congratulations, Rachel," Maggie said, looking at her friend.

The bell sounded, and Liam snatched another kiss from Rachel before he said goodbye to both of them.

"Crap, Rachel, you haven't told him yet?" Maggie scolded.

"I know, I will, I promise, I just haven't fully processed this whole thing. We are supposed to go and celebrate tomorrow night," Rachel explained. "Chelsea's flight is tomorrow morning."

Maggie released a loud sigh. "Yeah, I just ran into her, well, actually, she showed up at the shop."

Rachel smiled. "Really? Probably to see if Patrick was around. Boy, she thinks he's one of the best looking guys she has ever seen."

Maggie knew that Rachel had no clue about what went on with Chelsea.

"Patrick wasn't there, but she was there to see him for sure." Maggie took a seat at one the chairs in front of Rachel's desk as Rachel sank down into hers. Rachel looked happy and content; she didn't look like a woman who wanted to leave. "Rachel, have you told your parents about the baby yet?"

Instantly, Rachel's smile faded. "No, I haven't told anyone else besides you and Chelsea. I want to tell Liam next. I have an appointment at the clinic right after school today. I just need to make sure I'm pregnant before I drop a bomb on him."

"Okay, do you want me to go with you?" Maggie offered.

"Chelsea will probably tag along, if she isn't too busy trying to get her hands on Patrick."

"You promise you will tell Liam? Because honestly it's killing me not to tell him, Rachel," pleaded Maggie.

"Maggie, I want to tell him, but I just worry how he'll take it. I mean, we just started this relationship, and now I'm pregnant. I know he's going to want to do the right thing, he's that kind of guy, know what I mean?"

"I do, and that's why it's important that he knows so he can make that decision."

Rachel nodded. "I had a hard enough time letting my guard down to date him, and I'm not so sure I'm ready for the altar."

"It's hard for me to keep this from him, Rachel. Liam and I are very close. So you are going to tell him tomorrow?" Maggie asked.

"Yes, I promise."

At least that was settled.

***

Rachel

Rachel sat nervously next to Chelsea, who was flipping through magazines at a rapid pace. The office waiting room was empty, except for a child and her parent. She recognized the girl from school and gave her a small wave. The child smiled, then coughed and snuggled closer to her parent.

"I'm so freaked out, Chelsea," Rachel said.

Chelsea put the magazine down. "Maybe those tests were bogus."

Rachel nodded her head. "Part of me is kind of excited, is that weird?"

"What? Are you serious? Come on, Rachel."

Something was off with Chelsea, she had acted strange when Rachel picked her up after work to go to the clinic. She seemed a little cold and distant, and not her usual bubbly self.

"Is everything okay?" Rachel probed carefully, thinking maybe Chelsea was a tad envious about Rachel's possible pregnancy. They used to be in constant competition, always trying to outdo the other, well, it was more like Chelsea wanting to outshine anything Rachel was doing.

"I'm fine." Chelsea shrugged, her blonde hair

moved with her animated motion, "Actually no, I'm not. I went down and talked to Liam's sister today."

"Maggie?"

"Yes, I don't know why you are even friends with her, Rachel." Chelsea's voice became louder, her body stiffened.

"What happened?" Rachel was curious now. When she had seen Maggie today, the visit was unexpected. Perhaps her run in with Chelsea was what had spurred it.

"Well, I went to go see if Patrick was at his shop, and I don't know, she was kind of rude. She and I had a little argument…"

Rachel stopped her. "Wait, what? What did you guys fight about?" She was fully confused now, and wondered what they could have possibly disagreed about. When they hung out on Sunday everything had appeared fine. She actually thought Chelsea and Maggie seemed to have hit it off, which was a huge relief.

"Without rehashing every annoying detail, your little friend doesn't seem to understand some things." Chelsea kept being vague, and it started to irritate Rachel.

"Okay, look, I'm not sure what happened between you guys, but I've never seen Maggie be rude. Maybe it is just a misunderstanding?" Rachel asked hopefully.

"Oh, it was a misunderstanding, all right."

A woman with a clipboard entered the waiting room and called out Rachel's name. Gripping the handle on her purse tighter than necessary, she followed the woman back. Chelsea stayed behind in the waiting room, giving Rachel a weak smile.

***

Rachel discovered that peeing in a cup was more than difficult; it might have taken a trained acrobat to complete the challenge. The nurse laughed when Rachel had joked about the struggle she had. The nurse warned her that it would only get worse. After sitting in a tiny room, the nurse returned with a broad grin on her face and told Rachel what deep in her heart she already knew to be true. She was pregnant.

As she left the clinic with Chelsea, a prescription for prenatal vitamins, and a schedule for an ultrasound, Rachel actually felt a little excited.

"So, this is, like, for real, then?" Chelsea asked as Rachel slowly backed her car out of the clinic's parking lot.

"I guess so. I mean, wow, right?"

"Rachel, what are we going to do?" Chelsea's voice filled with panic.

Rachel almost felt the need to stop the car and give Chelsea a hug, her friend was struggling more with the reality of the situation than Rachel was. Granted, almost a week ago Rachel felt like someone tipped her world upside down, and then she remembered Mary saying that God doesn't make mistakes and that things happen for a reason. She found comfort in that, and now she was anxious to share the news with Liam. She wasn't completely sure how the rest of the O'Briens would take the news; she was worried more about Mary's reaction.

Rachel would cross that bridge when she got to it. Right then she just wanted to enjoy the magical feeling.

***

Chelsea sat on the couch next to Rachel, she had her bags packed and sitting by the door, ready for tomorrow's early flight.

"I can't believe you're leaving already. It feels like you just got here." Rachel frowned. "Will you come back up for the baby shower?"

"Rachel, maybe you should come down for that. I'm sure your mother would appreciate it."

Rachel groaned. "God, I'm dreading telling my mother. She is going to freak out."

"Well, can you blame her? I mean you go and move up here, and then like a minute later you get yourself pregnant."

Rachel stared at her friend. "I didn't do this on purpose, Chelsea. Remember how upset I was the first time I slept with Liam?"

"I know, but you should have been more prepared. Your mother doesn't even know you are actually dating Liam, so how do you think she is going to react when she finds out you are having his baby?" Chelsea's eyes were burning with anger. "Rachel, you never should have moved up here."

"Chelsea, I love it here. This place is really wonderful, and I have met the greatest people. I found everything that was missing in my life here in Birch Valley. Most importantly, I found Liam."

Chelsea snorted. "This isn't where you belong.

152

You should come back home, your parents can help you figure out this whole baby thing. You don't have to keep it, Rachel, you have options. Think about your future, is this really where you want to live for the rest of your life?"

Rachel's eyes grew wide. "I'm really surprised you are acting like this, I thought you supported me. You sound more like my mother than my best friend."

"I'm trying to look out for you, and you don't seem to be thinking rationally at all. I mean, honestly, you expect to work for the rest of your life? You think Liam can support you and this baby? He's a teacher, for Pete's sake. I've seen his truck, he obviously is not well off." Chelsea's disgusted tone made Rachel squirm uneasily. "Don't you think it's better you hear this from me, rather than your mother?"

"Chelsea, I appreciate where you are coming from, but honestly, I don't care how much money Liam makes, I love my job, and I love him. I don't give a flying crap what my mother has to say about it. She hardly speaks to me, I think she has to come to terms that I'm never going to be the daughter she wanted." Rachel raised her voice, as she hadn't expected this from Chelsea. "I don't want to marry some rich guy so he can throw enough money at me while he fools around behind my back and leaves me at home. No thanks."

"Not all guys are like your ex. There is nothing wrong with marrying someone who can provide you with a good life, one that you deserve."

"I'm not saying they are all like him, but what I

am saying is that I'm more interested in the life Liam could offer me." Rachel was beyond pissed. If Liam asked her to run away and marry him, she wouldn't hesitate. Her emotions were scattered all over the place, but right then the thought of being Liam's wife made her feel secure and loved. She wanted to run to him and have his strong arms hold her.

"Liam can offer you what, exactly? His tired, old pick-up truck, some crummy house in the woods, living here in the redneck wonderland?"

"First off, you can quit insulting Liam. He's been nothing but nice to you. His entire family was hospitable and kind. In fact, you were so anxious to get your claws in Patrick I thought maybe you liked it up here," Rachel retorted.

"God, I wouldn't marry Patrick, are you serious? He doesn't even own that shop. Besides, I could never live here. As far as Liam's family being so awesome, I'd have to disagree with you on that one too, his little sister sure is a piece of work."

"Chelsea, you ever think that maybe you pissed her off? Maybe you were acting rude? Maybe you said some disgusting things about her brother?"

"Rachel, I just don't get it. I don't know what has happened to you, but you are not the same person anymore." Chelsea spat as she sprang from the couch in anger and went to the guest room.

Rachel fumed, but a part of her felt broken and sad. Chelsea was her best friend, but so much had changed in her life, things were so different. She didn't want to lose their friendship. She needed Chelsea to see that she was finally happy, and maybe that's why she didn't seem like the same person anymore.

***

Rachel hugged Chelsea tightly at the airport terminal. "I'm going to miss you."

"Me too." Chelsea sniffled.

They had discussed everything on the way to the airport. Their friendship remained intact as they parted ways, still not fully seeing eye-to-eye, but Rachel hoped that Chelsea could eventually accept her decisions.

After one last wave, Rachel pulled her car slowly away from the drop-off point. Sadness sat in the car with her. She felt even more alone than usual in the empty car on the way back to Birch Valley, but a quick wave of nausea reminded her that she wasn't alone.

***

Rachel had invited Liam to come to her home that evening to celebrate the state testing results, as opposed to going out to dinner as originally planned. He happily accepted her offer, and arrived with a bouquet of flowers and a bottle of wine.

She reached up on the tips of her toes to kiss him. "These are beautiful."

"Just like you," Liam said. A hunger stirred in his green eyes that caused Rachel to melt.

He followed her inside the house. She continued

155

toward the kitchen to find something to put the flowers in.

"Smells great in here," Liam commented as he took a seat on her couch and waited for her to return.

"Don't get excited, I didn't cook, it's a pizza I ordered for us." Rachel laughed as she joined him, snuggling close. Liam had sat the bottle of wine on the table and suddenly Rachel realized she wouldn't be partaking in the delicious beverage.

"That's okay, I figured it wasn't your cooking."

Rachel playfully slapped his chest. They sat there quietly for a moment. Rachel savored being next to him, feeling his warmth from his body radiate to her. She looked up and studied his face. The sandy brown hair a little longer than she liked, his eyelashes were thick and shrouded his gorgeous eyes, and his strong jawline was freshly shaved. She inhaled the scent of his aftershave when a thought crossed into her mind. What would their child look like? Would it inherit the famous O'Brien eyes, or maybe her slightly upturned nose, which she hated? She needed to tell him.

"Liam…"

He bent down and planted a soft kiss on her lips, and electricity burned through her as it always did when his sensual mouth was on hers. *Focus, Rachel.*

Pulling away, she started to speak. "I have something I need to tell you."

Liam's gaze focused on her; she had his full attention. "Everything okay?" Concern laced his voice, and Rachel's stomach became a jumbled knot of nerves.

"Yes, well, that depends, I guess." The words she wanted to say didn't want to leave her mouth.

Liam seemed to sense her hesitation and fear. "Whatever you need to say, just say it." His hands moved from her shoulders to her arms, stroking them gently.

"God, I didn't think it would be so hard to tell you," Rachel managed to say.

"Let me guess, you are finally ready to tell me 'I love you', because honestly, it's not that big of a deal, I already know that you do, and if you don't now, you will," Liam said playfully as he kissed her on top of her head.

"Well, yeah, but no, that's not what I need to tell you. But yes, I do love you."

Liam pulled Rachel up closer to him, as if their bodies weren't already touching enough. "Well, what is it then?"

A loud shriek sounded, and instantly Rachel smelled something burning. "Oh no, the pizza!" Rachel removed herself quickly from the couch, and ran full speed toward the kitchen. She opened the oven door and looked at the blackened pizza staring back at her. Liam came up behind her, and he had already turned off the smoke alarm. He encircled his arms around Rachel's waist. "You managed to burn a pizza that was already cooked, impressive."

Turning around, Rachel had tears in her eyes. This was not going how she imagined.

"Rachel, what's wrong? Don't worry about dinner, we can go out." Liam rested his chin on her head lightly.

"Oh, Liam." Rachel cried, her words muffled in his chest as she started to sob.

"It's just a pizza, sweetheart." Liam cooed softly.

Rachel grabbed Liam's hand in her own and pulled him out the kitchen, the stink of the burnt pizza following them into the living room, making her stomach turn. "Liam, I need to talk to you about something important," Rachel said softly as she tried to steady her nerves.

Liam's eyes followed hers as he waited for her to speak.

She wasn't quite sure where to begin, finding herself searching for just the right words, Rachel slowly spoke, "Yesterday I went to the clinic after work with Chelsea." Liam's thick eyebrows raised slightly. "God, I don't even know where to start."

"Are you okay, are you sick or something? Is Chelsea sick?"

"No, Chelsea is fine. Well, I went in for me, you see I haven't been feeling well, and then I called Chelsea, and that's why she came up, and then I asked Maggie to come over…" Rachel rambled, and burst into tears, unable to say anything else.

Liam's arms swallowed her in a protective embrace. "Rachel, what's wrong? You had Maggie come over?" She could tell his head was trying to process what she had said, and he was more than a little confused.

"Liam, I'm pregnant."

Finally the words fell out of her dry mouth, and her throat hurt as she tried to swallow the uncontrollable sobs. She watched as shock replaced the confusion on Liam's face.

"I mean, how? We've been careful," he asked, running his hands through his overgrown hair.

"Not the first time, apparently. I wasn't on the pill then, and you didn't use anything."

"Wow, so are you okay? I mean…" Liam grabbed Rachel and held her tight, his tenderness and concern for her outweighing anything he was feeling.

Rachel shook her head. "Yes, I'm fine, just pregnant." She laughed uncomfortably.

He stared at her for a long while. It felt as though time was suspended, hanging over them as she waited for him to say something.

"Rachel, I want you to know that I plan to marry you," he announced finally.

She tried to catch her breath. *Marry?*

"Liam, I don't need you to make an honest woman out of me."

"Are you serious? Rachel, you're having my baby," Liam protested loudly.

She rolled her eyes. "I realize that, but we don't live in the Stone Age, and we don't have to get married just because I'm pregnant. I want you to ask me to marry you someday when we both are ready. I want it to be because of our love, not because of what is growing inside of me."

"No, Rachel, I have a certain responsibility to you and to our child. I want to marry you because I do love you."

Rachel absorbed what he was saying, but her brain only heard the part about his responsibility. She refused to get married based off of whatever obligation he felt.

"Can't we just wait and see how things play out with us first? I mean, Liam, we haven't even been a couple for more than two months. I take marriage very seriously, and don't want to rush into something like that."

"I take it seriously too."

"Then let's not worry about it right now, okay?" she pleaded as she reached for him.

"I'm sorry, I disagree. If we are going to have a child together, then we need to be together, simple as that. We need to be a family for that baby you are carrying. I want to be your husband, I want to take care of you." Liam scooped Rachel toward his lap. "I can't help but feel we were taken in this direction for a reason. I didn't expect to fall in love with you when I first laid eyes on you, God knows that, but here I am, hopelessly in love with you and our baby." Liam put his enormous hand over Rachel's flat belly.

"Liam, I don't want to rush into anything, maybe eventually we can get married," Rachel said, remembering her thoughts yesterday during her argument with Chelsea, when she was so quick to want to run away with him. Now that reality had set in, she wasn't just imagining some fairy-tale, and now Liam wanted to get married, and she wasn't quite ready for that. "It isn't something we even have to do. No one is telling us we have to get married."

"I don't want the town thinking I just knocked you up, I want them to know that you're my wife, Rachel."

"Liam, I don't want to fight with you about this.

You can't make me marry you." Rachel leaped off the couch and out of his arms.

"I'm not forcing you, but it's the right thing to do."

"Liam, just go home please," Rachel begged. She didn't need him guiding them with his moral compass right now.

"Rachel—" Liam tried to speak, but she raised her hand and stopped him.

"Please just go."

He left, and Rachel sank back down on the couch. She hadn't intended for things to get so out of hand. Part of her knew that he was going to suggest they get married, of course he would, Liam was as traditional as they came. He was a loyal man who stood by his promises and beliefs. But Rachel lived more of modern life and wasn't so sure she wanted to be captured and slung over some caveman's shoulder. She had already been asked before to become a domesticated housewife for her ex, and that hadn't ended so well. Whatever fantasy Rachel had before was long forgotten as she realized she wasn't cut out to be little Miss Betty Crocker, let alone a mother. What had she gotten herself into? Maybe Chelsea was right.

Chapter Ten

Michael

The bar was quiet. He could hear the clinking of heavy glasses in the background, but he was able to drown that out. Michael worked on his third drink, the amber colored liquid burned his throat as it slid down. He just hoped it would make him forget.

His life had been turned completely upside down, all of his work thrown away and dismissed. His brain couldn't erase the misery of the day's events. He had arrived at the firm, anxious, knowing that today was the day he would learn if he had made partner at one of the most elite firms in Seattle. He had been busting his back for them for several years now, he was at the prime age for the position he was drooling over. At thirty-five years old, he had goals and plans, all of which had fallen through.

More than a month ago his wife, Maggie, took their daughter, Melanie, and left for her old hometown, leaving him in their empty downtown condo. He hardly even slept there anymore, he would go there to shower and grab fresh clothes, but otherwise it was just a shell that held the contents of his life, their life. If learning that his wife was finally pregnant with their second child and leaving him wasn't bad enough, his father had died as well. He had to give the old man some credit; his father had left everything in perfect order, and Michael, as his parents' old child, inherited everything.

Since Michael was alone in the world, both parents dead, his wife and child, soon to be children, gone, he threw himself into work; it was all he had left. When that came crashing down, Michael found himself in an upscale bar that was home to many of the neighborhood attorneys. The expensive place could wet the palate of a lawyer who just won his first case, or lost it. The little bar was tucked in amongst the large skyscraping firms, with its overpriced drinks and pretentious customers, and it cradled Michael as he mourned everything that had gone wrong in his life.

Earlier that day, he was called into the firm's enormous conference room, the partners seated around the sleek mahogany table, with their steel faces, cold and unforgiving, staring at him. There were a couple in the group that eyed him with unspoken apology and sympathy, and he knew right then there was no making partner that day. Sudden anger, which had blended with his grief, erupted. He didn't bow down and accept their dismissal of his hard work and hours that he sacrificed, times he sacrificed with Maggie and Melanie. He hated that Maggie was right, but it didn't matter. He went to his office, gathering all of the possessions he had from practically living there for the last eight years, and then he had left.

He tapped his drink and signaled the bartender he needed another. He needed to forget that everything was crumbling around him. The world he had put his blood, sweat, and even sometimes tears, into was shattered.

***

Michael's back was stiff, he had been sleeping on the couch for the last couple of nights. The house was eerily quiet and felt empty. He didn't know what to do with himself now that he had quit the firm, there was no place to escape the loneliness he felt at home. For the past several days Michael would wander into Melanie's bedroom, her bed neatly made as if it was waiting for her to come home. Her toys were still scattered about the floor, he was tempted to clean them up, but seeing them almost looked like she had just played with them and would return to finish. Michael felt lost inside his own home, his own life. Nothing made sense to him anymore.

He tried to orient himself, as the room was fairly dark and his head spun as he eyed the partially empty bottle of whiskey. He rubbed his face, and he could feel the growth of stubble transforming into a beard. He hadn't shaved in days. Michael thought about calling Maggie, he would kill to hear her voice. He missed her more than he ever thought possible. Things were so screwed up between them, he realized that it was his fault. She never pushed him, never asked for anything, she only wanted him. He was the one that forced his tastes and way of living on her. He could feel his heart, bruised and broken, when he thought about how far away his wife was. He needed her. He wanted his family back. Michael rose off the couch and stared out into the traffic infused abyss, there was nothing left for him in Seattle. Through the fog that had settled in his brain, he found a lighthouse which illuminated the only possibility. Michael needed to go to Birch Valley. He needed to go to Maggie.

***

The span of highway that separated Michael from Birch Valley was quiet and nearly vacant at this time of night. Sober and showered, Michael had thrown together a duffel bag with some essentials and fled Seattle. He felt his body and mind work together on auto pilot, his thoughts free to roam as he cruised his black, sleek car through mountain passes and valleys. Michael worked out various scenarios, wondering if he could convince Maggie to come back home. Doubt plagued him, she had been more than firm that there was no going back, but at the same time he knew she loved him. He hoped that maybe he could convince her to return to their life together, especially since he had left the firm, things would be greatly different. His brain tried to wrestle with how he was going to handle that; it wasn't that he needed the money, especially after everything that was left to him by his father.

He contemplated opening his own practice. He loved law, he liked the fight and the challenges of working his mind around the cases and jumping through hidden loopholes. As a defense attorney in corporate law, he loved the strategy, the virtual chess game of the courtroom. It got his blood flowing; he loved swimming with all those sharks.

His brain reminded him of where he was headed as he saw the thick tree line of Birch Valley come into sight. He eyed the clock on the dash; it was a little after midnight. There was one place he knew he would be accepted that late at night with no notice: Liam's. Maybe he could get some inside info on Maggie from him as well, see how things were going with her. She always told Liam everything, and why not, he was laid back and not the least bit judgmental. Michael was closer to Liam than the rest of the O'Brien siblings. Patrick and Daniel were great guys, but they didn't share the same connection that Michael felt with Liam. So Michael veered his car in Liam's direction. He just hoped Liam didn't mind him showing up. Who knew what ill feelings Liam might harbor? Only one way to find out. Michael pushed the gas down and raced into the dark, shadowy night.

***

Michael's tires crunched over the gravel driveway as he steered his car slowly up Liam's driveway. He could spot the cabin and Liam's old pick-up truck. As he parked and got out of his car, he couldn't help but feel like he was surrounded in complete wilderness. There were no traffic lights, no street lights, no lights cast from neighboring houses, it was solid darkness. Michael wondered how someone could live so removed from everything, but a part of him was thankful to be so far away from the sounds and illumination of Seattle.

A low, golden light emitted off of a single light fixture guided him as he carefully walked up to the door. Knocking gently, he waited. He could hear movement and the sound of footsteps nearing the entrance.

As Liam opened the door, the sudden look of surprise on his face was priceless, "Hey, buddy," Michael said, standing there with his hands burrowed deep into his pockets.

"Michael, how's it going, man?" Liam stepped aside and invited Michael inside.

Michael instantly could feel the warmth generated from the fireplace that was burning a charred log. Liam added another piece of wood, stoking the fire, bringing it back to life.

"Want a drink or something? I'm going to get a refill." Liam waved his small glass that had some remains of what looked like whiskey or spiced rum.

Michael figured he had been sober long enough. "What are you drinking?"

"Some good Irish whiskey, you interested?"

"Absolutely," Michael said as he followed Liam into the kitchen.

Liam grabbed a heavy, small glass out of one of the hickory cupboards. He reached into his freezer and grabbed a little ice. "You want to mix this with anything?"

"Straight is fine, it's been that kind of week. Hell, it's been miserable for the last two months."

"I can imagine, and Michael, don't take this the wrong way, but you look like crap. What's with the beard?" Liam asked as he handed the freshly made drink to Michael.

Michael accepted the glass, and with his other hand felt the thick stubble. He had meant to shave when he showered earlier, but he didn't have the patience, and honestly didn't have the motivation or really cared. Usually he took excellent care with his appearance; he had to in his line of work. The prettier you were, the more likely the jury would trust you.

"Yeah, like I said, I've been having a rough time lately."

Liam ushered Michael back into the living room. He took the recliner, and Michael found a spot on the couch facing the crackling blaze. They sipped their beverages in silence, deep in their own troubled thoughts, each trying to drown the problems and find a solution at the bottom of their glasses.

"How's Maggie been?" Michael finally asked, shattering the quiet they were both so enveloped in.

Liam swallowed another sip. "Well, that depends, she is doing okay, I guess. She is working at the shop, as you know. Melanie is doing great at school, I see her all the time."

Michael nodded. "She ever talk about me?"

"I know she misses you and wishes things were different between you guys."

"Well, I'm here, and I'm hoping we can work on some things."

"That's good," Liam said, taking another swig of his drink, swirling the amber liquid, ice cubes clinking softly against each other.

"So, hey, why are you up and drinking?" Michael asked, realizing that Liam did seem a little different than his easy-going self. He was a little wound up, but appeared to be trying to fix that with the rich whiskey. He sure wasn't drunk yet, but who knew how much Liam had drunk already? The man could hold his drink as good as any Irishman.

"I don't even know where to begin," Liam replied, his eyes staring vacantly into the fire.

***

Michael woke up the next morning, his body sore, and his head pounding. One thing was for sure, Liam's couch was much more comfortable than his. He slowly tried to move into a sitting position, but the whiskey sloshed in his belly and his brain felt as parched as his mouth. They had stayed up and polished off that fantastic Irish whiskey as they shared their troubles. Michael was shocked to learn that Rachel was pregnant, even more surprised that Rachel didn't want to get married. Granted, they had only been dating for a couple of months, but Liam saw things the way Michael had when he got Maggie pregnant. The thought of a woman carrying his child and not being his wife bothered him. He knew he wanted Maggie when he first set eyes on her. She was young, much younger than him, almost a ten year difference in age. The firm had hired her as one of the new receptionists, and Michael had been instantly attracted to her. After charming her, it took only a short time before he was able to lure her to his bedroom. But it was Maggie who had the hold on him, with her magical eyes and gorgeous smile, and the tenderness and sweetness that seem to radiate from her. God, he missed her. His brain squeezed hard against his skull; he needed Aspirin and water. He heard heavy footsteps behind him as Liam shuffled into the kitchen.

"Ugh, my head hurts. You need any Aspirin, man?" Liam offered.

"Yeah, please."

Liam quietly grabbed two bottles of water out of his stainless steel fridge and carried a bottle of pain relief medicine as he rounded the couch and plopped down. Passing Michael the bottle after shaking out a couple of pills for himself, he groaned. "I haven't had a hangover like this in years."

"Thanks," said Michael as he accepted the Aspirin pills and downed them quickly. "I hear you."

"So what's the game plan for today?" Liam asked, his eyes closed as he rubbed his temples.

"Well, once we feel human, or as soon as I do, I need to go and see Maggie."

"I think I know the best hangover cure."

Michael looked at Liam. "What would that be?"

"Breakfast at Herrick's. Works every time."

Michael's stomach was a little unsure, but at the

same time it growled and gurgled, completely empty of food. He hadn't really been eating since he quit the firm, instead filling his hunger with liquid. It clouded the reality he found himself stuck in. But he was ready to face the day. Well, maybe after breakfast.

***

Maggie

Maggie washed the last remaining dishes from Sunday breakfast while the rest of the family had went to church. She stayed behind, as she needed the quiet time. The home was always so full of noise and distraction, it was nice to hear the thoughts in her head clearly. She was grateful to be living at her mother's, but the itching desire to find her own place was growing. Maggie scrubbed an oatmeal-encrusted pot that she had let soak for the last twenty minutes. Her mind wandered as she used a scouring pad to work the hardened oats off the rim of the pot. She felt the bubbly sensation of movement inside of her, which reminded Maggie she was far from alone. A sudden sadness washed over her as the image of Michael cropped up in her mind. She missed him terribly. They hadn't spoken at all the last week, and it had her a little worried. This was not the norm, granted, as she usually just passed the phone off to Melanie because it was too hard to hear his voice, but the fact he hadn't called bothered her.

She rinsed the suds off her hands when she heard

the loud commotion of the family returning. She stayed put, trying to savor her last bit of solitude when she saw her mother, who an odd expression on her face.

"How was church, Mom?" Maggie asked.

"Fine, dear. Um, you may want to sit down," Mary suggested, ushering Maggie toward the table.

"Why?" Then she had her answer. Michael stood in the archway of the kitchen, Liam tucked right behind him with a hopeful smile. "Michael, what are you doing here?" Maggie remained standing, though her knees had gone soft and weak. She tried to steady herself by placing her hands on her narrow hips. Seeing him made her heart race. His face looked worn, and the dark growth of a beard on his face made him look older.

Mary quietly pushed Maggie into a chair. "Sit, dear, I will start some tea." She turned to Michael and said, "You go join her." Mary looked at Liam, signaling that he should leave the room.

Michael crossed over slowly and took a seat next to Maggie.

"I can't believe you're here. I haven't heard from you all week," said Maggie softly.

Michael nodded. "I know, it's been rough. I had to see you."

"Did Melanie see you yet?"

"Your brother called your mom, and Daniel took her out for a treat. I wanted to talk to you first."

"Okay, when did you get in?" Maggie's head was swirling with questions. Why was he there?

"Late last night," he answered.

"How come you didn't tell me you were

coming?"

"Honestly, I didn't know I was going to."

Maggie looked at him with curiosity. "You didn't plan on it?"

"No," Michael said as Mary brought over two mugs of tea.

"Here you go. Now just continue your little chat, I'll be down the hall working on the laundry." Mary winked and quickly left the room.

Maggie felt awkward with Michael, almost like he was a stranger, especially with him donning the new beard. She wondered why he hadn't shaved.

"Maggie, I've missed you so much." His voice was tender, she could hear his longing.

"Oh, Michael." She felt herself on the verge of tears. Just being in his presence again was overwhelming.

He took her hand, his was warm as it covered hers. "We need to really talk. Can we maybe go to dinner tonight?"

Dinner? It was Sunday, so of course the entire family would be at her mother's house. It was their weekly ritual.

"What about you coming here for dinner? Melanie will want to see you," Maggie said.

"Okay, but we need to find some time to talk." Michael squeezed her hand lightly, and she felt her body responding to his touch. She had missed him more than she realized.

"That's fine. I'm sure Daniel will be bringing Mel back soon. You going to stay for awhile?"

"Of course, dying to see my little munchkin. How's my other one?" His brown eyes burned into hers.

Maggie swallowed. "I have an ultrasound scheduled next week. I have already felt the baby move."

His eyes widened. "Really, wow. Can I come with you to the appointment?"

"You'll still be here?" Maggie wasn't sure she understood him. Didn't he have to get back to work? It was strange that he was here now, but it was the weekend, after all.

Michael nodded. "Yes, I will be here for a while. That's why we need to talk, Maggie."

Things weren't any clearer, but somehow they made a little more sense.

***

Michael was stretched out on the couch with his eyes closed, and Melanie was asleep and completely draped over him. Maggie snapped a mental picture of them. Melanie could hardly contain her excitement when she came home to find Michael waiting. The two spent several hours together. Melanie showed him her room and sat next to him during dinner. He was attentive to their daughter, and he laughed with the rest of the O'Briens. The mood in the house felt peculiar to her, like she was living in some sort of dream. Just having Michael there with her and Melanie teased at what life with him could be like again. Maggie could tell that Michael was different, something had changed, and she was dying to talk to him and find out what was going on.

Then there was Liam. After getting over her shock of seeing Michael, when she saw Liam she knew that Rachel had told him. The confusing part was why Rachel wasn't there. Something didn't go as planned, and she intended to find out what. Maggie laid a soft throw over Michael and Melanie, covering them carefully so as not to disturb their nap. She snuck out of the room and went in search of Liam.

Liam was at the dining table, his head in his hands, his shoulders hunched over. This was not how she expected to find him, and her heart hurt for him.

"Liam," she whispered, taking a seat next to him. This was the perfect opportunity for them to talk. Patrick had already left with the boys, Daniel went to play pool with a couple of buddies, and Mary was meeting with her book club down at the Catholic church at the end of town. Grandpa Paddy wasn't feeling too well at dinner and had gone to lay down, and Pat was in the den watching a previously recorded taping of a rugby game. The house was still, and no one was around to bother them. "What happened?"

Liam looked up, his eyes tired, red, and little raw. "Rachel told me about the baby, but you already knew." His tone was flat and so unlike him.

Maggie nodded. "I'm sorry I knew before you, but I'm glad she told you."

"Glad? Why in the hell wouldn't she tell me?" He stared back at her, his eyes filled with questioning anger.

"I don't know, I mean, of course she would," she

stammered. She didn't expect him to be so upset with her. "Liam, what's going on?"

"Oh, nothing, I just knocked up a girl who has no desire to marry me. I haven't told Mom and Dad yet, but Michael knows."

"You told Michael? When?"

"Well, he showed up and I had already been drinking, and then we drank together, and I spilled the beans. I needed to talk to someone." The pain behind his eyes tore Maggie's heart. She had never seen him so wounded.

"Well, in that case, I'm glad that Michael went there first. You needed him," Maggie said in a quiet tone. "I guess I'm still shocked he's here, do you know what's going on?"

"Oh, Mags, I really think it's better if he tells you, it's important that you and him talk."

"Come on, you can tell me what's going on," Maggie persisted.

"Normally, I would. But you and him will talk tonight after you put Mel to bed."

Maggie let out a sigh. "Fine, but tell me more about this thing with Rachel. What happened?"

"Well, she had me come over, things were going good, and then she got all nervous and weird. She cried when she burnt this pizza she got us for dinner, it wasn't a big deal, but she just lost it, Mags, like full-on crying," Liam explained.

Maggie knew the wonderful perks of pregnancy hormones, the swinging emotions that come with it were not only fun to deal with on your own, but great for everyone around you.

"Hormones, Liam, hormones."

Liam looked past her with panic in his eyes.

"Hormones?" Mary repeated. Maggie's back was to her mother. She hadn't heard Mary come into the room, apparently neither had Liam, as they both sat there still and quiet, just waiting for the next thing Mary was going to say. How much had she heard?

Mary made her way to the table. "Liam Timothy O'Brien, please tell me that my ears deceive me?"

Maggie was scared to face their mother, so she remained with her back to the older woman. This reminded her of when they were kids, getting caught doing something bad. She only used their middle names when they were really in trouble.

"Mom," Liam started as Mary sat down across from Maggie. She watched as anger and something else flickered in Mary's eyes. Oh boy, she had heard everything.

"Son, please tell me what is going on," Her voice was flat, calm, and patient.

"Well, we were just discussing—" Liam explained, when Mary raised her palm, stopping him.

"Don't beat around the bush as you both usually do. Maggie, I'm assuming you know a little something about this matter?"

Maggie felt her mother's stare burning into her. She felt like a child again, and prepared for her scolding. She managed to shake her head.

"Liam, honestly, what were you thinking, son? Oh, Lord help us," Mary said loudly.

"Mom, I didn't mean for this to happen."

Mary squared her shoulders. "Hon, I understand that you are a grown man, but you haven't known her for but a moment. Oh, Liam."

Maggie watched as her brother digested her words. His head was bowed, and Maggie swore she saw his eyes well up with tears.

"I want to do the right thing, Mom. I love Rachel," he said, his tone soft as he looked at Mary. "I told her we should get married."

Mary shook her head. "You asked her then? Or did you just tell the poor girl that you would marry her?"

"I guess I told her that I think we should get married. It makes sense, I mean, I have never felt this way about another woman, and she's pregnant."

"Liam, love, that isn't how you propose the woman you want to marry, the woman you love."

Maggie looked at Liam. "Mom's right, you should make it special and make sure that is what you really want to do. There is no law that says you have to get married, Liam."

Mary snorted. "It is the right thing to do, he's just going about it the wrong way. It seems he has gone about it the wrong way altogether. Yes, Maggie, there is a law, God's law."

Maggie had no desire to get into a religious argument with her mother. She went through one before, when she found herself unwed and pregnant. Her mother had made it more than clear when she turned up home with Michael in tow with unexpected news. Mary insisted that they marry, and soon. Maggie felt terrible for Liam, because the pressure was on. She couldn't help but think of poor Rachel, that woman had no idea what was coming her way. Now that Mary O'Brien was involved,

God help them all.

Chapter Eleven

Mary O'Brien might be a lot of wonderful things, but when the woman was upset or disappointed, she was unlike anything anyone had ever seen. She had a way of making the guilt you were already carrying a lot heavier. Maggie watched as Liam finally left the house. She could tell he had been raked over the fiery coals. Mary O'Brien was not a happy woman.

Mary stood in front of the sink, staring out the window at absolutely nothing. Maggie waited, her mother was silent, but it was only temporary. She would definitely have something to say.

"Mom?" Maggie said softly.

"Yes, dear?"

Maggie got up from the table and went to her mother, putting her arms around her mother's soft and plump figure. "It'll be okay. Liam didn't mean for things to happen this way. He loves her, Mom."

"I know, it is just a bit of a mess."

"Mom, like you always say, God has a funny way of doing things sometimes, but things happen for a reason." Maggie tenderly held her mother.

"Thank you, dear." Mary reached around and encircled her arms around Maggie. "So two new babies for the O'Briens, there is so much to do."

Now that sounded more like her mother.

***

Maggie went into the living room to find Michael carefully lifting Melanie off of him. "I'm surprised she is still asleep. You guys had a nice nap."

Michael smiled. "Let me tuck her in, and maybe we can go and talk?"

She nodded. *Finally, some answers.* "Yeah, you want to maybe drive somewhere?"

"Yeah, that sounds good," he said as he carried their sleeping daughter to her room.

Maggie could feel a bundle of nerves tightening in her stomach. She was curious as to what Michael had to say, but she was also terrified. What if he was going to ask for a divorce? She didn't think so, but with how upside down everything was she had no idea what to expect. Maggie just knew things weren't normal, and she wondered if they would be again. She grabbed her sweater, which was strewn over the couch, and she waited for Michael

He walked toward her, his face almost foreign with the beard. His stride was off. Where was the cocky, arrogant swagger she had always seen him walk with?

"You ready to go?" Michael's voice was quiet.

Maggie nodded. She wasn't quite sure what she

was going to find out, but she hoped it would ease the hollow sickness she was feeling. She prayed that whatever he had to tell her wasn't going to completely shatter her already tattered world.

***

Michael sat behind the wheel of the sleek beast, with the glossy shine of its paint cutting through the beginnings of night. The sun was completely gone, and a soft quilt of stars had started to emerge from the sky. They sat quietly as he drove. Maggie could feel the vibrations of the tires hitting the road through the soft leather seats. The only noise was the growl of the engine as it purred on the empty streets.

"Where are we headed?" she asked.

"You live here, why don't you tell me?" She could still hear anger in his voice.

"Why don't you park by the church?" Perhaps it was a plea for a safe haven, as it was the location where they exchanged their vows. He couldn't possibly ask for a divorce if they were parked at the place where their marriage started. *Could he?* Maggie begged her brain to stop thinking.

They found themselves in the vacant lot near the church, which was a giant in the darkness with its tall copper steeple. Stained glass windows were illuminated from lights which remained lit inside. Maggie grew up in that church; it was home to many of their friends and family, a shelter of comfort, a place that harbored peace. Maggie didn't consider herself overly religious, but she kept her relationship with God on good terms, and faith often guided her through her confusing, complicated life. She had said her share of prayers over the last several months.

Michael turned off the car. She could smell the almost worn off hint of his aftershave, and her body reacted the way it always had.

"Michael?" She didn't recognize her own voice, it was uneven and wobbly.

His eyes remained on the windshield, looking up at the steeple that that reflected light from the street lamps. "I'm glad we are finally getting some time to talk."

"Me too." Maggie placed her hands in her lap, twisting them nervously.

"It's been rough, hasn't it?" Michael, still not looking in her direction, reached for one of her hands, gently clasping it in his. "There are not enough to words in the world to tell you how much you mean to me. I first want to tell you how sorry I am."

"Sorry?"

"Yes, for putting you second, for not listening to you."

She squeezed his hand "I know, you're so driven, and I love that about you."

"But I got lost, I was so focused on my goal that I didn't see that the thing I loved the most was crumbling."

"Oh, Michael." Maggie felt her eyes grow full of tears.

"Then for me to fail at our marriage, I didn't expect to fail at my career too."

"Fail at your career? That's the one thing you have been slaving over, you're brilliant and amazing at what you do." She felt a sudden need to defend him, an unexpected rush of sympathy filled her.

"I didn't make partner."

Maggie almost choked. How was that possible? He had been devoting his life to his career, enduring countless nights of working through cases. He was their golden boy, the man who won every time. The clients trusted him; they knew Michael could just about get them out of any pickle they had gotten themselves into.

Michael sighed. "I quit."

The shock from the first news hadn't fully settled in yet before she spoke. "What does this mean, Michael?"

"It means that I'm done. Well, done with the firm, I guess. Done with chasing the dream of making partner there."

"Wow, I guess I'm just a little surprised by all of this. First, why wouldn't they make you partner? You are the best weapon in defense that they have," Maggie said as she placed her head on his shoulder. "Second, what does this mean for us?"

"It means we need to be together, to be a family. When you guys were gone, I couldn't sleep in our bed without thinking of you. I could barely walk past Melanie's room."

"Michael, I'm so sorry."

"No, it was a lesson I needed. Being told that I wasn't good enough brought me to a new level of low. I saw that I had lost everything. I realized that I made excuses, saying that I was doing it all for you. Of course I wanted to provide the best things for you guys, but you never asked me to. You only asked for me, and I was so selfish and couldn't even give you the one thing you wanted." His voice trembled in the darkness that had settled around them.

Maggie undid her seatbelt and threw her arms around him. "I have always wanted just you. I know you worked so hard and gave us everything. But I just want you." Tears assaulted her cheeks. Maggie found Michael's mouth, the warmth of his lips on hers as she couldn't help but feel that her prayers had finally been answered. She hadn't asked God for a whole lot either; she just wanted Michael.

Michael held her by her shoulders. "Maggie, will you guys come home?"

"Come home? Birch Valley is our home now."

"I thought this was only temporary until I got my priorities straight, remember?" He raised his eyebrows at her.

She scooted back into her seat. "Michael, I can't go back. This is where I want to be. Where I want our kids raised."

"What about our life back home?"

"I had no life there," Maggie snapped. She crossed her arms over her chest.

"Please don't be upset." He tried to soothe her, but she pulled away.

"Can you take me home now?" She curled up closer to the door and looked out the tinted window and stared at the church. Had God just tricked her? She didn't understand what was happening.

Michael started the car. "Maggie, I wish you wouldn't be like this. I want us to be together, I just didn't think that we had to live here."

"And what is so wrong with here?"

"Well, nothing really, it's just that, well, hell, I don't know."

Maggie huffed out loud. "You don't know? Well, until you do, I suggest that maybe you go stay with Liam."

The moment the car parked in front of the O'Brien home, Maggie practically jumped out, leaving Michael behind. There was no point in running after him. She had made it more than clear that she didn't want him anywhere near her. He still had a few things to figure out.

***

Michael

He pulled away from the house after watching Maggie shut the door, and his heart sank. He had thought things were going well, they were kissing again, and she was in his arms. Suddenly, just because he didn't say he wanted to live in this tiny little place, she was pissed. Did she really think that Birch Valley had anything to offer him or their family? Granted, he could admit it was a nice enough place. But there was nothing there. Honestly, Michael just didn't see what Maggie saw. Of course her family lived here, and they were great, but could they actually live in Birch Valley? What would they do there? Could they be happy?

He owed it to her to try.

His car found its way to Liam's cabin, but he remained inside of his car. There were many things to consider. He rubbed his face, frustration ringing throughout his body. He hadn't slept well for what felt like weeks, months, maybe even years. He closed his eyes and let his worries rest. Not like there was a whole lot he could do right now. Tomorrow was a new day, and he hoped to prove to Maggie that their marriage meant everything to him.

Chapter Twelve

Maggie

Dew drops sparkled as the sun cast its morning rays brightly on everything. The day was already warm, the best kind of spring days, when everything is full of promise. Maggie had shoved away the dark, angry thoughts she had from last night. It was a new day. As she walked with Melanie, hand in hand, answering the silly questions that children ask, she couldn't help but appreciate the simplicity of their life. She wished Michael could see that and cherish it. This was why she had moved; things weren't so complex in Birch Valley. People just lived and pursued their basic needs.

Maggie could see the school in the distance, the outline of the aging brick building standing strong and waiting. She felt Melanie quicken her pace; she could tell her daughter was excited to get to school. Such a difference from over a month ago, when her daughter had been stomping her feet, defiantly refusing to enter the very grounds she was practically running toward. Then Maggie saw what Melanie saw. Michael. He stood there in a pale blue sweater and dark jeans, and his face still wasn't shaved. His hands tucked into his pockets, and a broad smile as he saw them approaching.

"Daddy." Melanie tore from Maggie's hand and ran toward him. He dropped down and scooped her up into his arms.

"My little ginger snap." He kissed the top of her head.

Maggie was standing there, more than a little surprised to see him there this morning.

"Good morning, Maggie," he said, his brown eyes looking up at her.

"Good morning."

Melanie reached for Michael's hand and started to drag him toward the school. She extended her other free hand to Maggie. "Come on, Mom." Maggie took her daughter's small hand, and the three of them made their way inside.

Michael let out an appreciative sigh once they were in the foyer, his eyes scanning everything. "Melanie, wow, what a great school."

"Thanks, Dad. Mom went here when she was a kid. Uncle Liam is a teacher here too."

Karen smiled at Maggie and rounded the counter quickly, extending her hand out to Michael, she said, "Hello, you must be Melanie's father, Michael. So nice to meet you. I'm Karen, the school secretary."

He shook her hand and gave her one of his killer smiles. Maggie almost laughed out loud as she took in the encounter. Her husband had the ability to charm just about anyone, and apparently Karen wasn't immune. "The pleasure is all mine."

The shrill of the bell echoed loudly against the walls. Melanie looked up at Maggie and Michael, reaching up on the tips of her toes to give them both a kiss and hug. It was a surreal moment, standing with Michael, watching Melanie hurry to class, just being together as a family in Birch Valley.

Out of the corner of her eye, Maggie saw Rachel making her way down the hall.

"Hey, guys," Rachel called out happily. She looked at Maggie with a curious expression.

"Good to see you again, Rachel," Michael said as he gave a slight wave.

"Likewise." Rachel turned to Maggie. "Do you think you can sneak away for lunch sometime this week?"

"Yeah, sure." Maggie tried to act nonchalant. She knew that Rachel had questions for her, and Maggie had some things she needed to ask Rachel herself.

"Well, I just wanted to say hello, you guys have a great day." Rachel's perfect smile beamed at them brightly.

They started for the exit. Maggie waved at Karen as Michael held the door open.

Once they were outside, Michael asked, "You want to get something to eat?"

"Actually, I need to get down to the shop." She glanced at her watch. "Lunch, maybe?"

He smiled. "That would be great."

It felt strange, almost like they were dating again.

"Can I give you a ride to the shop?" Michael offered.

"I like walking, it's good exercise and helps clear my head. But thanks."

"Okay then, can I walk you to work?" *Persistent devil.*

"Sure, why not, even if I told you no you still would anyway," Maggie said, feeling herself smile a little.

He grabbed her hand, and they set off in the direction of the shop. Neither of them talked. It was comforting just walking, keeping in a synchronized rhythm as their legs carried them. They used to always be in sync, what had happened?

"Maggie, I'm sorry about last night," Michael started to say as he switched from holding her hand to placing his hand on the small of her back as they crossed the street.

She relished the firm placement of his palm against her, the affectionate, yet protective gesture. Maggie felt the baby move, as if it acknowledged that its father was near, reminding her that there was so much more at stake.

***

Shutting down her computer, Maggie grabbed her purse and jacket when Michael walked in.

"I got a little caught up in something, sorry for being late."

"That's okay." She was curious what had kept him, after all Liam was at work so Michael hadn't been hanging out with him.

Michael leaned against the counter, and his body relaxed itself unintentionally into a sexy position. Maggie's insides stirred. Would she always have this reaction to him?

"So, where are we going to eat lunch?" His eyes stared quietly, consuming every inch of her. She could see the flame of desire licking inside of them.

"Um, H-Herrick's?" she stammered. Her throat was dry, her body tingled, betraying her as it quickly warmed to him being close.

"Wherever you want." The swagger and confidence had returned. She was dying to know just what he had been up to since that morning. Something had shifted, he was more like himself. The man she saw yesterday, that was the broken version. She felt herself smiling again as they left the shop. Maybe she needed to reconsider how stubborn she was being.

* * *

Michael

Just being around her drove him crazy. He wanted to take her somewhere other than Herrick's. Preferably somewhere with a bed.

He woke up early that morning with a plan, after weighing all the options life was offering, he figured on one option, truly the only one at that point that would solve everything. He set his plan in motion after he had walked Maggie to work.

He opened the door for her and waited as she slid onto the leather seat. She looked beautiful today, hell, she looked beautiful everyday. He had missed that when she was gone. Her chestnut hair was in a loose bun, several rebellious pieces straying and curling around her neck. He fought the urge to tug at a strand. The pale green skirt that swirled against her legs, the snug white v-neck shirt, it was a simple spring outfit, but to Michael it highlighted her gorgeous figure. He could see the soft outline of her belly protruding just a touch through the shirt. Knowing that she was carrying his baby inside that beautiful body of hers only increased the desire he felt for her. It also spurred on feelings of wanting to protect her. He loved her so much.

Michael walked around the car and let himself in, reclining in the comfortable seat. He started the engine. It purred down the road.

Maggie was quiet and looked to be deep in thought before she finally spoke. "You know, Michael, maybe I'm not being fair to you."

"How so?" Michael wondered where this conversation was headed. He eased up on the gas; he didn't want to blow his surprise.

"Well, about not giving you a choice in the matter about where we will live. I guess I just don't really want to go back to Seattle. I love being with my family, I like that Melanie is thriving here now."

"Yes, she does look happy, it has to be pretty neat to go to a school where your uncle teaches."

"But I'm sorry for just refusing to even compromise." She placed her hand on her curved belly.

Michael swallowed. What was she saying? That she wanted to go back to Seattle?

"Maggie, I want to show you something." He turned down a road in the opposite direction of Herrick's.

Pulling up to a vacant building on a corner, he stopped the car. The building was an older brick home, but had been converted into a piece of commercial property. Two large maple oak trees stood proudly on either side.

Maggie's brow creased in confusion as she asked, "Why are we here?"

Michael quickly hopped out of the car and raced around to open her door. She moved slowly, cautiously as he extended his hand to her.

They followed a sidewalk up to a porch where a thick wood door with frosted glass panes stood. Michael fished out a set of keys from his pocket, fiddling with them as he located the one he needed to open the door. He turned the key, and he felt adrenaline course through his veins. He tried to understand her expression after he let them in. Maggie stood still, looking as though she had missed the punch line to a joke.

"What do you think?" Michael wrapped his arms around her hips, bringing her closer to him, but her body was stiff and rigid.

"Michael, I don't understand."

"Well, I think it's safe to say we are going to stay here in Birch Valley."

Maggie softened and turned around, throwing her arms around his neck, kissing him suddenly. The heated friction surged through him as her warm lips grazed his. He could have only hoped for such a reaction.

***

Maggie

After leaving what would be the home of Michael's new practice, Maggie sat across from him at Herrick's. They were dining on club sandwiches as he explained his plans for the future. He told her how he planned to take his time even opening up the business, that they had more than enough money, especially since he had gotten his inheritance. He wanted to even possibly wait to start practicing again until after their baby was worn. She watched as excitement radiated from him, and couldn't help but be affected. The plans sounded great. It was everything she could ask for and more. Maggie just wasn't used to Michael wanting to be home and not work. Maybe he really had changed his priorities, and she silently sent a prayer of thanks to God.

"So now we need to look for a home here soon," said Michael as he took her hand in his own, dislodging her from her thoughts. "I guess that means we need to put the condo up for sale."

"Are you sure?" Maggie asked, still reeling from the shock that Michael had leased a building to open his own practice. She hadn't expected that at all. In all honesty she figured he was going to give her some long-winded argument and try to convince her to move back, so the whole thing had thrown her for a loop. She was worried it wasn't real, and she wanted to pinch herself.

"Of course I'm sure. Our life will be here now."

His stare burned into her, and she couldn't help but feel giddy and terribly attracted to him in that moment. These were all the things she had longed to hear him say. She was willing to compromise that day. After she had gone to bed angry and frustrated, she woke up and realized one thing: at least he had finally come to her. That was worth its weight in gold.

Michael went on to discuss the available properties in the area according to the town realtor, Cheryl. Maggie's head was swimming with all the details and various options. He showed her photos of the properties on his cell phone. There weren't a ton of listings, but the ones that Michael were entertaining the idea of buying were incredible. Some had a lots of land and were far too large for their small family, and a couple others were located right in the heart of town and completely adorable. She felt herself leaning more toward those possibilities because she enjoyed walking Melanie to school. Granted, a home on the lake would be amazing. She couldn't help but feel it was all a dream. It was too much to hope for, and she couldn't shed the feeling of waiting for the other shoe to drop.

***

After lunch was consumed and dreams of the future were shared, Maggie went back to work. She sat staring at the blank computer screen when Patrick walked in.

"Hey, Maggie," Patrick said, handing her a stack

of new invoices to process.

"How was the job?"

Patrick and Daniel had just been giving an estimate to a Russian-owned farm on the outskirts of town to possibly build an enormous shop. The Belsky family was well known in the community for the goods that came from their farm. They had two daughters; Maggie had gone to school with them. At fairs and open markets they sold canned preserves, and beautifully handcrafted garments and quilts. Recently, on a trip to one of the farmer's markets, Maggie had asked the older of the two, Hannah, about making a baby blanket for her. Hannah was kind and shy. Her sewing skills, with their bold and intricate designs, were flawless, and her creativity was impressive to say the least. There was a stigma about the Russians who had migrated to Birch Valley, that they opted to live outside of town, owning and operating their own farms, and that they kept to themselves in general.

"It went well. They have a nice piece of property out toward Lilac Lake."

"Where's Daniel, by the way?" Maggie asked.

Patrick smirked. "Oddly enough, still there. He got to talking to one of the daughters there. You know how he is, if he sees an opportunity he's all over it."

Maggie smiled. "Well, good for him. So, I had lunch with Michael today."

"Yeah, how did that go?" Patrick leaned against the counter, scanning through a thick pile of mail that had been dropped off. He didn't seem very interested in the subject of Michael, all things considered. Maggie didn't get into deep conversations about her life with Patrick; she never had. Liam was her confidant. Given that Patrick wasn't exactly keen on Michael at the moment, she proceeded with caution. He kept his thoughts to himself, but he wore them on his face. Maggie knew that Patrick played the part of big brother, protector and defender, very well.

"Well, actually, he leased a building here in town."

Patrick's eye went wide. "What? Seriously? So you guys are going to stay here then?"

"I guess so, he talked about selling the condo and looking for a home to buy here. He already signed the lease and got the keys. He's going to open up his own practice eventually."

"Wow, that was quick. Well, you know, I'm glad that he finally figured it out."

"You and me both." She laughed. Since she started to work at the shop, Maggie had learned more about the how her oldest brother worked. He was a complicated, moody guy who really had a heart of gold. She knew he still mourned Beth, but she hoped that someday he could find peace, and possibly happiness, with another woman.

***

Melanie giggled harder than Maggie had ever seen before. Michael sat across from their daughter and made silly faces at her as they shared a pizza at the only pizzeria in town. It was called Steve-o's, and they made killer calzones and had the most heavenly sauce. Maggie had never found a better pizza in all of Seattle, and she had tried. Pizza was one of her staples.

"Dad, you are so silly." Melanie squealed with delight.

Stringy cheese was hung out of his mouth, and he crossed his eyes. Michael's little performance was just for Melanie.

Maggie relished the moment; things were finally falling back into place. Melanie had her father, Maggie had the love of her life, and they were all together.

She was taking a sip of water when Michael asked, "So who is excited to go and look at houses?"

"I am!" Melanie exclaimed. "But will I still get to go to see Grams?"

"Of course, sweetie." Maggie chuckled as she patted her arm. "That is the wonderful thing about us all living so close. You will be able to even have your cousins come over to play."

Michael smiled. "Speaking of cousins, you going to have lunch with Rachel soon?"

Maggie raised her eyebrows at him, signaling that Melanie didn't know about Liam and Rachel's unexpected surprise. "She sent me a text, we are going to meet up this weekend actually."

"Liam asked me to go fishing, that okay?"

He was asking her permission. That was new. "Yeah, I'm so glad you are going to finally go. It'll be good for Liam too. You guys thinking of fishing on his lake?"

"Probably. I think I like the idea of being able to

finally relax. But honestly, it feels weird to not be working."

"I can only imagine, but we like having you around, don't we, Mel?"

Melanie nodded in agreement. "I'm so glad you are here now, Dad."

"Me too, my little ginger snap," said Michael as he reached across the table and stroked Melanie's cherubic face.

Chapter Thirteen

Rachel

Rachel prepared a simple lunch of a can of soup, as that was all that her stomach would allow. The nausea she felt was becoming more regular. She didn't understand why it was called morning sickness; it hit any time of the day, morning absolutely, noon positively, and night, of course. It was all day, every day. She heard a faint knock on the door. She wasn't expecting anyone, but Liam and her did have plans that evening to talk. Rachel opened the door without peeking first, and to her surprise Mary O'Brien stood outside.

"Hi, Mary, come on in." Rachel stepped to the side and gestured for her to enter.

"Sorry to bother you, dear, but I thought we might be able to have a chat."

"Sure, I was just heating some soup, you are welcome to some. Or maybe I can get you something to drink?" Rachel offered as she lead Mary towards the kitchen. Funny how much time

Rachel spent in that part of the house. Even at the O'Brien home, they were always in the kitchen, a room that Rachel never used except to make coffee and store fruit or veggies for salads. Cooking was not her strong suit.

"Tea would be lovely, if you have it."

"Sure, that sounds really good right now," Rachel said as she took two generous mugs out of the cupboard and started to fill a kettle to put on the stove. Rachel's mind churned. She was curious why Mary was there. Did she know about the pregnancy? Liam hadn't mentioned to her if he had told his family yet, but then again she had been avoiding him like the plague. Maybe Maggie slipped and spilled the beans? Or maybe she was just paranoid, she hadn't been herself for weeks now.

"Rachel, come and sit, please." The tone of Mary's voice set off alarms in Rachel's brain. She knew. She hurried back to the table, Mary's commanding tone partially scaring her.

She smiled, and Rachel took a seat across from her. Mary reached for Rachel's hand. "Dear, I'm not one to beat around the bush, I already know."

"You do?" Rachel asked cautiously.

"Yes, and though I don't agree with the speediness of this whole matter, it is what it is. However, my son loves you. I know that you love him as well, so, Rachel, my love, why won't you marry the poor boy?" Her eyes were slightly wet and pleading.

Oh, boy. Rachel let out a small sigh. "Mary, I truly care about Liam. Actually, I care about all of you, your family has made me feel welcome. It's just that this is all moving so fast."

"I know, but sometimes things happen, and they are meant to be. I can only imagine how scared you must be. This is a major, life changing thing, Rachel."

"When I moved up here, I had no intentions of getting involved with anyone. Then I met Liam. And, Mary, I do love him, but I hate the thought of us getting married just because of the baby." Rachel's hand traveled protectively over her flat stomach, and she felt on the verge of tears. "I never expected any of this."

"Well, think of this as a blessing. You are a blessing, Rachel, you have brought my son so much joy. As a mother, I couldn't have picked a better woman for him."

Rachel looked at the older woman and saw the sincerity in Mary's eyes. She rose from her seat and went over to Mary, wrapped her arms around the other woman, and started to cry. "Oh, Mary."

"It'll be okay, love. We are all here for you."

Rachel swatted away her bangs and wiped away her tears. "I know, and I appreciate it. I'm just so scared."

"Have you told your mother yet?"

Rachel shook her head. "No, I'm so terrified of what she will say."

"Well, we will get through this." Rachel moved back into her seat as Mary continued. "Are you happy at all about this baby?"

"Truthfully, yes. I didn't know if I ever would want to become a mother, but ever since I have been around you and Maggie, seeing what great mothers you two are, it has made me feel some maternal needs. Then when you add Liam into equation…he's such a great man. I have never felt this way about another guy before. I wouldn't want anyone else to be the father of my children." Rachel was shocked as the words tumbled out of her mouth. The honesty was liberating. To speak so openly and freely, especially to Liam's mother about such a sensitive issue, surprised her.

"Things will be fine, and you will make an excellent mother. I know you and Liam share something special, and God has put you in his life and in our lives for a reason. He is funny like that, but he doesn't make mistakes."

Rachel gave her a smile. "I left California in search of something. I just had this desire to go looking for whatever it was that was missing in my life. I'm just shocked I found it so soon."

"Well then, dear, it looks like we have a lot of planning to do."

The tea kettle screeched loudly. Somehow Rachel felt like Mary was right; things were going to be okay.

***

Liam

The sun sat in the east as Liam and Michael cast their fishing poles out into the dark water. The boat was small but perfect on the calm lake on Liam's property. Canadian geese honked overhead, and the morning was alive with several deer drinking from the lake in the distance. The fish were already biting. It was going to be a good day.

Liam took a sip from his travel mug, enjoying the dark flavor of the roasted beans. He sighed. "Can't beat mornings like this."

Michael grinned. "I can't tell you how relaxing this is. I'm having a hard time getting used to it."

"Well, this is life here in Birch Valley. No skyscrapers or traffic, just these birds and animals. It's slower here."

Michael reeled in his line slowly, dragging it delicately through the water. "So, how are things going with Rachel?"

Liam huffed and reeled his own line in, recasting it out to the glass-like water. He heard only the soft *plop* as the line dove into the water. "We are getting together tonight to talk."

"Yeah, Maggie is going to have lunch with her today. They sure have gotten close, it's really nice for Maggie to have a friend here. And then considering they both are pregnant, pretty cool for them, I would think, to have someone to share that with."

"Rachel really likes Maggie. I just hope her and I can figure things out. I didn't mean for this to happen, well, at least not so soon."

"You know, you aren't the only one. Why do you think Maggie and I got married so soon?" Michael said with a knowing gaze.

Liam raised his eyebrows. "Really? I thought you guys got married and then got pregnant with Melanie."

205

"Oh no. I remember how scared Maggie was to tell your mom, and then when she did Mary insisted that we get hitched and then say we got pregnant. She worried about Maggie and just wanted to protect her. Best decision ever, though. I would have married her the second I met her if she'd let me. Didn't matter that she was pregnant."

"That's how I feel about Rachel. I just want her in my life, the fact that she's pregnant makes me want her even more. But it wouldn't matter, she's so different than any girl I have ever been with."

Michael took a sip out of his travel mug and sighed contentedly. "You ever really look at how beautiful this is? I mean, look at the fog lifting from the water over there. I think I want a house on a lake."

"Yeah, I love this property. When are you guys looking at some houses?"

"Tomorrow we meet with Cheryl and go over our wish list. Maggie thinks she wants to be in town so she can walk to the school and work. But man, I love it out here. It's so quiet and hidden, a man can actually think."

"Yeah, I wonder where Rachel will want to live if we get married. I love this place."

A bald eagle flew by them. It ran its talons through the water, trying to catch a fish for breakfast. "Well, no matter what our women tell us, don't ever sell this property, this needs to be our retreat."

Liam laughed. "I'm never getting rid of this place, trust me."

***

Maggie

It was a little after one in the afternoon as she headed toward Rachel's home. Maggie was eager to sit down and really chat with her friend. She wanted to see how Rachel was doing, and was dying to share her good news. The sky was a pale blue, with white fluffy cotton ball clouds that floated happily along. The sun was warm and shining brightly. Maggie let out a breath. She was content and happy. Things were finally in place, or at least headed in the right direction. The next day Maggie and Michael would be meeting with the Realtor to discuss properties. The very thought of making things more concrete thrilled Maggie. She could actually relax; she knew that it isn't just a dream or wish, it was her life now.

She parked her car and had a little more pep in her step as she practically skipped up the walkway. She happily knocked on Rachel's front door.

Rachel opened the door and greeted her with a smile. "Come on in."

Maggie hugged Rachel and entered the home.

"You look happy," Rachel commented as she plopped down on the couch, where she her legs under her body.

Maggie joined her on the same couch. "I am. Oh God, I have so much to tell you. But first, I want to know how you are doing."

"Well, I'm doing okay, actually. Your mom stopped by yesterday, and we had a nice chat."

"Are you serious? What did she say?" Maggie grew concerned, but she had faith that her mother would only be kind to Rachel.

"Well, she helped me realize that things are meant to be, no matter how outrageous they might seem. She's happy about the baby, which is a huge relief. Granted, she feels the way I do, it's a little soon, but she was super supportive."

"That's good. I know she is a little thrilled to be having two brand new grandbabies coming her way." Maggie paused and reached for Rachel's hand. "But what about you and Liam?"

Rachel rolled her eyes. "I'm going to see him tonight, we had planned on talking. I feel horrible, I have been avoiding him."

"So what do you want to do about all of this?"

"Honestly, crawl into a hole." Rachel laughed loudly and playfully slapped at Maggie. "Seriously, Liam and I need to talk more and really decide what we both want."

Maggie released out a loud sigh. "What do you want?"

Rachel pursed her lips thoughtfully. "Well, I love Liam, simple as that. As much as I try to fight it, it's always there. I guess part of me just feels like, how did I end up here, and so quickly?"

"Um, I can tell you if you are really confused." Maggie laughed.

"I mean, it's just wild to think I'm going to have a baby, something I wasn't sure would ever happen. And then to fall in love with someone like Liam, who frustrates me but makes me feel things I never knew were possible. Without getting into too much detail, I know how I got into this mess. But I'm glad it's with him."

"Ah, that's so sweet. So do you think you guys might get married?" Maggie asked hopefully. She really hoped that Rachel would be open to the idea. She loved the thought of her friend becoming her sister in-law, especially with having babies near the same age.

"Ugh, that is where it gets all weird, you know? Like, of course I want Liam, but I hate the thought that we are just doing it for this baby."

"Trust me, it isn't just for the sake of the baby. Liam has shared with me how much he loves you. You have changed his life in so many ways."

"Well, especially now."

"Good grief, Rachel. You know, I was you almost seven years ago. I found myself tangled up with this gorgeous man, then pregnant."

"You got pregnant before you guys were married?" Rachel asked, her eyebrows raised high in surprise.

Yeah, so trust me, I get where you are coming from. I had only been with him for a couple months, but I knew I loved him and wanted to spend my life with him. Do you feel like that with Liam?"

"I do, I hate that we don't wake up together. I wish he were around all the time, even though I love my space, it feels empty when he's not around. It's been hard not seeing him lately." Rachel's eyes became watery with tears that threatened to spill.

"Trust me, it doesn't get any easier, you'll see." Maggie ran her hand along the couch, she realized how hard it had been not having Michael around.

She switched the topic a little. Maggie asked, "So, how are you feeling? Morning sickness getting any better yet?"

"Like the thought of food grosses me out," Rachel said, putting her hand to her mouth. "Is it always this bad?"

"Well, I was really sick with Melanie, but this one, oh boy, really amazed me. But I'm feeling good now, I actually have energy again. When is your ultrasound?"

"Like in a couple weeks, I think the second week in May. I'm glad to hear that there is a light at the end of the tunnel."

"That's exciting. I am having one next week. Do you see the irony of having an ultrasound right around Mother's Day? That's kind of special, isn't it?"

"It is, I know. I just can't wait until I start feeling more human, and I think seeing the baby will make it feel a little more real," Rachel said as she picked at something on her jeans.

"Oh yeah, and then wait until you are starving all the time. Speaking of which, what do you want to do for lunch?" Maggie's stomach gurgled.

"Ugh, the thought of food. But yeah, let's go somewhere."

"It will get better, Rachel, I promise. It will all be better."

***

Liam

Liam tapped the steering wheel of his truck along to the song that blasted out from his radio. He was in a great mood; hanging out with Michael and fishing had done him a world of good. Just being out on the water, the simple act of casting the line and hoping for a bite, was a great distraction. They didn't catch a single fish, but Liam took so much away from it. He saw Michael differently. Liam already liked Michael and knew that he was good guy, but their time on the water showed Liam a relaxed version, a changed man. He looked forward to spending more time together, and raising their children together. Liam sighed as he got closer to Rachel's home. What was he going to do about her?

The little yellow house appeared, and Liam parked his truck next to her Silver BMW. They were so different, complete opposites. How they ended up together still surprised him. He strolled to her porch, knocked lightly, and found himself smiling.

Rachel opened the door slowly, and once she saw it was him her eyes flickered with a new light. Liam enjoyed how they changed shades of blue, depending on her mood. She reached up to him, looped her arms around his neck, and rose up on her toes to meet his mouth with her own. She tenderly kissed him, and it sent a shock of heat through him as he pulled her closer.

"Well, hello," said Liam as the kiss ended and they broke apart.

Rachel touched her lips. "Hi, yourself."

Liam followed Rachel inside. He hoped that kiss was the start of a much more entertaining evening. The day already turned out to be great all the way around. He watched her move, her jeans snug against her legs. Her v-neck shirt hugged her torso, the gray material set off a pattern of blue in her eyes he hadn't noticed before. She was plain delectable. He groaned. Being away from her had been frustrating, he wasn't sure how more he could take. She had been avoiding him and keeping her distance for the last week or so, and being unable to touch her was killing him. He needed her kiss more than she realized.

Rachel went into the kitchen, and he trailed after her, enjoying the view from his angle. "You want something to drink?"

"Sure, whatever you got is fine."

"Iced tea okay?" Rachel offered.

Liam nodded, and he crept closer. He linked his arms around her as she busied herself at the counter filling the glasses. He nuzzled her neck and breathed in her floral aroma. "God, I've missed you." He could lose himself in her softness.

"Oh, Liam." She moaned.

He ran his hands down her sides until they were flat and gently resting on her tummy. "How have you been feeling?" Liam asked carefully. He didn't want to turn their discussion into an argument, but he was genuinely concerned. He had been thinking about their situation every day since she had told him about the baby.

Rachel laid her hands on top of his. "I feel like hell, but this feels nice right now."

"Is that normal, I mean, feeling so bad?"

"I talked to Maggie, she says it's totally normal." Her voice turned breathy. "I've missed you too."

Liam reluctantly pulled away. He could have held her for the rest of the evening.

Rachel turned around. "Let's go sit in the living room." She guided them to the couch and placed the drinks on the coffee table. She sat down.

Liam joined her on the opposite side, and he reached out for her. He had to touch her, to feel the connection that had been absent. His fingers curled gently along her neck as he started to stroke her exposed collarbone.

"Liam, what am I going to do with you?"

"Love me." He moved in for the kill, smothering her words with his mouth. Her hands flat on his back, she braced herself as he seductively attacked her mouth. He could hear her moan against him. They couldn't keep away from each other. Liam needed her to understand that him wanting to marry her was for so many more reasons than the life that was growing inside of her. He needed her like he needed air. The swelling of his heart threatened to burst from the love he felt for her. And by the way her body responded to his touch, he had the sneaking suspicion she needed him just as much.

Chapter Fourteen

Maggie

The cold sensation of the jelly on her stomach sent a shiver down her entire body. It had been over six years since she had been through such a procedure, and a mixture of nerves and excitement coursed through her. She had asked Rachel and Mary to come with her and Michael. She wanted to share the experience with her mother, and wanted to show Rachel what to expect when she had her ultrasound. Michael held her hand from where he was planted, right by her side.

A woman dressed in colorful scrubs smiled sweetly at Maggie. "Sorry, it's a little cold."

Maggie felt her roll the device along her stomach, traveling closer to her pubic bone. Her stomach was fully exposed, and she felt embarrassed. She had noticed her belly starting to grow, her jeans had grown tighter, and she knew she would need to switch to maternity clothes soon.

A grainy image flickered on the screen mounted

on the wall and on the computer monitor. Maggie squinted to make out the image. The quiet room let out a collective gasp as they heard the heartbeat of the baby echo loudly. Maggie felt tears stream down her face. She looked over at Michael, his eyes shiny and wet. They squeezed their hands together more tightly. Maggie saw Rachel's reaction. Her friend was smiling wide, and had her arm wrapped around Mary. That special moment would forever be imprinted in Maggie's mind.

After her belly was wiped down and she was given some print outs from the scan, Maggie felt happy and reassured. The baby was active from what they could all tell. The baby's movements were becoming stronger and more regular.

Michael ushered Mary out the large glass doors of the medical building, and Maggie and Rachel walked together.

"I bet you can't wait now, Rachel," Maggie said as they crossed the large waiting room in the clinic.

"It was really something. Just seeing the way Michael was looking at you. Oh, Maggie, it's so exciting. Thank you for including me." Rachel hugged Maggie tightly.

"Just keep that in mind when you have yours next week."

Rachel nodded. "Of course I want you there."

They all said goodbye in the parking lot. Michael and Maggie set off together to his car. They sat as they watched Rachel and Mary drive off.

"That was incredible. It was nice having your mom with us," Michael commented as he started the car. "Do you want to get anything to eat? Maybe go look at houses?"

They had visited a couple houses and narrowed down their choices, but it was so difficult to decide on which one to purchase. Michael was anxious and wanted to make an offer soon, so they could go through escrow and be all moved in long before the baby arrived. Both of them were anxious for their own space, even though they appreciated being able to stay with Maggie's mother. Maggie loved being near her family, but staying with them for the last two months had started to take its toll. She hoped they figured out which home they could agree on purchasing, she wanted their new life to begin, and soon.

***

Rachel

Liam had his arm around Rachel as they snuggled on the couch finishing an old Western movie. As the credits started, she felt herself growing tired. Liam's couch was far too comfortable. Things had been pleasant with him the last week since he came over to her house, granted, they didn't do a whole lot of talking, but things were at least back to normal. That night they were tucked away inside his cozy home, where they dined on chili and cornbread and then decided to watch a movie.

"You ready for bed?" Liam asked, his eyes twinkling with desire.

"I bet you are."

"Hey, I'm only saying it because you look tired. We can stay up, if you want," he offered as he peeled Rachel off of him and removed himself from the couch. Rachel eyed him. He was such a gorgeous man. He stretched his long arms above his head. She watched as the shirt he wore lifted slightly, exposing his strong and lean stomach. A light trail of dark hair spread across his belly, and she couldn't help but wish that her fingers were touching his skin. Her attraction to him just kept increasing, and she couldn't explain the effect he had on her.

"Let me help you clean up," Rachel said as she got up and grabbed a large bowl, which still had some kernels of popcorn in it.

Liam carried their empty glasses and led the way into the kitchen. Rachel couldn't help but think how ordinary it seemed, how simple and completely wonderful at the same time. Being with him in his domain had been intimidating at first, but she somehow felt like she belonged there. If they did decided to marry, his house would be her new home. That spare room near his bedroom could even maybe be the nursery. Her head started to spin when she considered how drastically her life was going to change. Fear crept inside, rearing its ugly head as it always did when she started to have happy fantasies. She wasn't sure why such feelings kept happening, she supposed a lot of it had to do with the guilt she carried for not telling her family about Liam or the pregnancy. Her shoulders carried a heavy burden, one she knew she would have to deal with before too much time passed.

Rachel put the bowl in the sink, and Liam put other remnants of dinner they had left out away. She stood, doubt digging its way deeper, clawing at her mind, and the worry penetrated her core when she felt Liam's arms wrap around her. He bent down, nuzzled her neck, and kissed her softly by the ear. "Let's go to bed." All the negativity had vanished. How was it possible that he could have that affect on her, every time?

***

The sun was barely rising above the small mountains behind Liam's cabin when Rachel prepared coffee, taking in the view out of his kitchen window. She wore one of his shirts and padded around barefoot. The wood floor was cold against her feet. Liam still slept deeply. Rachel had admired him before leaving the warmth of his bed, his eyes closed, long lashes feathered out delicately against his skin. Dark stubble was scattered along his jaw, and his lips were soft and tender, slightly swollen from all of the kissing the night before. She had been tempted to plant her mouth on his, but hadn't wanted to disturb him, he looked so peaceful. He had a subtle masculine beauty that made her want to touch him, to trace the outlines etched on his face. There was no mistake that Rachel loved him. She needed to throw away her fears, confront everything head on, and since the following day was Mother's Day, she decided she would tell her family.

The smooth flavor of the coffee sent a quick

buzz through her. She curled into the breakfast nook. Deep in thought, she set out her plans for battle when she heard the distinctive, heavy shuffle of Liam's feet headed into the kitchen.

"I woke up and you weren't there." His voice was seductive and rough from sleep as he helped himself to a cup of coffee.

"Sorry." Rachel smiled as Liam slipped into the nook with her, and he planted a soft kiss on her cheek.

"Have I told you how gorgeous you are?" Liam asked, his eyes surveying her.

Rachel blushed. He made her feel so sexy, intelligent, and well-loved. Would it always be that way? They both climbed out of the nook.

"So, I was thinking today we should go out on the lake." Liam said as he sipped his coffee and staring into the distance.

"Sure, that sounds like fun. We going to fish?" Rachel still had not been fishing, or, well, ever.

"Yep, it is a beautiful day to go. Also, Mom asked if you were going to come to the house tomorrow."

Rachel nodded. "Sure, I have a gift for her, actually. I can't believe I have been here for over five months now."

"Incredible."

She snuck closer to him, placing her head on his shoulder. "I never thought I could find this kind of happiness, Liam. Thank you."

"No need to thank me, I'm the lucky one." He brought his head closer to hers and lifted her chin to meet his lips. "You want to get dressed and get out on the boat?" His voice sounded different, nervous almost, his eyes darted away from hers.

***

The air was crisp, cool, and dewy as Liam led Rachel down to the dock. He carefully placed their poles and tackle in the boat before helping her in, treating her like she was made of glass. He untied the small metal boat, and turned the motor on low. The boat vibrated quietly along the water, cutting through the smooth surface. Rachel instantly felt sick, she sucked in the breeze, trying to calm her stomach. But even with the slow movement, her body was not happy. She was used to boats, but hadn't been on one since becoming pregnant.

Liam stopped the humming motor once they were in the center of his lake. Rachel could hear the cry of several birds, the solitude and quiet was striking.

Liam readied her pole. "Have you ever fished before?"

"Well, one time my dad took Ethan and I out on a boat in the ocean, but I have fished a couple times off the pier with Ethan. So I know the concept, I've never actually caught anything though."

"Well, it's simple enough, and I can show you how to cast your line if you want?" Liam offered as he reached into his tackle box.

"Sure, I wonder if I will catch something today," Rachel said excitedly.

"Maybe." Liam's voice was quiet as he fed the line. Rachel stared out into the water. Her stomach settled down, and she could actually enjoy herself. She took in the varied shades of green, the trees sheltered against the hills and small mountains. There was tall grass surrounding the shore of the lake. The water spoke to Rachel. It had a completely different beauty than the ocean, but it was majestic and mysterious all the same. She loved the water and its ability to calm and seduce her. She felt tranquil as she gazed at the ripples dancing along the surface, admiring the bubbles from the life that lived just below.

"Rachel, here's your pole." Liam handed her the long wooden pole. She was about to cast it as she slung it behind her, ready to hurl it into the water, when he suddenly stopped her, fear covering his face.

"What?" Rachel was confused. Had she done something wrong?

His eyes followed the length of the line, and she looked down and saw something glitter against the morning sun. Her heart stopped. Tied delicately to the end of the white line was a stunning ring.

"Marry me." It was more of a command than a question.

Rachel admired the gold band encrusted with smaller diamonds and one large stone, and when she slipped it onto her finger it fit perfectly.

She looked up into the hopeful green eyes of her soul mate. "Yes." Rachel felt the word slip out of her mouth. She had no control, no hesitation, it was what she truly wanted. Her heart sang. She was getting married!

Chapter Fifteen

Maggie

Mother's Day started early at the O'Brien house, with the sky a perfect baby blue and lacy clouds that looked like pulled apart cotton. The day promised to be beautiful. Mary had requested everyone attend church services and come to her house to celebrate the day.

Maggie hugged Melanie in the kitchen as all the women were fluttering around. Preparations for the special Mother's Day dinner had begun right after church. The home smelled lovely, scented from all the bouquets of flowers that Mary and Maggie had received in their honor. Melanie had created several fun Mother's Day cards, which were proudly displayed on the fireplace mantle in the living room. Rachel kneaded dough for homemade bread as Mary was busy preparing vegetables for cutting.

The mood was happy when Mary asked, "So, Rachel, how are you feeling, dear?"

Rachel looked up from her task, her hands

dusted in flour. She clapped them together lightly to remove any excess of the white stuff. "Well, I feel good right this second." She laughed and then added, "But, for the most part, I am praying to the porcelain god."

Melanie crinkled her nose in disgust. "That sounds gross." She turned to Maggie and asked, "Mom, can I go play?"

"Sure, sweetie," Maggie answered, covering her mouth with her hand to stifle a laugh as Melanie scooted out of the room.

"How about you, do you still have morning sickness?" Rachel asked.

"Not really, you will start feeling better soon, I promise."

Mary scrubbed some potatoes and commented, "I remember being terribly ill with you kids. Oh, it was awful. But I would do it all again in a heartbeat." Mary turned and squeezed Maggie, who stood next to her.

They continued to work together. They laughed and shared more details of their lives. Maggie and Mary shared the joys of motherhood, reassuring Rachel of the joys of the experience and what she had to look forward to. Mary removed the roasting pan from the oven as she asked that Maggie call everyone in to eat. Rachel had finished setting the table, and followed Maggie as she left the kitchen.

"Maggie," Rachel called to her in a near-whisper.

"Yeah?"

"I wanted to tell you something." Rachel's cheeks flushed a soft pink.

Maggie searched her friend's eyes, trying to get a glimpse if there was something wrong. "Everything okay?"

Liam rounded the corner as soon as Rachel opened her mouth to speak, but she quickly closed it, stopping the words from coming out. He put his hand on her hip and pulled her close to him. He asked, "Dinner ready yet?"

"Yes," Maggie and Rachel answered in unison.

Maggie would have to wait until the coast was clear to ask Rachel what she wanted to say. There was nothing like being left hanging.

After a collective "Amen" was said by everyone, they started dining on a dinner of roasted chicken, vegetables, and sliced homemade, buttered bread that no one could keep their hands off of. Compliments were doled out to the ladies for providing such a delicious meal. The children gobbled up their food quickly and begged to go play outside. It was still light out, and the air was warm, what child could resist?

Maggie watched Liam and Rachel. They were all touchy-feely and giggling, as if they shared a secret between them. She reached under the table and squeezed Michael's thigh. He turned and gave her one of his smiles, one of the ones that completely melted her insides.

Liam cleared his throat loudly. "Hey, guys, I have an announcement."

Eyes quickly moved toward him; he had their attention. Maggie smiled encouragingly. *You got this, Liam.* He stalled for a few moments. He glanced at her and then back at Rachel, then at

Mary, the only ones that already knew.

"Out with it, lad," Grandpa Paddy ordered.

"What's the big announcement, son?" Pat asked softly. He turned his eyes to Mary, who only shrugged.

Liam held Rachel's hand, stroking the top of it with his thumb. "Well, guys, Rachel and I have decided to get married."

Daniel's eyes grew wide. "Whoa, I wasn't expecting that."

Pat looked at Mary again. "I know congratulations are in order, but why the rush?"

"When you know, you know," Grandpa Paddy said. He chuckled. "They are probably anxious to give some wee ones to ol' Mary there."

Maggie watched, she saw her mother turn a new shade of pink. Liam broke out into uncomfortable, nervous laughter. "Funny you should say that, Grandpa Paddy, because Rachel is pregnant."

Maggie could feel everyone room pause in shock, other than the few that already knew the secret. Daniel's eyes grew even wider. He gaped. Patrick stared blankly as he digested the news. Michael moved to Maggie's ear and leaned in, whispering, "I knew." She wanted to smack him. *He knew?* That must have been what Rachel wanted to tell her. Maggie looked over at her friend. Rachel met her gaze and nodded with some slight tears in her eyes—not sad tears, but ones of pure happiness.

"Aye, Mary, looks like we'll be having a double blessing of babes." Grandpa Paddy's thick brogue shattered the silence.

Pat smiled and said, "Welcome to the family,

Rachel. Hope you're ready to deal with this lot."

Mary beamed, a wide smile on her face. "I'm so happy." She dabbed the corner of her eyes with a cloth napkin.

Maggie felt her heart swell with joy. She was honestly thrilled that Rachel agreed to marry Liam. She looked over at her brother. The sheer giddiness that oozed out of him was not lost on anyone. "I'm so happy for you both, this is incredibly exciting!"

Grandpa Paddy tapped on his glass. "I want to say cheers, good health to these babes, and a job well done, my boy." Liam blushed as he turned to kiss Rachel on the cheek. Grandpa Paddy steered his eyes to Daniel and Patrick, who were seated near him and joked, "Looks like you fine lads are next."

Daniel shook his head. "I'm too young, these guys are crazy to get hitched." He paused. "No offense, Rachel, you're awesome. But damn, Liam, baby and a wife, you are going to be a full-on family man now."

"Language, son," Mary reminded him.

Patrick rose from the table. "Congrats, you two." His coloring looked off to Maggie as he muttered, "Will you guys excuse me? I need some air." He fled the dining room.

Maggie stole a glance at Liam, who returned a confused look.

Pat drank from his glass and said, "Not easy for him, I'm sure."

Liam sat his napkin down, eased out of his seat, and left the room, probably in search of Patrick. Maggie felt numb, she had been terrified of telling

Patrick about her own pregnancy. Liam wasn't as hesitant. She couldn't blame him, he was excited and wanted to share the news with the entire family. The hard part was that, in matters pertaining to family, walking delicately around Patrick had become common practice. A piece of Maggie wished her brother could move on and eventually find happiness again, but something blocked him, kept him from opening his bruised heart. Maggie sent out a silent prayer that he could be helped.

***

Liam

Liam closed the front door after he caught up with Patrick, who leaned against the wooden rail on the front porch.

"You okay, man?" Liam asked cautiously as he stood next to his brother. Patrick gripped the railing.

His brother released a sharp sigh. "I mean, I'm happy for you, but damn, Liam, you don't think you're rushing into things?"

"I know it's crazy, but I love her."

"You hardly know her." Patrick's bitter words bit at Liam.

Liam grunted and exhaled hard as he tried to be patient and understanding with his brother. "I know that she is unlike anyone I have ever been with or wanted. You encouraged me to see her."

"Yeah, but I didn't tell you to knock her up and marry her."

"Patrick, that was not intentional, but whether

she's pregnant or not, I want to be with her."

He turned and looked at Liam. "I just think you are getting into something you aren't even prepared for."

"Patrick, I know it's gotta be hard, seeing everyone here married and having kids. I can't even imagine losing Rachel, so I know you have to be hurting, man."

"That's right, Liam, you can't imagine. There's no way you love Rachel the way I loved Beth, you don't know how it feels." Patrick growled and pushed past Liam, leaping down the several stairs to the driveway and to his car. Liam watched as the anger and hurt took over his brother. He felt terrible for Patrick, and he wished that his brother could somehow find peace; he had suffered long enough. Would his brother ever be able to move on, to find love again? God, he hoped so.

***

Maggie

Maggie carried a stack of dirty glasses to the sink, where Mary ran the water to rinse several plates, after which she placed them inside the dishwasher. Rachel was quiet, her head down as she wiped the counter of imaginary crumbs. The jovial mood had shifted after Patrick left. Everyone sort of went off into different directions, which left the ladies alone in their favorite room.

"It's hard on him, all this talk of babies and marriage," Mary said, breaking the silence.

"I know, Mom, but Liam didn't look so happy when he came in. I think they got into a fight, I mean, look, Patrick left." Maggie stood near her mother and leaned against the counter.

"I think Liam just wanted to share with everyone. We should have thought it out better, and taken Patrick's feelings into consideration."

Rachel swatted her overgrown blonde bangs away from her eyes. She looked like she was about to cry; her blue eyes had a sad sheen, and her lips were turned into a frown. Maggie could see that Rachel genuinely felt terrible, and it was a shame that the happy day had to have such an ending.

"Of course Liam is excited to share this important part of his life, we're his family. I just wish Patrick could have understood."

Mary stopped the water. "Patrick will come around, Maggie, have patience with him."

"Mom, I just feel bad that Rachel is upset. This is an emotional thing for her." Maggie glanced over to see tears streaming down Rachel's cheeks. "Rachel, you okay?"

She nodded. "You know, I feel awful about all of this. I'm so happy to be with you guys, and I truly care about everyone in this family." She began sobbing loudly. "I told my parents."

"Oh, Rachel, what did they say?" Maggie moved toward her friend and pulled Rachel to her chest in a close embrace. Mary rubbed Rachel's back soothingly, hushing her and assuring her it would be fine in a delicate whisper that only a mother could.

"They are so upset. I called my mom first, and she is just livid. My dad, beyond disappointed."

"Give them time, dear, they will come around," Mary looked over at Maggie and shook her head. They both knew the kind of relationship Rachel had with her family, and it was far different than that of the O'Briens. That was part of the draw for Rachel when she met them, and they had gladly adopted her.

Maggie pushed Rachel away just enough to see her face. "Things will be okay, and if nothing else, Rachel, you have Liam, and you have us." She saw a faint smile appear.

"When Liam proposed yesterday, my heart and brain were in sync for the first time. I didn't even hesitate." She pulled out of the embrace completely and dried her cheeks with the sleeve of her shirt. "I know I disappointed my parents, I can't blame them for being upset with me. They don't know Liam or you guys, but I hope one day they can meet everyone here and see how great you all are."

Maggie and Mary squeezed her, sheltering her from her obvious pain. The three women stood huddled when Liam walked in.

"Everything okay?" His eyes were dark with concern.

Maggie looked up at him and offered a weak smile. Rachel moved out of the embrace and quickly went to Liam. He circled his long arms around her as she buried her face in his chest. Maggie sighed as she remembered the hurtful things Rachel's friend Chelsea had said. When she watched Liam and Rachel, no soul could doubt that they were in love and that they belonged together.

***

Maggie said goodbye to both Liam and Rachel as they got into Rachel's car. Michael stood next to her with his arm slung gently across her lower back, and he as they pulled away from the house.

"So, wow, huh?" Michael said as the silver BMW pulled out of sight.

"I know." Maggie had wrapped her arms across her chest, and felt a shiver run down her spine as she thought about the emotional evening.

Michael rubbed her back. "You cold?"

"No, not really," she answered. The sun was starting to set, the sky a mixture of orange and red, which swirled together like sherbet ice cream. The air was still warm, and Maggie inhaled the delicate scent wafting from the lilac bush.

"Maggie?"

"Yes?"

"I love you," Michael said as he kissed the top of her head. "Thank you for being such a great mom to our babies." He placed his hand on her growing belly. Maggie covered his hand with hers, and they both felt an incredible hard, swift kick from inside her womb.

"Oh my God, did you feel that?" Michael's brown eyes were wide and excited.

"I did. Pretty neat, huh?"

"I guess our baby just wanted to say happy Mother's Day." Michael planted a kiss on Maggie's mouth, which sent a tingle straight through her.

"How did I get so lucky?" Maggie asked, looking up at him.

"Sweetheart, I'm the lucky one."

Maggie almost couldn't remember the lonely past several months, the tears that had soaked her pillow, the knotted up anger she felt. It all seem so distant. As she stood alongside the man she loved, she felt complete. It had been a hard path which led her and Michael to the road they were traveling on now, but she was glad they were together.

Chapter Sixteen

The alarm shrilled loudly. Light filtered into her bedroom as she slowly, very regrettably, started to inch off the bed. She peeled Michael's arm off, and Maggie slipped out from under the weight of it. She instantly missed the feel of his arm over her as she wrapped herself in her robe and headed down the hall to wake Melanie.

She tapped lightly against the solid door with her knuckles, then carefully opened it. Maggie whispered, "Melanie, time to get up, sweetie." She heard her daughter stir beneath her covers and agree to get out of bed. Maggie left her and went to start breakfast.

Standing at the stove, she pushed the eggs together in the skillet. Maggie felt arms circle her waist. "Where did you go?" Michael's lips found her neck.

"I have motherly duties, you know," she said as her body responded to his touch. She raised her lips to his.

"I guess you're right." He released her and

started for the coffee pot. "So, you want to go check out a couple more places today?"

"We need to. I will go to the shop after we are done. I really want just the right place. I don't know why you want to live outside of town."

"Have you seen Liam's property? It's amazing. The land will be worth a fortune someday." Michael sipped his black coffee.

Maggie stirred the fluffy eggs and added a little pepper to them. "I like the idea of being in town. I love walking Melanie to school. I don't think you will like driving in the snow when winter hits."

"We need to think about getting an SUV or something, I was talking to your brothers about that just the other day." Michael sidled closer to Maggie, and she forked a small helping of eggs into his mouth. "Those are hot!"

"Sorry." Maggie heard little footsteps headed toward them, and Melanie appeared. "All ready for breakfast?"

"Yep, I'm hungry." Melanie took a seat at the dining table as Michael went to pour her some juice.

Maggie filled plates with food and served them as Daniel shuffled into the kitchen. His reddish hair was wild from sleeping, and he yawned loudly before greeted everyone.

"Daniel, there's plenty of eggs, you want me to make you some toast?" Maggie offered as she sat Melanie's plate in front of her daughter.

"Thanks, but I got it," he said as he threw some slices of whole wheat bread into the toaster and started to pour himself some juice. "You didn't make bacon?"

"No, sorry." Maggie laughed. Her brother loved his bacon, hell, the guy loved food in general.

He grunted and served himself some eggs as his toast popped up. He buttered it quickly and went to sit down next to Melanie. "How's my little Mel this morning?"

"Good, Uncle Daniel. Sorry Mom didn't make you any bacon."

"That's okay, I think she'll make some next time." Daniel winked at Maggie as he shoveled eggs into his mouth. "Good eggs, though."

Maggie grinned at him and then turned her gaze to Melanie. "Better hurry, we need to get ready for school." Melanie nodded as Maggie got up to get dressed.

A bit later, Maggie locked the door behind her as Melanie ran to the car. Michael was already in the driver's side. She reluctantly slid inside. The weather was lovely. She would have enjoyed walking tat morning, but they were on a mission to find their perfect home. Not a cloud was to be found in the perfect blue sky, and Maggie took that as a good omen.

After they dropped Melanie off at school, Michael steered them toward the real estate office on the main street. As they cruised slowly, Maggie saw cheery, giant baskets with a mix of bright flowers hanging off each lamp post. Michael found a spot a few doors down from the office and parked.

"So, let's keep an open mind, really weigh in on everything to get exactly what we want," Michael said as he turned off the car.

"Well, quit being so settled on living outside of

town," Maggie responded with a teasing laugh.

"As long as we are under the same roof, I don't care where the house is." He leaned over and kissed her cheek before opening the door to get out.

Hand in hand, they made the short walk to the real estate office. Michael held the door open for her. Janice, the receptionist and close friend of Mary's, greeted them with a broad smile. "Good morning, you two. Isn't it pretty as a picture out there?"

"Remarkable," Michael answered as he ushered Maggie inside.

"Is Cheryl in yet, Janice?" Maggie asked.

"She just called, and she is on her way."

"Well, that's no problem. We will wait here, if that's okay?" Michael asked, flashing Janice his charming smile as he headed toward the small sitting area near a large window.

"Of course, you guys make yourselves at home. How's your mother doing, dear?"

"She's well, thank you," Maggie responded as she sat down next to Michael. Janice rounded her desk and came to join them.

Janice sat across from Maggie, and placed her hand on Maggie's knee. "How about you, love?"

Maggie looked over to Michael and smiled back at Janice, "We are doing great. Starting to feel really good, no more morning sickness."

"Good thing you two are looking to buy your home now, before the baby comes. Plenty of time to set up the nursery."

Maggie nodded in agreement. "Absolutely, we're so excited and really hope we find the perfect place today." She pointed at Michael and continued, "This one wants a place out of town like Liam's, but I want to stay right here in town."

Janice sighed. "Well, both are lovely, but I know Mary would rather have you and those babies close to her."

"I keep telling him that driving into town in the winter is not a whole lot of fun. But he seems to think he wants to live out in the country." Maggie laughed as she rubbed Michael's leg.

"Hey, you can't blame me, it's beautiful out there."

They heard the distinctive clicking of the high heels that belonged to Cheryl. Cheryl was in her late forties, Maggie guessed. She was always sharply dressed and ready for business. She didn't really exude warmth, but she did have a kind way about her.

"Who wants to buy a house today?" her voice sang out loudly.

Michael got up quickly to shake Cheryl's hand. "Good morning, and yes, we are hoping to find the perfect one today." He pulled Maggie close to his side.

"Well, I have several properties I think would be a great fit for what you are looking for. So why don't we get this show on the road?" She turned on her heel and started for the door. She meant business.

***

Maggie stood in awe. This was it, the home she wanted. Located on a large corner lot just a few blocks from the school and Michael's office, it had everything she wanted. The outside was almost as grand as the inside. There was a wrap-around porch, and a beautiful, green, sprawling yard, which was landscaped with precision and love. The two-story home was a muted gray, black shutters graced all the large windows, and a bright red door matched the equally bright red metal roof. The kitchen was incredible, not that Maggie spent a great deal of time in them, but when she lived with her mother she found herself appreciating the space. Stainless steel appliances sparkled, and granite countertops with veiny ribbons of gold sat on top of dark cabinets. The home was modernized beyond any home in Birch Valley that Maggie had ever seen. Gleaming cherry wood floors spread throughout each room, crown molding gripped along the seams of the ceiling. There were too many incredible features to list, but when Maggie and Michael locked eyes as they explored the master bedroom and bathroom, they knew they had found their home.

They stood near the kitchen island, Maggie running her hands over the smooth stone surface as Michael confidently penned his name on the offer. When it was Maggie's turn, she nervously tried to sign her name. The home was not cheap. Michael hadn't blinked an eye at the asking price. She knew they were sitting well from his father's inheritance and would be in great shape once they sold their condo. But Maggie felt her head spin when she saw numbers that large.

Michael must have sensed her discomfort, as he took her hand in his. "This is going to be our home."

"I know, but Michael, it's so expensive."

"Maggie, I would pay any sum of money for the smile that has been on your face the last hour. We are getting this house." Michael's lips touched hers softly, and his hand gingerly stroked her cheek.

***

Maggie sat at her desk sorting invoices when she heard Patrick walk by. He had been quiet since she had arrived. Daniel rolled his eyes at her when she walked in, signaling that their brother was not in the best of moods. Surprise, surprise. That was Patrick, after all. He had always been moody, granted, the last three years were extreme, not that anyone could fault him. He had lost a great deal, and was still grieving. Time moved in slow motion for him. He wasn't growing or moving on from Beth's death. Granted, not that Maggie completely blamed him. If she lost Michael, she imagined she too would be a shell of her former self. It was just hard to watch it on display. With all the new life budding around them, she knew he was suffering.

"Patrick," Maggie called out from behind her computer monitor.

"Yes?" he answered from his office. The door was wide open.

"Do you want to grab lunch together?"

"No, thanks, I have a lot to do here." His tone

was flat.

Maggie sighed loudly. "Ah, come on, we can go to Herrick's."

"I'd rather not today, Maggie."

Well, she tried. Maggie hoped to get him to get out of the office, as getting a little fresh air would do him a world of good. She'd had a great day with picking out the house, and the weather had been gorgeous. The only thing that dampened things was Patrick's sour mood.

She felt her cell phone buzz and saw that Michael was calling. "Hey, hon."

"Babe, they accepted the offer." Joy vibrated from his voice, and pure excitement filled Maggie as she let out a happy squeal.

"Are you serious?"

"Yes, ma'am. We need to go over to Seattle and start getting things in order over there. We even got a short escrow because we're paying cash."

"Paying cash? Michael, what do you mean?" Her guts twisted at the price tag on the house.

"Well, babe, it made sense to offer a little lower than asking, and cash, that way we don't have to wait as long to close. We need to be in our own place."

"But, Michael, that's a lot of money we're talking about."

"We can afford it. I just wanted to make sure we got that house. I know how much you love it, and we are going to raise our kids there. It's perfect." His voice was gentle, soothing her of any worries.

"It is perfect, but I didn't think we could afford to pay it all at once."

"Well, we can, and we just did. So do you feel like celebrating tonight? I figure we can drive Melanie by the house and maybe get dinner?" Michael suggested.

"Sounds great. I'm so ecstatic." Maggie felt the thrill travel through her. They had found the most beautiful home, Michael was going to open up his own practice, and they were all together. Life was good.

"Well, I will see you this evening, love you."

"Love you too." She hung up and practically raced to Patrick's office.

He glanced up from his desk and removed his reading glasses. He dropped the pen hard against the notepad. "What's up?"

"We got the house!" Maggie scooted over to her brother and squeezed him. She needed to hug someone.

"Congrats!" Daniel called from the doorway. "What house did you guys put an offer on?"

Maggie ran to Daniel and circled her arms around him. "Oh, it is just the prettiest place ever."

"I'm glad you guys found something, and it's here in town?"

"Yes, it's the gray house on Lincoln, near the school, and sort of by Michael's building."

"Dang, no way! That place is amazing." Daniel's eyes grew large. "Patrick, remember that one with the black shutters, we helped them with that shop and deck a couple of years ago?"

"Oh yeah, wow, Maggie, you guys bought that one?" Patrick's face wrinkled in surprise.

"I know, it's wild, huh?" She could hardly

241

contain herself, her mind had already started decorating the large home.

"We should all go to lunch and celebrate, maybe drive by it?" Daniel offered with a grand smile.

"I tried to convince Patrick to go to lunch with me, but he wasn't having it." Maggie pouted and placed her hands on her hips, eyeing her brother.

"Oh, fine, I'll go."

Maggie was thrilled he had surrendered. "Let me grab my purse and let's go."

Lunch with her brothers turned out to be wonderful, even Patrick managed to smile and laugh a couple of times. Patrick and Daniel were amazed that the beautiful home was going to be Maggie's. Lots of hugs were shared as happiness overflowed. They joked all the way back to the office, and the light mood followed them for the remainder of time at the shop. Just as the perfect blue sky had promised that morning, the day had turned out wonderful.

***

Rachel

Rachel sat on her couch. Her eyes were red, swollen, and sore from hard crying. She had just gotten off the phone with her mother, who was still livid at the whole mess. She demanded that Rachel return home so they could figure things out together. Her brother, Ethan, had called and tried to talk sense into Rachel as well, and that had completely thrown her for a loop. He explained that

242

she didn't need to go through with this, and that she had options. Oh, she knew what options they meant, and she refused to even consider them.

She heard her cell phone ring, and expected it to be her mother trying to wage war once again, but was surprised to see Chelsea's number on the screen. "Hello?"

"Hey lady, wow, you sound awful. Are you sick?" Chelsea asked.

"No, I've been crying. I just got off the phone with my mom and Ethan," Rachel replied, sniffling and trying to dry her runny nose.

"Ah, I'm sorry. I know my mom had lunch with yours. She isn't happy at all, Rachel."

"Yeah, I kind of got that when we talked. But there isn't a whole lot that can be done, I'm marrying Liam, I love him, and we're having a baby," Rachel said defiantly.

"I know, Rachel, but come on, you've got to admit it isn't really fair, or well thought out. But you're right, there isn't a whole lot that can be changed."

"Thank you."

"So, how are you feeling? Still yucky?"

Rachel huffed loudly. "Well, there are good days and bad days, but for the most part I'm better. I have an ultrasound this week, so I'm pretty excited for that, but nervous too."

"Wow, how neat! Have you felt the baby move yet?"

"No, nothing yet, at least I don't think so." Rachel laughed. She had no idea what to expect with the pregnancy. Her emotions were all over the place, and when she wasn't hugging her toilet, she was starving. She hoped things would become a little more even keel, and soon.

"So, tell me about the ring? I know you sent me a picture of it, but are we talking like huge rock or what?"

"It's stunning, to be honest," said Rachel as she glanced down at her finger.

"You really love him? I mean it's so soon, Rachel," Chelsea said sternly.

"I do, I can't explain how he makes me feel, I have never ever felt this way before. It's truly incredible."

"You sound happy, I can't deny that. I just wish you were here. It's hard being so far away."

"You could always move here," Rachel teased.

"Yeah, I think I'll pass, no offense. Will be happy to visit you, of course, but living there in Birch Valley, um, no thanks." Chelsea paused as they both laughed together before continuing, "So, this wedding of yours, when is it going to be? Before or after your baby?"

"Well, Liam and I really think it would be nice to get married this summer. We are thinking maybe around fourth of July weekend. It would be the perfect time. We are thinking of getting married on his property by the lake."

"Ah, that's sweet."

"Yeah, we just want something simple and beautiful. Maybe an evening wedding and reception. Chelsea, would you be my maid of honor?" Rachel quietly asked.

"Was kind of waiting to be asked. Of course I

want to be, been waiting my whole life for this!" Chelsea's voice was loud over the line.

"That means a lot to me."

"Well, you mean a lot to me. I may not totally agree with the shenanigans you got yourself into, but I support and love you. You better make me the Godmother to that precious baby."

"Who else could live up to that role?" Rachel giggled.

"True, I sort of like the idea of being Auntie Chelsea...that does have a nice ring to it, don't you think?"

Rachel was happy that Chelsea was finally warming up to everything. Their relationship had been strained since Chelsea's visit, and she hoped that eventually her friend could make amends with Maggie.

The two continued to chat about various baby names and what the gender would be. Rachel smiled as her world began to fall into place. The tears from earlier had dried, and they were now replaced with laughter, lots of laughter.

Chapter Seventeen

Maggie

Maggie sat next to Rachel, who tapped her foot nervously. Liam had his arm around her, but looked equally sick. She remembered the first time Michael and her gone to her ultrasound, but each appointment after the first was a treat, they could see their baby.

"It's going to be okay, this is the fun part. Getting to see your little baby is the best thing in the world," Maggie tried to reassure her friend.

"I know, I'm just worried, what if things are messed up or…"

"Stop, don't borrow trouble."

Mary looked up from the magazine she flipped through. "That sounds like something I would say." She smiled at both Maggie and Rachel. "But Maggie is right, dear. You needn't worry, things will be just fine. God has a way of making sure."

A woman dressed in bright blue scrubs ventured out to the waiting room and called for Rachel.

Maggie and Mary trailed after Liam and Rachel, they were led to a darkened room, and Rachel was given a gown to dress in.

"I feel sick," Rachel announced, holding her hand over her mouth. Liam rubbed her back, whispered into ear, and kissed her head.

Maggie remembered the feeling, the nerves and fears of the unknown. "It's going to be okay, I promise you." Everyone stepped out for a moment to let Rachel change.

Rachel poked her head outside in record time. "Okay, you guys can come back in."

The nurse returned with a soft smile and told Rachel to relax. "Sorry, hon, this is a little cold." She smeared a thick jelly on Rachel's tanned, flat tummy. The screen on the wall came alive, and instantly a grainy image appeared. Everyone tried desperately to make it out.

"I have to go to the bathroom so bad," Rachel complained as the nurse rolled the device closer to her pubic bone, pressing hard. Maggie laughed. She knew that pain. They always demanded you come in with a full bladder—pure and utter torture.

A weird mixture of noises filled the room as they waited, holding their breaths for the sound that they all wanted to hear. The nurse's face twisted in confusion, her eyes perplexed as she ran the wand over Rachel again.

"Excuse me, I'm going to get the doctor real quick." The woman hurried out of the room, leaving Rachel and everyone with their mouths gaped open.

"Oh God, something's wrong." Rachel started crying, Liam rubbed her arms and kissed her forehead. Mary immediately pulled her rosary out of her purse, bowed her head, and began to pray, her words a whisper as she worked her rosary, running it through her fingers tightly. Maggie felt the room spinning. Could there actually be something wrong? It could change everything. Guilt started to swell inside her heart. She had done nothing but assure Rachel all was fine, when it very well might not be. She closed her eyes and began to pray.

It felt like time was suspended. The only sound that could be heard were Rachel's muffled sobs.

Moments later the nurse returned. She looked over at Rachel and said, "Oh dear, don't be upset. Everything's okay. I'm sorry, it's just I needed to have Dr. Salinger come in and take a look."

A woman with an overly large mouth and dark hair in a tight knot on top of her head stood in the doorway. "Hello, I'm Dr. Salinger. You must be Rachel?" She extended her hand. Rachel managed to give the doctor's hand a weak shake, as did Liam.

"Well, let's have a look here," Dr. Salinger said. Her eyes were pretty, a pale blue, shrouded by long black lashes. Maggie didn't recall if she had met the doctor before, but enjoyed her calm presence. "Okay, nurse, you were right. Rachel, I want you to close your eyes, listen very carefully."

Maggie watched the panic set into Rachel's face, and gave her an encouraging smile.

"Rachel, listen, do you hear that?" Dr. Salinger asked, her voice mellow and slow.

A rapid thumping sound emerged. It was dancing with another beat. Mary and Maggie looked at each other, then stared at Rachel and Liam.

Rachel wore a confused frown. "I don't understand?"

Liam kissed her forehead. "Babe, I think we're having twins."

Dr. Salinger nodded. Maggie felt tears of relief stream down her face. The rest of the ultrasound was a daze, everyone still reeling from the shock. One moment they were certain that something was terribly wrong, but a double blessing banished all those fears once they heard those two little heartbeats.

***

The family had gathered around the large wooden table, as per usual for their ritual of sharing Sunday dinners together. Smiles were plastered on everyone's faces; there was a lot to be thankful for and excited about. Only one face looked sullen—Patrick's. Maggie kept sneaking glances at him. His mood had been sour the moment he and his sons, Finn and Connor, had arrived.

After dinner was consumed, the children ran outside to play in the backyard. Grandpa Paddy and Pat retired to their favorite spot in the home, the den, where one could always hear a soccer game on and smell sweet tobacco hanging in the air. Daniel excused himself to go and play pool down at Antlers with some good buddies of his. Liam and Rachel remained at the table along with Michael, Patrick, and Maggie. Mary had started a kettle for tea.

Maggie smiled at Rachel and asked, "So, are you still in shock?"

"You have no idea. I called my mom and told her. She was completely surprised."

"How's that going? Any better?" Maggie was worried that this news of twins might upset Rachel's mother even more.

"Actually, she is finally warming up to the idea. She has accepted she is going to be a grandmother, and now plans to be a fabulous one. So we shall see." Rachel laughed as Liam slipped his arm around her shoulders.

"Well, that's good, I'm happy to hear she is finally coming around."

"So, that house, you guys, wow," Rachel said to both Maggie and Michael.

Michael smiled. "It's great, isn't it?"

Rachel's eyes grew wide. "Um, amazing is more like it."

Patrick cleared his throat and asked, "Liam, are you guys planning to keep the cabin or buy another home?"

Maggie was glad that he was joining in the conversation. He had been quiet most of the afternoon. She knew he was struggling with everything that was going on; the news of Rachel being pregnant with twins really sideswiped him. That brought things to the surface for sure, and he seemed to carry a worried expression on his brow.

"We are thinking that since Rachel's lease is up next month, she will move in with me. We love the house, don't we, babe?" Liam looked at Rachel. Maggie could see the love in his eyes. It made her so happy that he had found love, and with such a great woman. She adored Rachel.

Rachel nodded. "I love Liam's place, granted, it would be nicer if we were in town. It's great being so close to work."

"See, I told you. Being is town is great, you can walk everywhere, be close to work. I tried telling this guy that." Maggie pointed at Michael and laughed.

"Yeah, and look who won that argument," Michael replied as he swooped in for a kiss.

Patrick actually had a slight grin on his face. "Yeah, that house is incredible, but Liam's place is awesome. I love my house. I have the best of both worlds I suppose. I'm right outside of town, but not out in the country."

"Your house is gorgeous, Patrick," Rachel commented. She had been invited over there a few times for a movie or pizza with Liam. She also babysat the boys for Patrick one time, and had fallen in love with the house. It was a two-story home, classically beautiful, and charming was an understatement. It still had some of Beth's touches throughout, but overall it was a man's house. Rachel hoped that someday Patrick would meet a woman who could bring in that feminine sparkle that she felt every home needed.

"Thanks, we like it." His tone lacked a lot of light or life to it, but Maggie was thankful that he was even talking to them.

"So Finn and Connor have their birthday coming up soon, right?" Rachel asked. Instantly Maggie's stomach bottomed out, and she stared at Patrick. His eyes grew dark as he simply nodded.

Maggie tried to give Rachel a signal to indicate that topic might not be a good one to start with. She was thankful when she saw her mother enter the dining room with a tray filled with tea.

"Sorry I took so long, I brought Dad and Grandpa Paddy their tea first, and they insisted on having some shortbread cookies with it." Mary smiled as she placed the tray on the table, quickly turning around to fetch cups. She returned with several dainty cups dangling from her fingers as she gave one to each of them, and started to pour the steaming hot liquid from the kettle.

Maggie held her cup, savoring the warmth that radiated from the fine china. She inhaled the fragrant scent of the herbal blend. She sipped slowly, the heat scorched her tongue and mouth.

They continued to sit and dine on cookies and sip their tea. The conversation had steered away from anything to do with Patrick, babies, twins, or anything that might upset him. They kept the topic light and general, mainly on the weather and other happenings in town.

"Well, I'd better get the boys home. Thanks again for dinner, Mom," Patrick said as he grabbed his cup and rose from his seat. He paused and looked at Liam and Rachel. "I'm happy for you guys, but it's just a little hard, I hope you two understand."

Rachel frowned sympathetically. Liam got up from his own seat and went to hug his brother, whispering something in his ear that Maggie couldn't quite make out. They just needed to take things slowly with Patrick. They needed to show him love and support. They would get through it, they were a family, and they stuck together.

***

Rain, lots and lots of crummy rain. Maggie looked outside the window of the shop. Sheets of water fell from the dark gray clouds, and the ground held pools as more splashed down, soaking everything. Maggie held her mug filled with hot tea, a slice of lemon bobbed on the top of the brown liquid's surface. She could taste the sweetness of the honey she had added, and she watched the sky release its torrent of precipitation as her mind wandered. Michael and her planned on driving to Seattle that weekend to begin the process of putting their home up for sale, and to start organizing everything. Their new home would be closing in a little over a week, and there was still so much to do to prepare. Maggie was excited and a little overwhelmed. If only the awful weather would change back into the glorious sun-filled days that brought light and warmth to Birch Valley. She didn't care for things being drab and just plain yucky. After she took another sip of her tea, she moved back to her desk. She heard Daniel and Patrick arrive.

"Hey, guys," Maggie said as she plopped down on her chair.

"Don't pretend to be working, Mags," Daniel teased. His hair was wet, and his jacket stuck to him like a second skin.

"Ha Ha, so funny."

Patrick headed toward his office, his black hair plastered to his head. He gave her a curt wave and nod as he passed. Once he had closed the door, Maggie crinkled her finger at Daniel. "Come here," she whispered.

Daniel approached slowly. "What's up?"

"How has Patrick been all day?" She kept the volume of her voice low.

Daniel started taking off his coat, and ran his hand through his rain-soaked hair in an attempt to tame his wild tresses. "I don't know, pretty quiet. You know the twins' birthday is coming up, so I'm sure that's got him a little upset."

Maggie made a tight-lipped smile and nodded. "You're right, maybe we can try to do something fun with him to cheer him up?"

"Actually, funny you should say that because us guys are taking him out this Friday. Figure get some beers into him and he might loosen up a bit."

"That's a great idea, Daniel."

"I better go dry off, but don't worry, Mags, he'll be okay."

"I know, he's made of some pretty tough stuff. I just want him to be happy, that's all."

"He will be someday. I got to get out of these wet clothes." Daniel started towards their shared restroom, where there was a shower and extra towels.

Maggie turned her attention back to the work that was in front of her. Her brain wasn't able to focus on the task at hand. As she stared at the bright screen of her monitor, it finally hit her, a fantastic idea. But she knew she couldn't do it alone. She also hoped Patrick didn't kill her when he found out, but it was for his own good.

***

Rachel

"Mom, you aren't even listening to me," Rachel practically shouted into her cell phone.

"You seriously expect us to allow you to get married to this man without meeting him first?" Evelyn Montgomery declared loudly.

Rachel rolled her eyes. She hadn't told her mother that she couldn't meet Liam or his family, she had only suggested that maybe she should wait to come up a little closer to the wedding. Rachel feared that her mother would do try to pull some kind of stunt in order to stop their nuptials, but that didn't mean she was forbidding her mother from coming to the wedding. Heck, she even said she could come up and help a little, possibly a week before the wedding. But that was not enough for Evelyn, the woman who always got her way. It was the various forms of manipulation that often shocked and confused Rachel. Her relationship with her mother was dicey, to say the least. They didn't share a tight bond. The only thing she had inherited was her mother's petite frame. Besides that, they were complete opposites.

"Mom, I said you could come up and even help. I want you to meet Liam and his family."

"Rachel, do you think it's wise to be planning a

wedding while pregnant, let alone with twins? Weddings are highly stressful, and you need to think more about the babies than yourself." Evelyn's voice was sharp; she was going to try to guilt Rachel into not marrying Liam. Rachel could sense her mother's attack coming on, and silently prepared for battle. Why did it always have to be that way with her? Most of the time they weren't speaking because Evelyn was too wrapped up in her own life, and when she got the sudden urge to play mommy it simply drove Rachel insane. There was no winning with her mother, but yet Rachel continued to try, even if it usually ended with her in tears.

"Seriously? I think what you are trying to do is stop us from getting married," Rachel stated coldly.

"I don't see why you feel like you have to rush into marrying someone you hardly know. Rachel, you really should have thought things out a little better, now look at the mess you are in."

"There is no mess, I love him."

Evelyn let out a loud huff. "You mean to tell me that if you hadn't went and gotten yourself knocked up, we would be planning a wedding right now?"

Rachel considered that. She knew exactly what tactic her mother was using, and she didn't like it one bit. She knew that the pregnancy had spurred the quick proposal, but she did love Liam. Rachel wasn't entirely sure that she would be racing down the altar if she hadn't ended up pregnant. She had even insisted that they wait, that marriage wasn't a requirement in her eyes. Doubt had started to weasel its way into her mind. But something inside her shooed it away, and she had to admit the security of knowing that Liam was going to be her husband and the father to their children did feel wonderful. Of course it seemed ridiculously old fashioned when Liam had first suggested they marry, but that was Liam, that was the O'Brien way. Once she stepped back and realized that Liam wasn't only marrying her to keep her from being an unwed mother, or the talk of Birch Valley, but because he actually loved her with all of his heart, she started letting some of her guard down. She had been fighting the very idea of such a commitment, but if Rachel was actually honest with herself, she knew that she loved him all along.

"Are you just going to ignore me?" Evelyn snapped as she became aggravated.

"We obviously don't agree. I'm getting married, we are having twins, and so if you want to be involved, great, if not, well, that's your call," Rachel snipped back. She could feel anger starting to boil in her veins.

"I just can't see you settling. There is still time to fix this, Rachel," Evelyn cooed, reshaping her tone into something delicate and almost soothing.

Rachel shook her head, her mother was unbelievable. "And by fix, you mean…?"

"Well, you got yourself into a lot of trouble, I'm just suggesting you consider all of your options, especially some that need to be decided in a timely manner."

"I'm sorry that you want me to even consider any options that don't include having your grandchildren." Rachel bit her lip hard to keep herself from crying; she could taste the metallic taste of blood.

"Do not turn this around on me. You should never have gotten involved with this man, you should have stayed here, none of this would even be happening right now, Rachel."

"You're right about that, none of this would be happening, and I am so thankful that I came here. Liam was exactly what was missing from my life. Now, we're going to be having children, another thing that I never thought would ever happen in my life back in California," Rachel spat, pausing to readjust her anger, to focus on the good in her life, before she continued, "I can see how this happening so quickly would upset you, and for that you are entitled to be upset with me. But now that I have two babies due in November, and a wedding in July, I can only hope that you can accept it and actually, just maybe, support me."

"Rachel, your father and I have always supported you."

"Not when it came to something that mattered. Like when I decided to move up here, you two were dead set against it. I don't recall there being any kind of support."

"Perhaps you forgot that check I gave you right before you left," Evelyn quipped nastily.

The same check that she received every Christmas. It wasn't heartfelt or thought out.

"I'm not talking about financial support when you know very well I don't ask anything of you or Dad." Rachel felt insulted. She could afford her own life, granted that Beemer that was sitting in her driveway was another story. Rachel wasn't a spoiled brat, unlike her best friend Chelsea, who completely lived off of her parents' wealth. Even her brother, Ethan, who had made his own fortune, was happy to receive "monetary love," as he called it. Money in general made Rachel uncomfortable, it always had. People acted different whether you had a lot or a little of it; it just seemed to cause a lot of problems, and Rachel had seen it with her parents' marriage. That was the main reason for its collapse.

"I swear, Rachel, I don't know why I even try with you." Evelyn had apparently become bored of their fight, and was ready to depart.

"On that note, we should probably just leave the conversation here." Rachel felt tears threatening to spill. It was rare enough to get a call from her mother. Unfortunately, most of the time they ended the same way. Rachel heard the line go dead, and that was enough for the final push. She grabbed the tissue box off her end table. *Investing some stock in this tissue company might not be such a bad idea.* Rachel let out an awkward laugh as she wiped away the tiny rivers trailing down her cheeks.

Chapter Eighteen

Maggie

Melanie hummed a tune that Maggie didn't recognize as they walked hand in hand to the school. The early morning sun was chilly but bright. It would warm up, and the sun would cast its glorious rays on Birch Valley, and everyone would complain that spring was already becoming a little too warm for their liking. That is what the residents of Birch Valley did. There wasn't a whole lot else to be upset about, so weather was fair game.

"It looks like it's going to be a nice day," Maggie said as she looked down at Melanie.

"It's pretty." Melanie paused and stopped right in her tracks "So when are we going to move into our new house?"

"Soon, very soon, like by next weekend I think." Maggie felt a surge of excitement flow through her. They were closing on the house on Friday, and that was only a few short days away.

"Are we ever going back to our old home in

Seattle? What are going to do with that one?"

"We are going to go there very soon and get all of our stuff, and then we are going to put the condo on the market." Maggie smiled. It dawned on her how long it had been since she had been at the condo.

"Market? Why is it going on the market? What does that mean?" Melanie's eyes grew curious as her brow furrowed with concern.

Maggie laughed. She probably should have simplified her answer. What six-year-old would understand what the market was, besides thinking that is was like a grocery store? "Not like a grocery store market, but it's this…" Maggie tried to think of how to explain such an imaginably intangible, yet completely important thing.

"Oh, it's okay, Mom. I just figured it out, you and Dad are going to sell the house."

Maggie was quite impressed and happy to have such a bright child.

Maggie held the door open as Melanie slipped inside the school, and they both caught sight of Liam as he stood by the counter chatting with Karen.

"Good morning, you two lovely ladies," Liam greeted them with a cheerful smile. Her brother had been beaming with happiness over the last couple weeks.

Melanie ran to Liam. "Uncle Liam," she said as she wrapped her arms around his waist.

"How's my favorite niece in the whole world?" Liam looked down at her. Maggie watched the special interaction between them. That was one of the reasons why she wanted to come back to Birch Valley.

"Mom says we are getting our house soon."

"I know, isn't that so cool?" Liam looked over at Maggie and smiled.

Melanie shook her head in agreement as the bell sounded. She waved to Maggie and gave Liam one more quick hug.

Liam walked over to Maggie. "That is pretty cool about the house, you guys excited?"

"Oh yeah, we are going to go to Seattle, I think next weekend or the one following, to start packing it up and putting it up for sale."

"What about Michael's dad's place?"

"I'm not sure what we are going to do with that, I haven't wanted to bring it up to him." Maggie frowned softly.

"I imagine it's still pretty hard for him. Let me know when I can help move stuff. I'd better get to class, I'll catch up with you later." Liam jogged toward a hallway and disappeared.

Maggie stood for a moment, she thought she heard her name being called.

"Maggie." Rachel quickly approached her, and her friend seemed to be glowing. Rachel's eyes were bright and happy.

"Rachel, how's it going?" Maggie hugged her.

"Great, how about you? You guys close on the house this week, right?" she asked.

"Funny, I was just talking about that with Liam. But yeah, we close this Friday."

"That's so wonderful, congrats! So, how are you feeling?" Rachel held her own belly as her eyes traveled to Maggie's growing stomach.

"Pretty good actually, morning sickness is gone, and now we feel the baby moving more."

"Wow, how awesome. I'm still getting sick, I feel exhausted, I find myself napping any chance I get."

"Totally normal. Besides, you are having twins, so you get double the pleasure of the pregnancy experience." Maggie laughed as she teased Rachel.

"Ha Ha, very funny. But I couldn't be happier. Liam is being so wonderful, no surprise there, of course. He comes over and helps with dinner, half the time I can't eat it, but just him being there is great." Rachel's gaze seemed distant and far away.

"Well, I'm glad. And it will get better, I promise. You will feel human again, but by the end of it you will be more than ready for these babies to come."

"Ah, there is so much to do. I'm starting to plan the wedding. I want you and Mary to come dress shopping with me. Not sure what I will fit into by Fourth of July. I'm already growing out of my favorite jeans." Rachel pouted.

"All part of the joy of pregnancy." Maggie snapped her maternity pants, showing Rachel the elastic waist of the jeans she was wearing.

"Wait, what? Those are maternity pants? They are so flippin' cute and look like real jeans." Her eyes grew wide in surprise.

Maggie nodded. "And they are super comfy. Like literally almost as good as yoga pants."

"We need to go shopping soon."

"Sounds like fun, there are some really great stores in Spokane. Let's try to go soon," Maggie suggested.

"For sure. Well, I'd better get back to work." Rachel gave Maggie another hug. Maggie was so glad that Rachel was going to be her sister-in-law. Maggie adored Rachel. They were not only becoming close friends, but there was almost a sisterly connection, as neither of them had a sister, only brothers. There was something special about having a sister. At least, that was what Maggie had always assumed, and she knew that there was something special about Rachel.

***

Friday morning arrived swiftly, and Maggie woke up feeling tired, just plain tired. She had tossed and turned the night before, which hadn't allowed her to get much sleep, and she had been plagued by weird and strange dreams the entire night. Michael didn't move an inch, and she envied his sound sleep every time she looked over at him. Maggie let out a frustrated breath and removed herself from the bed. She shuffled to the kitchen, where she quickly prepared some much needed caffeine. She stood, watching it drip too slowly for her liking into the glass coffee pot. The rich and seductive aroma teased her. Maggie heard footsteps behind her, and then the warm arms of Michael encircled her waist. He nuzzled her neck and whispered, "Good morning." He left a trail of kisses along the side of her throat. Normally it would completely turn her on, but not that morning. She was cranky.

"Morning." Her tone was flat.

Michael backed off, looking a little confused and disappointed. "Didn't sleep well?"

"Nope. I tossed and turned all night." Maggie's hand was on her hip, and she stared at the coffee pot, which still didn't have enough brown, precious liquid to fill her mug. *Good grief, did it normally take that long to make coffee?*

"I'm sorry, hon. I will take Mel to school this morning, maybe you should try to go back to bed," he offered as he leaned casually against one of the counters, his arms crossed over his chest, concern in his soulful brown eyes. Seeing him standing there almost changed her mood. The man was a pleasure to look at. But even her husband's good looks couldn't change her mood.

"Nah, I can't. I need to go to work for a little while, and then we have the signing later with Cheryl."

"Well, I will still take Mel." Michael moved toward her and planted a kiss on her forehead. "Even when you are terribly cranky, you are still very sexy." Maggie playfully slapped at him as he strolled off laughing to get Melanie up and ready for school.

After she packed Melanie's lunch and sent her daughter and Michael off with a decent breakfast, Maggie showered and got ready for her day. She felt a little better after letting the hot water beat hard against her shoulders and back. When she emerged dressed in maternity slacks—which were a charcoal gray—and a flowing, turquoise-colored blouse, she felt almost normal. Her hair, however, was threatening to make her day a disaster. It had grown wavier over the last couple months; the same thing had happened when she was pregnant with Melanie. But it was becoming unmanageable, so a ponytail was the remedy for the day.

She walked back into the kitchen and contemplated a second cup of coffee to help correct the last remains of her sour mood. Maybe another cup would also hopefully help defeat her sleep deprivation.

"Good morning, love," Mary's sweet voice called out from the dining table.

"Morning, Mom," Maggie answered as she filled her mug again, adding a little extra sugar.

"So, today is the day, you and Michael must be so excited." Mary raised her teacup and nibbled on a buttered scone.

Maggie yawned and said, "Yes, we are."

"Why are you so tired, dear, did you not sleep well?" Mary's furrowed in concern.

"No, didn't sleep well at all, but hopefully, with a little help from my old friend coffee here, I will be able to make it through the day," Maggie said as she raised her mug. She took a hearty sip and enjoyed the slight burn as the coffee traveled down her throat.

"Oh, you poor thing, you need your rest. Well, tonight your father and I plan on taking Melanie out to that new movie she's been wanting to see." A flicker of mischief sparkled in her eyes, and Maggie grew curious. Her mother was a terrible fibber, and could hardly contain herself when it came to a secret. Mary's eyes always gave her away. Maggie didn't have any desire to investigate further. If there was something up, she was sure she'd find out soon enough.

"Well, I'd better get down to the shop." Maggie downed the last bit of coffee, and placed her dirty mug in the sink. Maggie hugged her mother and gave Mary a small peck on her soft, wrinkled cheek. "Have a good day, Mom."

"You too, sweetheart." Mary patted Maggie's lower back as she pulled away to leave.

***

Maggie could hear Patrick, Daniel, and Michael laughing as they sat in Patrick's office. She was finishing some last minute things when her husband had arrived earlier. Soon they were going to sign the papers on their new home. She gathered her purse and walked to Patrick's door and peeked in. The three men all looked comfortable. It was great to hear Patrick's laugh and to see him smile. The only thing missing from the picture was Liam; when the guys all got together, they were loud. Maggie already knew that Michael had plans to make the finished basement in their home a man cave so he and her brothers could have a safe haven just for them. Maggie didn't mind, she loved being around her brothers, regardless of how rowdy and crazy they got. She was thankful that they were getting closer with Michael. Liam had always been kind and got along great with her husband. Patrick was a little slow to warm up, and especially after Maggie had left Seattle earlier that spring, he grew cold toward Michael in order to protect her. Daniel was easygoing like Liam, but didn't share as much stuff in common with Michael, but they were finding they actually did have a great deal of similar interests. Maggie just wanted to make sure Michael felt comfortable, especially with them starting their lives in Birch Valley.

"You ready to go, Michael?" Maggie asked as she poked her head through the door.

"Sure," he answered. He stood up from the chair across from Patrick's desk and told the guys that they needed to get together for a poker game soon. They all agreed and wished them well with the signing.

Once outside of the building, Michael opened Maggie's door and waited for her to slip in before closing it. Michael got in the driver's side and started the car, the gentle purr of the engine humming quietly as he drove them toward the realtor's office.

"You excited?" Michael reached over and squeezed her left knee.

"Well, of course, but it's just so much money."

"It is, but we'll be here for the rest of our lives, and that makes it worth it. Making you happy, us being together, totally worth every last cent." He flashed her the perfectly charming Trembley smile that made her go weak at the knees every time.

"Do you know how sweet you are?"

"Not really, just as long as you think I'm sweet, that's all I care about."

Maggie rolled her eyes. He sure was laying it on thick today. She couldn't help laughing out loud.

She tried to stifle it as she covered her mouth with her hand, but why try?

"Why are you laughing at me?" Michael's smile only teased her more.

"Ah, what am I going to do with you, Michael Trembley?" Maggie asked.

"Love me." He winked and gave her a slanted, lazy grin. The sex appeal that easily oozed from Michael drove her crazy. He knew exactly what her buttons were and how to push to them, and she could tell he enjoyed every second of it.

***

"Sign right here, Maggie." Cheryl pointed to a line that was marked with a sticky note. Maggie could feel her hand cramp as she tried gripping the pen tighter, sweat causing it to slip, she had already signed and initialed her name so many times the whole process was becoming a blur.

They were seated across from Cheryl's large, sleek desk that was a little too big for the small office. Maggie felt claustrophobic, packed in like sardines, she felt herself grow hot and sweaty.

"You okay, babe?" Michael asked, eyeing her with concern.

"I'm fine, it's just a little warm in here." Maggie knew that seeing the numbers for how much they had spent was partially to blame, but the stuffy, cramped office was making it nearly unbearable.

Cheryl looked up at Maggie and said, "Only a couple more signatures, and then the house is yours." She dangled the keys in front of them.

Michael tossed Maggie a reassuring grin as Cheryl slid the last of the paperwork in front of her. Maggie gripped the pen with all her might and signed away. She needed to get out of that office.

Before much longer, they were outside. The fresh air never felt better as it slapped against Maggie's skin, which was wet with perspiration. The pure relief of being outside consumed her as she inhaled deeply, letting the cool air travel inside her. Maggie let out a breath and said, "I'm so sorry, I thought I was going to die in there. I was so overheated."

"Probably the pregnancy hormones," Michael suggested as the walked to a nearby bench and took a seat. A little foot traffic passed them, but they had a great view of the movie house across the street and of the beautiful hanging baskets of flowers on the antique lamp posts.

"Yeah, or the insane amount of money we just spent."

"Oh, Maggie, please get over that, we can afford it, okay? I don't want you stressing over it anymore. It's done, and we now own a beautiful home in Birch Valley." Michael kissed the top of her head, his arms slung over her shoulders.

They sat quietly, and Maggie reflected on how drastically different her life was. Only a few months ago, her world was crumbling. Michael was right; it was worth every cent being here with him and Melanie, and with the baby growing inside of her. She placed her hand gingerly on her belly, feeling the swirling movements of the life inside her. He, or she, was also starting to get a little cramped.

Michael positioned his large hand over hers; together they felt the strong kicks, which reminded hey how blessed they were in so many ways. She relished the moment. Maggie closed her eyes and thanked God for everything He had done for her.

Interrupting her prayer, Michael asked, "You ready to go back to work?"

"Yeah, I'd better." Maggie reluctantly got up from the bench.

"I will be buying new locks for the house, and I have a couple of errands to run as well."

"Mom said she and Dad were going to take Melanie to a movie tonight. Maybe we can go to the house and work on cleaning it or something?" Maggie suggested as she stretched and yawned.

"Well, I'm going to change the locks and do some things around the place, want to meet me there a little later?" Michael's soft, brown eyes twinkled.

"I will feed Melanie, and then when they get ready to leave I'll head over, sound good?"

"Perfect." Michael stood up, took hold of her shoulders, and lowered his mouth to hers. Maggie sighed inside of his mouth, savoring his kiss.

He broke away and grabbed her hand, leading her to their car. The ride to the shop was quick. She said goodbye and left him, feeling content and pretty darn happy.

***

The house stood tall and proud at the corner of the street as Maggie pulled into the driveway and parked next to Michael's car. She still couldn't believe that it was their new home. Melanie had been torn between going to the new home or to the movie with her grandparents. Even Grandpa decided to join them when he heard they would be going out for ice cream afterwards. Mary made sure that Melanie decided on the movie. Maggie found her mother's behavior a little odd. Maggie loved that her parents took Melanie out and spent so much time with her, so she didn't question her mother's motives, but it seemed like something was up.

Maggie out of her car and popped the trunk, loading her arms full with bags of cleaning products and some basic toiletries. She followed the brick walkway to the magnificent front door. She knocked, but then laughed. This was her home now.

She could make out Michael's figure coming to the door, and once he opened it he saw that her arms were loaded. "Here, let me help you," Michael said as he started removing some of the bags that were tangled all around her arms. He let Maggie in first, trailing close behind her.

Maggie gasped loudly. Her hand covered her mouth as her eyes feasted on the sight before her. There were candles lit on the counters and built-in shelves, which cast a soft, romantic glow. A bottle of champagne was sitting in a bucket of ice, two glasses next to it.

"Is that…" Maggie started to ask.

"It's cider," Michael answered quickly as he placed the bags on a neighboring counter.

Her eyes absorbed every detail. A silver vase with red roses sat on the kitchen island, and delicate petals decorated the floor, leaving a trail of the velvety flowers. Maggie followed the trail to their formal dining room, where she saw a large blow up mattress sat on the floor. It was decorated with a silky looking sheet and soft comforter, both in a beautiful green.

She wasn't prepared for such a night. She grimaced as she glanced down at her jeans and old Seattle Seahawk football shirt. Hardly sexy. But considering the surrounding atmosphere, she highly doubted she would be dressed for long.

As she stood in awe, Michael came up behind her, his lips finding the soft skin behind her ear. "Oh, Michael," Maggie whispered. The room was full of shadows from more candles that were placed around the bed. The floral smell mixed with the aroma from the scented candles was inviting, and she inhaled it deeply. Could it get any better?

"Welcome home, Mrs. Trembley," Michael said, his voice saturated with arousal and desire. Maggie felt herself grow warm, and her knees went weak. He was there to catch her should she collapse or melt, both of which were very likely.

She around to face her husband and anchored herself to him, looping her arms around his neck. She couldn't take her eyes off his mouth, she needed to feel it against hers. Maggie lunged for his sensual lips, crushing her mouth on his, pressing away any space that was between them. She cherished his taste, it was a cross between mint and a flavor that was solely him. She pulled back, licking her lips, which ignited a fire in his eyes that was burning bright against the candle-lit room.

Their hands explored each other, sliding across smooth skin, mapping out every inch.

Michael guided her toward the bed, where he slowly started to undress Maggie. He carefully lifted the faded t-shirt over head, his hands instantly drawn to the swell of her breasts, which were cupped in a plain bra, nothing fancy.

"You should have told me you were doing this. I could have come dressed to impress." Maggie giggled, thinking how ridiculous she must look.

"I don't care, you would end up the same way if you had dressed in the sexiest thing you own." Michael's mouth had found the top of her chest, kissing the milky flesh. She could hear him moan into her skin. Maggie arched her back, pulling his head closer, feeling her own breath escape, leaving her body starving for more of Michael's touch.

He nudged her backwards, the powerful weight of him hovering over her as he stared at her. His eyes were hungry. Maggie swallowed, she felt almost nervous from the way his mocha-colored eyes were devouring her without even touching her. He ran his tongue across his lips, and growled before he pounced on her mouth, nipping at her bottom lip, probing his tongue inside, staking his claim. The electric current that burned through her as they connected left her feeling hot and wild. Their kiss deepened, which spurred her to bring him closer to her, eliminating any gap between their bodies.

Michael resisted, but only for a moment as he shed his gray v-neck shirt, exposing his toned chest with the fine spray of black hair dancing all the way down his waist. Maggie partially sat up on her elbows to get a better view of his abdomen. It rippled under her touch as she extended her fingers and lightly grazed the smooth skin. He let out another groan, which was deep and full of frustration, almost animalistic. In a swift movement, their clothing had mysteriously and effortlessly been removed and she soon found herself writhing under his touch, begging him to help her find release.

His hands moved down the length of her body, pausing at her belly. "You're beautiful," Michael stated as he bent down and swept his lips across it, leaving goose bumps on her skin.

Passion flowed through her as Michael carried both of them to a lust filled haze and an afterglow so sweet and unmatched that Maggie felt tears developing. He cradled her in his strong arms, the skin to skin contact drawing heat. His hands ran along the lines and curves of her body, and he sighed appreciatively. They lay quietly, basking in the light from the candles and the beauty of the love they shared for one another.

"God, that was amazing," Maggie managed to say, her voice hoarse. Her body still throbbed and tingled, and sensations still vibrated through her. That had been one of the most incredible love making sessions they had ever shared. *Well, that was one way to christen the new house.*

Chapter Nineteen

"What do you mean, you don't think it's a good idea? I sure think it is," Maggie argued. Rachel and Mary looked at her like she was crazy for even suggesting it. It was a modern world, and people did the online dating thing all the time, it was nothing new, and in Maggie's opinion, it was an option for Patrick.

The women were seated around the dining room table in the O'Brien home. Mary released a loud sigh. "It's a step up from a mail order bride, Maggie. Patrick will be livid if he finds out, you know how he is," Mary pleaded.

Maggie could see that Rachel was on the fence. "Rachel, come on, you know that it's a great idea."

"Well, I mean, I know people do it all the time, so it's not a crazy idea."

"How else can we get Patrick to meet someone? I don't see you guys coming up with a game plan." Maggie grabbed her mug and another cookie.

"It's a good idea, but Mary's right, he will be so pissed."

"Good grief, of course he will. But this is for his own good. I even started setting up a profile for him on a free dating site I came across." Maggie got up to retrieve her laptop.

Mary let out another huff. "Oh, dear Lord, Maggie, you don't think that's going a bit far?"

"No, Mom, I don't. He has been alone now for almost four years," Maggie said, returning to the table and opening up her computer. Her fingers quickly typed in the website's address.

"It needs to be in his own time, dear." Mary took another sip of her tea.

"But as we learned with Beth dying, you never know how long you have. I just want him to be happy, that's all."

"I know you have no ill intent, love. It might be best if you don't meddle in his love life."

"Wow, really, Mom? You are the queen of meddling, I learned from you." Maggie stuck her tongue out, causing both Mary and Rachel to giggle.

Maggie figured her mother would be all over the idea, that she would probably have spear headed the project herself. Maggie pulled up the profile she had created for Patrick.

"The only thing I'm really missing is a picture of him where he isn't scowling. I think I got everything covered, but wanted to go over everything with you guys just in case I forgot something."

Rachel and Mary moved behind Maggie and started to read the profile.

"Just from how you describe him I can only imagine the flood of emails you are going to get,"

Rachel commented as she returned to her seat.

"You did a fine job, Maggie. You really know how to sell your poor brother."

"So what else should we add?" Maggie asked. Her fingers hovered over the keys, ready for dictation.

Rachel looked up to the ceiling before returning her gaze on Maggie. "Did you mention he is widowed?"

"Well, see, I didn't exactly put that. I wasn't sure how people might perceive that. What do you think?"

Mary raised her eyebrows and said, "Best to be as honest as possible, a good woman will appreciate that. Need to weed out the crummy ones."

That was more like it. Maggie listened as her mother explained more about the importance of providing an accurate profile for Patrick. The women laughed as they tried to come up with clever things to say about him. They were so deeply involved in their project they didn't hear Patrick walk in.

"What are you ladies up to?"

They all turned. Maggie could only imagine her eyes were as big as Mary and Rachel's. *Talk about getting caught in the act.*

Patrick's face grew curious. "Why do you all look like you are up to no good?"

Maggie stumbled over her words. "Um, well, we were just working on…"

Rachel was apparently quick on her feet. "Wedding dresses. We were looking to see which one would work for a pregnant bride." She shot

Patrick a frown, as if she were trying to gain some sympathy from him. *Good job.*

"You could show up in a sheet or a garbage bag and Liam will think you are the most beautiful woman in the world," Patrick said, attempting to reassure Rachel.

"That's sweet, never considered a garbage bag. Thanks for the suggestion, Patrick." Rachel put on her best serious face.

"Well, I will leave you guys to it then. Mom, I'm taking the boys home, see you guys tomorrow for dinner." Patrick disappeared quickly.

Maggie let out the breath she had been holding. "God, that was close. Wow, Rachel, pretty darn impressive."

Mary patted Rachel's hand. "Yes, dear, quick thinking there."

Rachel offered them a weak smile. "I felt horrible, but had to think of something."

"Well, it worked. So where were we?" Maggie's eyes scanned the monitor. "Ah, here we go, what you would say is his most attractive feature?"

Rachel bit her lip. "Probably best not for me to answer."

"Oh, come on, we know you love Liam." Maggie swatted at her. "We need an outside opinion, so, Rachel, that leaves you. I can't really say because eeeww, you know?"

"True, like when Chelsea goes on and on about Ethan, I'm like, yuck." Rachel pretended to gag, which caused Mary to frown at her. "Sorry, Mary, but you get what I mean."

Maggie thought back to Chelsea's visit earlier

that spring, she recalled how interested she had been in Patrick. "What about Chelsea? What did she find so appealing about Patrick?" Maggie found it difficult to hide the sarcasm in her voice.

"Well, she loved his eyes. You guys all have them, they are beautiful and mesmerizing. She just thought he was gorgeous, like, all of him." Rachel laughed.

"Oh my," Mary said as she took another sip of her tea.

"Mom, you know how all the girls around here have always been in love with him, they practically throw themselves at his feet," Maggie explained.

Rachel asked, "So why are we needing to even set this up for him?"

"Because he's difficult and we need to help him, whether he likes it or not."

They all nodded in agreement.

*　*　*

Maggie looked down the hallway to make sure no one was in earshot as she quickly ducked into the kitchen where Rachel and Mary were getting Sunday dinner ready to serve.

"You guys won't believe it," Maggie announced in a whisper, keeping her voice low just in case. After the close call with Patrick the day before, she wasn't taking any chances.

"Believe what?" Rachel asked as she stirred a simmering pot on the stove. Maggie almost laughed at how domestic Rachel looked as she wore one of Mary's floral print aprons, holding that wooden spoon like her life depended on it. She was steadily becoming quite a good cook. Maggie wasn't sure if there was much hope for herself, but her family was hardly starving.

"The hits on Patrick's profile."

Mary turned around, carrying a handful of silverware in her hands. "Really? What did the ladies have to say?"

"Oh, that he's super hot and they all want him, and that is the condensed version." Maggie laughed.

"I'm not all that surprised, are you?" Rachel said as she continued stirring.

"Well, I was shocked he got so many responses in less than twenty-four hours."

"How many?" Rachel's blue eyes grew curious.

Maggie stepped closer, and quickly looked behind her to make sure no one else was around. "Try close to a hundred women, even a couple men were interested."

Mary's mouth gaped open. "Oh, dear Lord, you can't be serious."

"Oh, I am. It's crazy, isn't it?"

"Which part? The number of women, or that men are even throwing themselves at your brother?" Rachel let out a soft squeal.

"I'm going to show you guys after dinner, you won't believe me until you see it with your own eyes."

Maggie retrieved several plates and started to set the table. She was itching to show them the progress that they had made. She had to figure out how to get Patrick to go out on these dates, once they sifted through the contenders and really made sure he didn't get stuck with some weirdo, or a man. Then he would kill her for sure.

Maggie stole glances at Patrick as they all sat and ate dinner. She was trying to gauge his mood, seeing if it was possible to even broach the subject of dating. Maggie could feel eyes on her, and caught her mother and Rachel both looking at her. They would turn away and try not to giggle. Maggie was having fun with their secret project.

Dinner was its usual loud chatter-filled ceremony of feasting on something delicious that Mary had cooked. Maggie was more than relieved when everyone started to excuse themselves from the table. The children, as usual, were the first to beg to go outside and play. Grandpa Paddy and Pat retired to the den, eager to puff away on their pipes and catch up on their nightly reading of the newspaper. They especially loved the Sunday paper. Michael looked at Maggie as if asking permission to go play with her brothers. She sent him away and received a kiss on the cheek as he and the guys set off towards the basement. It was finally quiet, and Maggie raced to grab her laptop to show Mary and Rachel the site.

"Rachel, try to keep watch, okay?" Maggie asked as the site started loading.

Rachel took the chair facing the archway that led into the kitchen. It was the perfect spot to see if anyone came in.

Mary took a seat next to Maggie. "So, tell me, how do we get him to date some of these women?"

"I think once we really go through and find the best ones, we should probably sit him down and explain. What do you guys think?" Maggie asked.

Mary moved her head closer to the screen, a surprised look on her face.

"What?" Rachel asked.

"He has over two hundred people now interested in his profile," Mary answered.

Maggie was astonished. *How could that many people be interested?*

"I think we need to start sorting the creepers from the keepers, sound good?" Maggie said as she started to click on the profile of the first woman who had made contact.

"She seems lovely," Mary commented as she stared at the screen alongside Maggie.

Maggie moved a little closer to Rachel so she could see what they were seeing.

"That one does seem pretty."

They continued to view and delete ones they felt were not even a remote possibility for Patrick. Rachel excused herself to go to the restroom. Mary and Maggie were engrossed in their project, huddled together as they reviewed more candidates.

"What the heck are you guys up to?"

Maggie felt the hairs rise on the back of her neck, her stomach dropped as she felt Patrick behind them. He bent lower to get a closer look. He immediately wore a confused expression, which was swiftly replaced with anger.

"What is this?" Patrick asked as he pulled away.

"Patrick, don't be upset. We were going to talk to you about it," Maggie said, trying to defend their action of deceit.

He rubbed his jaw, and she could see a little muscle ticking away near the dark stubble. She had seen that before; he was pissed.

"Is that some kind of dating site?"

Maggie nodded. She caught a glimpse of Rachel entering, and Liam was trailing behind her, completely out of the loop.

"What dating site?" Liam asked.

"Oh, just one that Maggie has apparently signed me up for," Patrick replied angrily as Liam went to have a look for himself. He looked at Maggie, disappointment filling his eyes.

"We were just trying to help," Maggie explained.

"So you all are involved?" Patrick looked at each of them. Rachel hung her head, Mary kept her stare on him, and Maggie couldn't face the icy glare from him.

"She meant well, son. She was only thinking of your happiness," Mary tried to reason with him.

Patrick rolled his eyes as he started pacing the dining room. "I don't care if she meant well, she never should have gotten involved."

"If you would just calm down and take a look at this, you might actually find this very interesting."

"No, I wouldn't because I have no intention of meeting any of those damn people. I can't believe you would do this. You really crossed the line." Patrick fumed. Maggie didn't know what else to say to him, other than she was sorry.

"I shouldn't have, but I'm trying to help you."

"No, you are not helping. From now on, please stay out of my business. Just because your life is suddenly all roses again doesn't give you the damn right to try and fix mine. You might want to focus on your own issues before trying to work on other people's problems."

"Patrick, that's not fair." Maggie tried to push back the tears. That was a low blow, and it stung, especially coming from someone who always protected her.

"Hey, man, I think she really was trying to help. It's been almost four years." Liam placed his hand carefully on Patrick's shoulder, only to have it quickly shrugged away.

"You don't think I don't know it has been four years, Liam? I live with it every day, every morning I wake up, and Beth's not there. Every time Finn or Connor look at me, I see her. Do you know what that is like?" Patrick's stance was solid, his eyes narrowed on Maggie.

"I can't even imagine…" Liam started as Patrick raised his hand, stopping him.

"Then don't. Because you can't. I wouldn't wish that on you." Patrick shoved past Liam and headed out of the kitchen.

The room was silent, everyone digesting what had happened. It was moments before Mary spoke. "Perhaps it's time to call it a night. We need to give him some time to cool down." She hugged Maggie and said, "You tried to help him, dear. But he's just not quite ready yet."

***

Work was unbearable. Patrick hadn't uttered a single word to Maggie. Daniel was the translator, anything that Patrick had needed done, he sent Daniel to ask.

285

"Can't he just flippin' talk to me like a normal person?" Maggie complained as Daniel handed her a stack of invoices to file.

"Mags, he's pissed."

"I know, but still, it's pretty unprofessional to act like such a jerk and give someone the silent treatment all day." Maggie raised her voice loud enough for it to carry to Patrick's office. She knew very well he could hear her, and she hoped he would quit being this way. Of course she felt awful, but at the same time she didn't, she felt justified in what she was doing. Maggie wanted to bring a little love into his life, was that such an awful thing to do?

"Let it go, he'll get over it…eventually." Daniel gave her a lopsided smile.

Maggie rolled her eyes as Daniel started to head back to his office.

The day didn't get any better, Patrick still wasn't speaking to her, and she'd had about as much as she could handle. If he continued to act this way, then she didn't know how much longer she would be working there.

The rest of the week was more of the same, Patrick ignored her and continued using Daniel as his messenger. Maggie was leaving for Seattle that weekend, and hated that things were unresolved between her and Patrick.

She was sending an email when Patrick and Daniel came in, and she looked up and smiled at both of them. "How was the job?"

"It went well, we will be there most of next week," Daniel replied, throwing Maggie a look of caution.

"Great." Maggie turned her gaze to Patrick, who was sorting through the wire basket that was loaded with mail. "So, Patrick, still not going to talk to me?"

She watched her brother frown as he eyed Daniel and said, "Daniel, I'll be in my office if you need me." He took the stack of envelopes and went to his office, shutting his door a little harder than necessary.

That was the final straw. She jumped up from her chair and stormed to Patrick's office. Daniel trailed after her, and Maggie caught a glimpse of panic in his face. She swung his door open hard, and took an assertive stance in front of his desk.

She pointed her finger at him, anger flowing freely inside her. "This ends now. You have been rude to me all week."

The smirk on his face made her even more upset. "Rude? I haven't said a single thing to you until now."

"Exactly, and that's rude and you know it."

"Hardly." He rolled his eyes toward the ceiling and let out a snarky laugh.

Daniel entered and stood next to Maggie. "Okay, enough, you guys, come on, let's just calm down," Daniel pleaded.

"He's been a jerk all week to me, Daniel. I don't deserve to be treated like this, like I don't exist." She narrowed her eyes at Patrick.

"Oh, trust me, it's well deserved," Patrick rebutted and matched her stare. "You had no right, Maggie. You should have come to me first."

"You would have said no."

"Exactly, so if you already knew my answer, why did you think it was okay to do it then?" His eyes never left hers.

Daniel let out a large huff and said, "Patrick, she didn't mean any harm." He turned to face Maggie and continued, "You have to see where he is coming from, Mags."

Maggie threw her hands up in the air. "I give up, all I was trying to do was help you, Patrick."

"I didn't ask you to." His voice was cold.

"I know you didn't, you would rather mope around for the rest of your life, instead of trying to be happy."

He raised his eyebrows, and cocked his head to the side. The muscle in jaw was ticking again. Oh boy, she had really pissed him off.

"You don't get it, and hopefully you never will. I pray to God that you never ever go through the hell that I live through everyday. Something so awful and cruel, no one should have to bear it."

His words penetrated her, causing her to feel an overwhelming sense of guilt, but her anger still burned. "Patrick, people die. People grieve, and then they move on. You deserve to be happy again, to love someone, to find a mother for your boys."

"Maggie, you need to just stay out of it. Leave it alone."

Daniel put his hand on Maggie's shoulder. "It's okay."

"No, it's not."

Patrick let out an arrogant laugh. "Maggie, I didn't do anything wrong, you started this. Daniel, you don't need to get involved, man. She's a big girl, she got herself into this mess, she can most certainly figure her way out."

Maggie's mouth dropped open. "That's it, I'm done. I can't deal with this anymore. There is no talking to you, you are impossible, Patrick O'Brien." She stomped out of the office and went to get her purse. She was done trying to defend her actions, he was being unreasonable, and she needed some space.

Daniel followed her out as she was nearing the front door. "Maggie, don't leave like this."

"I'm sorry, but I don't think I can work here anymore, not with him, anyway." With that, she closed the door behind her. As she got into her car she saw Daniel looking somber as he watched her from the enormous window.

Maggie sped off. She had a plane to Seattle to catch with Michael that evening. Flying made her nervous as it was, and the irritation she felt was only going to make her more anxious. Looking back in her rearview mirror, a twinge of guilt sat in her stomach, but it was too late, she needed some space. She refused to go back and make amends with Patrick. She pressed the gas pedal down a little more, eager to get far away from Birch Valley for the first time since she had returned.

***

Liam kept his eyes on the road as he drove Michael and Maggie to airport. Maggie sat in the front seat and looked out the passenger window.

Storm clouds moved in, gray and white swirls, and it matched her mood perfectly. She still felt the residual remnants of her argument with Patrick.

"Mags, you can't really blame him for being upset," Liam said. They had been discussing the fight during their drive to Spokane. Maggie felt alone, no one seemed to agree with her.

"Honey, you were a little out of line. Your heart was in a good place," Michael called out from the back seat.

"So you guys think it was perfectly fine that he gave me the cold shoulder all week?"

Liam shook his head and replied, "I'm not getting involved. Do I think he needed to act like this, not really. But he's Patrick, come on, you know how he is. And you should have thought about that."

"Ugh, are you serious?" Maggie threw Liam a disgusted look.

"I'm not saying that you aren't looking out for him and don't have his best interest in mind, but Patrick's difficult."

Michael leaned forward to get in between the front seats. "You tried, but now it's best to just drop it. He'll come around, I promise."

"I just want him to be happy like us." Maggie reached for Michael's hand and smiled at him.

"He was once, with Beth. I know if I lost you, I wouldn't be so quick to replace you." He kissed her hand and winked at her.

"It's been almost four years though. You don't think that's long enough?"

"You know, it's hard to say for someone else. I

don't know if I could ever remarry, or, who knows, I might only wait like a month or so," Michael teased, causing Maggie to slap at him.

Liam laughed. "Yeah, hard to say when it's the right time. But he'll figure it out."

"Well, I'm done trying to help." Maggie folded her arms across her chest and pouted.

"Oh, Maggie, don't be like that. You love him, and of course you will try helping again, maybe next time he will more receptive." Michael tried to reassure her as he ran his hand down the length of her arm.

Liam pulled in the terminal. The traffic had been light, and there were only a few travelers outside of the airport. He parked behind a shuttle bus and popped the trunk as he went to grab the single suitcase they had packed.

"You guys have a safe flight. See you two soon." Liam hugged Maggie tightly before giving Michael a handshake that turned into a quick hug.

"Be careful with my car," Michael teased as he patted Liam's shoulder.

Liam waved as he hopped back into the luxurious car and cruised slowly away from the curb, leaving Michael and Maggie behind.

Maggie could see that Liam had enjoyed driving Michael's sleek sedan, but she appreciated him driving them to the airport, so it was an equal trade off. They would be returning to Birch Valley in a couple of days with a fully loaded moving truck. Her parents were going to watch Melanie, and Liam and Rachel even offered to take her to school the following week, Maggie was more than grateful, she wasn't quite sure what snags they might encounter once they got to Seattle.

"We better get inside, looks like might rain soon," Michael commented, picking up the suitcase and grabbing Maggie's hand with his other hand.

They made their way inside, past the large glass doors to a well lit, but quiet foyer. There were lines for each airline to check in, and there were only a couple of people standing patiently. Maggie loved how this airport was never overly crowded, the customer service was stellar, and it made her appreciate the small town feeling even in a city as large as Spokane. She secretly dreaded having to arrive in the congested Sea-Tac airport in a couple of hours. She wasn't excited about going to Seattle at all, except that she didn't have to deal with Patrick. Maggie knew that the flight to Seattle held a lot of meaning; it was the closing of a chapter in her life, in their lives. She looked up at Michael, watching his brown eyes take in the surroundings of the airport. She wondered what he was thinking about. He was quietly assessing everything, but when he turned to look at her, he flashed a broad smile.

"Just think we will be moving all of our stuff into our new home by next week," he said as he squeezed her hand a little. That's right, they were coming back. Maggie felt the tension that had been building melt away, she'd just needed to hear him say it. She was eager to get back to Birch Valley to start living in their new home, to start their new chapter.

Chapter Twenty

It was already dark when they landed, but the bright lights of the giant city illuminated everything. Maggie and Michael hurried to the baggage claim area and retrieved their single suitcase. Michael had called for a cab to take them to the condo, but he hadn't really said much after they touched down. Maggie felt her nerves balling up in her gut, she knew coming back here would feel weird, but it was more than that. The last time they were here together, she and Michael fought, and she had left with no intention of returning. Now she was back.

Michael was staring out the window of the backseat of cab as rain splattered hard against the glass. Maggie sat close to him but felt like he was miles away.

"Michael, you okay?" Maggie asked quietly.

"Yeah, I'm fine." His tone was anything but fine; it was flat and distant.

Maggie sighed and looked out her own window. The Space Needle was in the distance as they neared their old home. The rest of the ride passed in complete silence. The driver parked near the entrance to the parking complex. Michael paid the driver and grabbed their suitcase. He walked hard against the pavement of the parking garage to the elevator. His steps echoed loudly, and Maggie trailed close behind him. She still couldn't quite understand his suddenly cold behavior.

Seeing their door made Maggie's stomach feel ill, she hadn't realized just how difficult this was going to be. Michael unlocked it, and they both entered. Standing side by side in their living room, they stared at their old life. Everything was still as it had been when Michael arrived in Birch Valley. Nothing had changed since Maggie had left. Everything felt foreign. The home itself felt cold and strange. Maggie became eager to start packing away any leftover memories. She wanted the house emptied and sold.

Michael reached for her and quietly said, "It's weird being here, huh?"

Maggie agreed and nodded. "Yeah, I didn't think it would feel like this. This used to be our home, but it doesn't feel like it anymore."

"I know. The sooner we pack it up and get it sold, the better. We still have to go my dad's place, that's going to be hard."

"It will be, but we will get through this together." She slipped her fingers through his, clamping her hand tight against his, giving it a tender squeeze.

***

The gray morning light filtered in through the large living room window. Maggie stood looking into the open fridge, it was completely empty. *So much for breakfast.*

"Sorry, I cleaned it out when I left, I didn't want anything to spoil. I didn't have a whole lot in there to begin with," Michael explained as he peeked inside the cupboards, finding them practically bare.

"Should we go out and get coffee and something to eat before we get started?" The beauty of living in the downtown district was that everything was within walking distance.

"Yeah, we'd probably better. We have our work cut out for us today."

The outside air smelled of a mixture of raw ocean and damp city streets. Maggie sniffed the scent, it was so different than Birch Valley, but Seattle used to be home. Now she felt disconnected, like she was only a visitor to a place she had lived at for almost eight years. They walked to a small coffee shop only a couple of blocks away from the condo, the rich aroma a pleasant distraction from the air outside. Maggie inhaled it deeply, savoring the smell of roasted gourmet beans.

The ambiance was trendy and modern, the customers were a blend of uptight looking professionals en route to their downtown offices, and hipsters wearing thick reading glasses and scarves and beanies, even though the temp was warm. Maggie, who once dressed sharp and just as chic as everyone in that room, now felt utterly out of place, like a fish out of water. She was no longer a Seattleite.

295

"What do you want to order?" Michael asked, interrupting her observations as she was taking in the scene.

"Probably just a mocha, and maybe a scone or muffin, if they have it," Maggie answered, tucking her hands into her jeans as they waited in line. She felt her body bopping to the pop music that was a little too loud, especially for this early in the morning.

Michael looked all around as well. Maggie wondered if he was missing Seattle; it was all he had ever known. These were his stomping grounds, this was where they met and started their life together. Maggie felt a shred of guilt that she didn't feel a little regret in leaving. She was anxious to pack up the house and get home.

As the line moved efficiently, they placed their order and found a table next to a large window with an expensive view.

Holding onto her large paper cup, letting the warmth travel through her hands, Maggie sipped the hot drink and let out an appreciative sigh.

"Good, isn't it?" Michael asked, his eyes still not quite connecting with hers.

"So good. Michael, what's going on with you? You've been so quiet since we got here." Maggie held onto her cup as she waited for his answer.

He shrugged, the muscles in his strong arms bulged with the casual movement. Michael was wearing a Seattle Mariner t-shirt that a little snug against his broad chest and shoulders, and the bold, blue color looked great against his naturally tanned skin.

"Come on, something's up, what is it?" Maggie reached across the tiny table for his hand.

Michael's fingers played lightly against the supple skin of her palm as he answered, "I don't know, it's so weird being here. A part of me misses it, to be honest. But, at the same time, there are almost too many memories."

Maggie frowned sympathetically. "I know. You know, we can always come here to visit."

"What would be the point? There isn't anything really here for us now."

Maggie shook her head, she knew this wasn't easy for him. "That's not true, I'm sure we will need to come and catch a Mariner game at some point." Michael laughed unexpectedly, it warmed Maggie to see him smile.

***

They had been working on packing up their belongings for most of the day, sorting things that would need to be donated. How did they accumulate so much stuff in such a tiny place? Michael carried another box and lined it up against the wall with the others that were to go into the moving truck. Maggie sat on the couch to take a break, she was beyond exhausted, and her body had no problem telling her it was time to take a rest. They worked great as a team; together they tackled the living room first, clearing a side for all the boxes to go to Birch Valley, and a separate area for donations. Melanie's room a little painful, sorting through toys, clothing, and her art projects.

So many memories flooded Maggie, thinking about the last eight years was hard. There were happy times throughout those years, but for the most part Maggie had felt lost and alone, that she didn't even know her husband. He wasn't the same person who now stood only a few feet away from her. Michael had changed so much over the course of time; things were different, he was now more like the man she had first fallen head over heels in love with.

Michael stretched, raising his long arms over his head before he asked, "Are you getting hungry yet? I was thinking maybe we could order a pizza or get a little fresh air and walk to somewhere, see what we find."

"That sounds good, I could use a break from here." Maggie got off the couch and walked toward Michael. She looped her arms around his torso, her cheek flat against his chest, and she inhaled his scent. He wrapped her up in his arms, laying his head on top of hers. Maggie felt content for the first time since arriving. "I love you."

***

Maggie laughed so hard she almost choked on a thick noodle from the delicious pasta that filled the large bowl in front of her. She reached for the glass of lemon water to wash away the culprit, and wiped the tears from her eyes. She hadn't laughed that hard with Michael in a long time, and it felt great.

Earlier they had walked in search of food and remembered a little hole-in-the-wall Italian place that they had always wanted to try, but never did. The food was amazing, the flavorful sauce and the aroma of garlic with hints of basil wafted through the air. The tables had red and white checkered table cloths, with jarred candles in the center, casting a lovely glow. The restaurant was cozy, soft music played in the background, the decor was traditional old country Italian, and yet there was a modern flare. The giant cans of olive oil neatly lined up on the shelves on the walls reflected the candlelight and soft track lights on the ceiling.

"God, this food is so good." Maggie slurped another noodle, feeling a little splash of sauce hit her chin. Michael noticed it too; he gingerly used his thumb to remove it and put it in his mouth. Just seeing him do that sprouted all sorts of tingly feelings; she knew what his mouth was capable of.

"You ready to go home?" His eyes were dark like coal under the shadow of the low lighting, but his gaze held unmistakable desire.

"Eat your food, if you are good, we can order dessert," Maggie playfully scolded.

He gave her a sexy grin, and his voice, utterly seductive, said, "I'd rather have you for dessert."

Maggie laughed again; her sides actually were starting to hurt now. All night he had been joking and endearing, it reminded her so much of when they were dating. Maggie could feel herself falling in love with him all over again.

***

After dinner last night, they went home and had

dessert, which certainly didn't involve food. Michael and Maggie woke up early, grabbed a coffee, and packed up the remaining items. The local charity center had already come to accept the donations. They had accomplished a great deal, and it wasn't even noon yet. The game plan for that beautifully warm Sunday was to grab the moving truck, drive over to Michael's dad's home, and then meet the hired loaders by five that evening.

The sun bounced off the glass skyscrapers in downtown Seattle as they took a cab to the moving truck rental lot just outside of the city to pick up, what seemed to Maggie, a truck that was way to large for the task at hand. Michael assured her they would fill it. She knew she needed to trust him. She was just more concerned about him driving it through the tight and narrow streets of Seattle. She was sure they could fill it, her worry was more about side-swiping cars when they actually had to drive the beast.

The drive through Seattle to where Michael's dad's house was terrified Maggie. With the sharp turns and the narrow passages, she found herself gripping the dash and holding her breath. Michael begged her to relax, he seemed completely at ease behind the wheel of the monstrous truck. Maggie let out a large breath as relief flooded her when she saw his father's home. Michael parked along the curb in front of the home and turned off the truck. He grew quiet and stared at the house.

Maggie reached over and put her hand on his thigh, she patted him softly and said, "It'll be okay." She could imagine what thoughts were spiraling out of control in his mind.

Michael hadn't mentioned his father's death since coming to Birch Valley, it was as though he was escaping all that had troubled him in Seattle. Now his left over emotions had bubbled to the surface.

He gave her a tight lipped smile. "I know, thanks, babe."

Maggie was happy they were closer, and that she could be his pillar of strength. When his father had passed early in the spring, their marriage was cracked and just about ruined, and as disconnected as they had been, she tried to be a loving support for him. She wanted to hold him up during his vulnerable time of sorrow, but that wasn't how it played out. They fought, and she left shortly after the funeral, thinking that their marriage was over.

Michael got out of the truck and came around to open her door and help her out. She felt like she was exiting a monster truck, the tires were enormous, heck, the entire truck was gargantuan. They walked hand-in-hand along the stairs leading to a large double front door. Michael fished the keys from his pocket, slid them into the locked door easily, and opened it.

The entrance was just as Maggie remembered, with a dark slate stone floor. The house displayed wealth and taste, but it was empty of light and life. She had only been to the house a few times. Maggie never recalled it feeling warm or comfortable, it was so different than her parents' home. It was the type of place where you sat straight on the couch, no slouching or actually cozying up, and you

301

certainly didn't put your glass down for fear of leaving a ring on the fine wooden tables. It was not a house for children; the interior was decorated with rare artifacts, at least they seemed that way to Maggie. Tall vases of varied sizes were everywhere, sculptures and art strategically placed in perfect lighting for proper viewing. This was more of a museum than a home to raise a son in. But it was Michael's childhood home. The wooden and stucco shell held all of his memories growing up, and she knew from what he had told her most of them weren't very happy.

Maggie rubbed Michael's lower back as they stood in muted breath taking in the residence. She could sense the tension in his body as she asked, "You okay?"

When he turned to meet her gaze, she could see the wetness pooling at the rim of his eyelids, threatening to spill over. It broke her heart witnessing the pain he was undoubtedly experiencing. She pulled him to her and held him.

Time stood still; it hung in the balance, waiting. Michael wiped his eyes and cleared his throat. "I just wanted to do a walk through again before I call the agent to list the property. I've already hired a team to come in and move everything into storage for us to handle later."

He started moving toward the expansive living room with the giant fireplace, which seemed to be crawling up toward the high vaulted ceilings with the exposed beams. The room was breathtaking. Maggie followed closely behind him. He was walking with purpose, a business-like pace, his jaw tight, and his eyes focused and serious. He looked every inch the attorney he used to be. Michael paused, as if taking mental inventory of the prized possessions. It wasn't as though he wanted anything, there were no childhood mementos that he would cherish. His parents had quickly gotten rid of all the effects of his young years once he was a teenager. His old bedroom was promptly remodeled into a showcase guest room. Maggie couldn't imagine her mother ever changing anything. Her room was still the same as it had been when she left for Seattle. Over the last six years, it had been Maggie's suggestion to make it a little more suitable as a guest room, but Mary insisted keeping it fairly reminiscent of Maggie's life there.

Michael's stride was quick as he leaped up the wide staircase. He glanced back at Maggie and said, "You don't need to come up, I won't be long." He continued up the stairs.

She was curious why he didn't want her to follow him. Maybe he needed space to sort the jumbled emotions he was going through. Maggie strolled back into the living room, examining different art on the wall. His mother had had an excellent eye; the pieces were colorful and simply exquisite. Maggie, who enjoyed painting, and had been fairly good at it at one point, wished she could have been closer to her husband's mother. They could have talked about their favorite artists and maybe went to a gallery, but she wasn't that kind of woman. She barely tolerated being a parent and didn't have much room available in her heart. It wasn't until Melanie was born that Maggie had seen her warm a little, but she was tragically gone too soon. Her death had crushed Michael and his father, but it brought them closer, which in its own way was a blessing. Michael had been basically shunned by his father, but once his mother had died they leaned on each other, changing their relationship for the better. Maggie knew that his sudden death had torn him up. But with death came life; such was the full, ever-changing circle. She felt that change kicking and stretching inside her as she placed her hand over her belly, cradling the moving lump under her skin.

"They would have loved you very much," Maggie said to her baby. She didn't hear Michael return, but caught a glimpse of his figure as he stood watching her.

"They really would have," Michael said as he went to her and placed both of his hands on her belly. He kneeled down and kissed her stomach. "Hey, you in there, Daddy loves you."

Maggie released a giggle, she knew Michael would continue to grieve, but the little life inside her would carry on their memory, pieces of them would live on, as they did with Melanie. That was the beauty of family.

***

Maggie stood in the center of their nearly empty living room. The movers were loading the last bit of boxes and furniture. The place felt so odd; it looked a lot bigger with everything removed. She swept, mopped, and scrubbed every surface from top to bottom, her body ached, but the deep clean smell was worth her efforts.

"This is the last of it," Michael announced as he picked up a couple of boxes. Two younger men dressed in matching uniforms used a hand truck to load another tower of boxes that were stacked near the hall by the entrance. Michael followed them out, but not before winking at Maggie and flashing her a half grin.

Maggie grabbed a leftover roll of paper towels and sprayed window cleaner on the large living room window. She wiped the surface, ridding it of any streaks or smudges and then watched the traffic roll past. She had spent many nights staring out this same window, waiting, wondering, and worrying. The day had been a rollercoaster of emotions, highs and lows. Maggie felt drained. She was thankful that they had accomplished what they had set out to do.

After the movers had gone, Michael leaned against the counter, surveying the space.

"I'm so glad that's over," he said, covering his mouth as he tried to stifle a yawn.

"Me too." Seeing him yawn caused her to release one of her own. Both were worn out and near starving.

"Sleep or food?" Michael asked as he rubbed his face hard, a feeble attempt as he tried to shake away some of the exhaustion.

"Well, we haven't eaten much, but God, I'm so tired too."

"It's our last night here, and you know what sounds fantastic right now?"

Nothing sounded fantastic right then, they were hungry, dirty, and tired. They were planning on sleeping on a blow up mattress so they could easily load it into the truck the following morning. She hated sleeping on those things, but Maggie was a trooper and was willing to suffer to get the whole moving process over with. Right then, showering and sleeping was high on the priority list, but she entertained Michael's question.

"Hmm, not sure, what?" Maggie feigned interest.

"A bread bowl with the best clam chowder in Seattle," he stated very matter-of-factly.

That did sound delicious and wonderful: the creamy concoction, with its bits of tender clam meat, roasted corn, chunks of potatoes, and the perfect blend of seasonings. She drooled as she envisioned the warm, crusty bread that was served with it.

"Yes!"

"Let's clean up, and I'll call a cab," Michael offered.

***

A light drizzle tapped against the roof of the cab as they drove toward the waterfront. The cab driver dropped them off within walking distance of Pike Place Market, home of Seattle's best chowder. They had used the last bit of their energy getting out of the cab.

With bread bowls in front of them, each let out a satisfied moan. The evening lights danced on the surface of the water, and the pungent, salty scent of the sea hovered around them. The rain had passed, everything was damp, but they located a covered patio area outside with a great view that had remained partially dry. Michael and Maggie sighed in unison as they consumed the warm soup, taking in the sights of the popular tourist area.

The waterfront was a well known boardwalk, with little shops and eateries that was usually packed full with out-of-towners during the warmer months. Locals knew the right time to visit and to shop in order to avoid the heavy foot traffic. Maggie had enjoyed taking Melanie shopping or going to visit the aquarium. She had enjoyed looking beyond the harbor, out into Puget Sound. Maggie suddenly felt a bit homesick; she would miss that part of Seattle. She wouldn't miss the fast pace of living or the thick slough of people in rush hour traffic. But knowing the vast ocean was just beyond the line of boats that trailed in the distant horizon was almost magical.

"You almost done, babe?" Michael asked as he gathered his trash.

"Sure," Maggie replied, scooping the last little bits of chowder out of the bowl. "That was so good."

"You're welcome." A playful, smug look was on his face.

"Hey, it was a great idea, I'll give you that."

"Well, I aim to please." A wicked smile appeared on his lips.

Maggie rolled her eyes. Her husband had an insatiable sexual appetite. "What am I going to do with you?"

"I think you know the answer." he winked as he grabbed the trash from her and threw everything away in a trash can a few feet away.

"Is that all you think about?" Maggie asked as she watched him jog back to her quickly.

"Pretty much, and food." He leaned in and kissed her on the lips.

***

Maggie flipped over to her side, the squishy air mattress heaved and moved. She grunted in frustration; she hadn't slept well, but she had expected that. They had a long drive ahead of them, and would easily be on the road for six to seven hours. Maggie figured she might as well get up, no point in wallowing in her discomfort any longer. After pushing herself off the bed in a near gymnastic stunt, she was upright. She eyed a sleeping Michael, the sheet draped haphazardly over his body. She knew that he had next to nothing on, and the thought sent a zing through her. Apparently she wasn't much better than him when it came to having insatiable desire. Maggie made her way to the bathroom to shower and dress for the day but couldn't empty several naughty thoughts that were running wild in her mind.

Emerging from a steamy shower that felt almost heavenly, she entered their bedroom and saw Michael sitting up in the blow-up bed. He threw her a happy smile.

"You are up early," he said as he yawned and stretched naked arms over his head. His dark, nearly black hair was messy and incredibly sexy. His brown eyes still sleep heavy.

Maggie sighed as she took in the sight of her gorgeous husband. "I think I'm just anxious to get on the road." She crept closer to the mattress as she spoke, still drying her hair in a thick towel and tightening the one that covered her body. Michael reached for her and pulled her down to his lap, causing her to squeal and playfully slap him away.

"I'm surprised you didn't sleep after how last night went," Michael responded, wiggling his eyebrows.

"Good grief, you know how much I hate air mattresses. They are just so darn uncomfortable, and you always take up most of it." She poked him playfully in the chest.

"Well, you shouldn't have tried to sleep so far away, spoon with me next time, and you will have a lot more room," he suggested as he started kissing her bare shoulder.

"If I did that, you wouldn't let me sleep. I know better than to spoon with the likes of you, mister." Maggie grabbed his face and planted a soft kiss on his mouth.

Michael let out a laugh. "The likes of me? Oh now you're in trouble."

Maggie felt like they were on a second honeymoon, constantly touching, kissing, and basking in their love. She remembered when things weren't that way, when she slept alone wondering where he was or when he would be home. That was all behind them, and their marriage was stronger and better than ever. The love had always been

there, but now it shone brilliantly above everything
else.

***

The truck rattled and shook; it was heavy and
weighed down with everything they wanted to bring
to their new home. Seattle faded into the
background as they headed east out on the freeway,
crossing a bridge over a small body of water. The
sensation of departing from their past life and
moving in the direction of their future brought a
sense of excitement and joy to Maggie.

Their surroundings kept changing as they
traveled, walls of mountains on either side of them
becoming rolling hills, which turned into desert
canyons as they inched closer to home.
Washington's landscape varied drastically, offering
different terrain across the state. The drive along
Interstate 90 was actually smooth, the traffic almost
nonexistent, even with their late start and several
rest stops along the way, they made remarkable
time and were able to enjoy the trip. Michael and
Maggie spent most of their time chatting about how
they were going to decorate their new home and
plans for Michael's practice. They tossed around
different baby names, and wondered what gender
the baby might be. The future was open to so many
possibilities.

They cruised through the large city of Spokane;
they were on the final push, the last leg of the tiring
journey. Michael had driven the entire time, but
Maggie's body was starting to complain. They

stopped in Spokane for something to eat, and the rest had been much needed. Once they felt rejuvenated and ready to conquer the road, they loaded themselves back into the massive truck.

Birch Valley was a little more than an hour north of Spokane. The single lane highway that would carry them home had very few drivers on it. They sailed through several small towns along the way, with lakes on one side, shimmering with the sun's beautiful light, and large fields with ancient looking barns standing alone on another. Homes lined Highway 395.

As Maggie stared out her window, she took it all in, the sky cloudless and perfect, the best shade of blue, and the kind that painters dream of. Lilac bushes were in full bloom, lavender, magenta, and white flowers hung from hardy branches filled with thick, glossy green leaves. They only flowered for a short time, but their delicate fragrance was incredible. Wispy wildflowers speckled the surrounding hills; everything was brilliant, the colors bold and gorgeous. That was why she loved the area; the natural beauty was unmatched.

Maggie could see the thick line of evergreen trees as they coasted down the hill that would lead them to Birch Valley. Maggie looked over Michael, and they both wore the same expression, happy to finally be home.

Epilogue

Patrick

Patrick tapped his fingers hard against the steering wheel of his SUV. There was no music playing, no beat to drum them to. He was fidgeting purely from annoyance. The O'Brien women had crossed the line, and the main culprit was his sister, Maggie. He didn't appreciate them sticking their nose in his business. Setting up an online dating profile just went against everything he was about. He knew Maggie, Rachel, and his mother all meant well; they were only trying to help. But the fact remained that he was still hurting. He missed Beth with all the last remaining broken shards of his heart. She had been gone almost four years. He would never forget, especially since the day she died was the same day Finn and Connor had been born.

He could see something coming up in the road and started to reduce his speed. He had wanted to go for a drive. He wasn't headed anywhere in particular, but just wanted to clear his mind. People hardly traveled on the old country road, and as he pulled up he noticed that a car with a small trailer had its hazard lights on. A woman stood by the side of it, one arm extended high towards the sky, not to flag him down, but by the looks of it trying to get a signal for her cell phone. *Well, good luck with that.*

Rolling his window down, he cautiously asked, "Excuse me, do you need any help?"

What Patrick wasn't prepared for was the most incredible eyes that stared back at him: they were a deep, sea green, helpless and lost. Her face had a hint of something familiar, but he couldn't place it. Her long black hair laid against the middle of her back, and several strands were flying wildly with the swift breeze that was blowing.

"Hi, thanks so much for stopping. We blew a tire on that trailer." She pointed at the small rental trailer that was connected to the car.

"Do you mind if I take a look?" Patrick offered.

"I'd be very grateful."

He maneuvered his own vehicle off the road and parked behind the trailer. Patrick hopped out and met her by the shredded tire, bits and chunks of rubber were scattered nearby. He knelt down to see if there was a spare, luckily there was.

"I can change this and get you back on the road," he said as he assessed the situation. "I'm Patrick O'Brien, by the way." He extended his hand to her after wiping it on the back of his jeans.

Her mouth opened wide into a pleasant and grateful smile. "I thought that was you. I'm Amber Mills," she said, but then shook her head as Patrick gave her a confused look. "I mean, I was Amber Herrick, my parents own the diner in town. You and I went to school together."

That's where I know her from. I knew she looked familiar. Patrick was floored with how gorgeous she was. He didn't remember her looking like that in school, he would've remembered her for sure.

She stood a lot shorter than him, her curvy figure hugged in dark wash jeans, and a soft, red, cotton shirt. Patrick couldn't explain the sudden attraction he felt toward her as he tried desperately to pull himself together. This wasn't like him at all, easily stirred up by a woman.

"So what brings you back to Birch Valley?"

Amber bit her lip. Patrick tried hard to resist staring at her full mouth as she said, "Well, I'm moving back."

Damn.

About the Author

I was born and raised in southern California and relocated to beautiful eastern Washington state. The rural small towns that speckle this vast area have inspired my ideal setting for most of the stories I write. The pine and tamarack trees covering the towering mountains, the shimmering lakes and rivers, the abundant wildlife and a feeling of a time forgotten, stirs so many of my creative juices. I can't thank my parents enough for dragging this city kid on long roadtrips up to this rugged foreign area, because now it is my home and I truly love my life here.

Reading was something that spurred me to begin writing at a young age. I enjoyed creating characters, different settings, and describing anything and everything. Storytelling, I have found is something I have inherited from both of my parents. I love attention to detail, using words to fully bring the picture alive, that is something I got from my dad. Creating characters and figuring out their story and how to achieve their happy ending comes from my mom. Then there is the smell of a book, new or old, the weight of it in your hands as you balance it open, seeing all those beautifully typed words spun and woven into sentences, this was created by a writer. I knew that was what I wanted to be when I grew up.

Over the years I fiddled with a story here and there, but it wasn't until 2015 that I realized it was time. Time to get those dreams down on paper (or my laptop) and so The Cloverleaf Series was born.

Coming from a family that is focused on being involved in each other's lives as much as possible created a great deal of inspiration and ideas for The Cloverleaf Series. My family is one that has weathered several terrible storms and still somehow keeps propelling forward. During those sunny times we can be seen gathered around, eating good food, sharing memories, and laughing until we can't catch our breath. We fight hard and love hard.

Romance, I simply love it, that's why I write it. I remember my mom giving me my very first paperback romance novel. It was a pretty exciting one filled with suspense and an overall excellent storyline, she had just read it and she felt it was suitable for my teenage eyes. That was it, I was hooked. I began to devour these romance stories that varied over the years from sweet to sultry, I consumed thousands of books and stories over the years. Each time I finished reading a novel, the desire to write my own grew stronger. As ideas for books swirled in my mind, it always had a romantic element to it, and I suppose it always will. What is there not to love about falling in love and finding that special person to share your life with? Who doesn't wish for passion, butterflies in your stomach, and that happily ever after?

As a reader, I can't even begin to thank all of the writers that have created so many emotions for me, falling in love with characters, mourning their loss, sighing as I close the final chapter or smiling when everyone lives happily ever after. As a writer, I just want to do the same.

Facebook:
http://facebook.com/authorgloriaherrmann

Twitter:
http://www.twitter.com/@gloriaiswriting

Website:
http://www.gloriaherrmann.com/

Goodreads:
https://www.goodreads.com/authorgloriaherrmann

Instagram:
http://www.instagram.com/authorgloriaherrmann